Prisons of Fate

By
Sandi Zambarano Griffin

PUBLISH AMERICA

PublishAmerica
Baltimore

First printing

Text and cover design
by author.

ISBN: 1-4137-0150-7

PUBLISHED BY PUBLISHAMERICA, LLLP

www.publishamerica.com

Baltimore

Printed in the United States of America

For Chet,

the song in my heart

Prison

any place or condition of confinement

Chronology

1872   Haddie Kelly McFee, born in America of an Irish mother

1900   Haddie, 28 years of age, marries Oliver James Halloran, 38

1901   Daughter born; Heather Rose

1911   Hallorans moved to Red Brick on Benefit Street
        Providence, Rhode Island (Heather, 10)

1913   Son born, Oliver James Halloran (Haddie, 41, and Oliver, 51)

1925   Heather Rose, 24, marries John J. O'Shay. They bore 3 sons
        1927   John Jr.
        1929   Michael
        1932   Patrick

1929   Stock Market Crash

1950   Korean War

1951   Patrick enters college

1953   Summer at Sweetmeadow Cottage in Narragansett, Rhode
        Island

Oliver James Halloran
weds
Haddie Kelly McFee
("Grams")

Daughter	Son
Heather Halloran	James Oliver Henry
weds	
John Joseph O'Shay	

Sons
John Jr, Michael, & Patrick

Bart and Violet Moore
Daughter
Guinevere

Thaddeus Tilton Huntingwell III
weds
Prunella Catherine Cooper

Estate staff:

Molly: Prunella's personal maid
Nigel: Thaddeus' valet and butler
Cook: Head cook
Max: Chauffer
Angelo: Gardener
Tillie: Maid

Ireland
(A secluded farming town)
1872

"She's n'better than a common whore!"
"Shameless!"
"A Strumpet!"
"Disgraceful!"
"Saucy little thing!"
"Sinful."
"The horror of it all."
"...and her uncle a holy priest!"

Gossip spread like volcanic lava over the secluded little township, belching out an inferno of empty accusations and vicious untruths. Hot coals of hatred scorched the minds of all in it's path, singeing even the wisest and most revered among them.

A scandal in this serene meadowland was rare enough, but one of such assumed magnitude had, indeed, pierced the armor of the impoverished little farming community. As innuendoes festered, seeping into every crevice of the small society, it's mendacity grew more distorted and ugly. The fever of slander had become so contagious that even those good God-fearing people had become unwitting victims of herd mentality. They were unable to divorce the passions of the mob, from simple logic. These good citizens were rather skillful at masking their own indiscretionary habits behind the cloak of holiness but were quite ready to accept the failings of others.

The truth was that Sarah, the fourteen year old innocent in question, had nothing to do with the rape, except to be terribly young and irresistibly virginal. The truth was that she had not flirted with, nor encouraged, the whiskey besotted plow boy to pursue her in the barn. The truth was that Sarah had been unaware that she was being watched every afternoon as she escaped to the hayloft to devour her "forbidden books."

The tragic irony was that the ol' barn had always been Sarah's safe haven, her magical world, a place where she could unashamedly vent her love of literature. As young and sheltered as she was, she possessed an innate quest for knowledge and an insatiable thirst to read and study older authors. The beloved barn had offered her this sanctuary. She had been helplessly drawn to the enormous weathered structure now sagging with age like a dowager matron, since she was a tiny tot. Sarah loved to explore the barn for hidden treasures, and she would become giddy with pleasure when she stumbled on an unusual find among the rubble. She delighted in the rough-hewn beams, the patina of well worn, handmade tools, and faded overalls haphazardly skewered on rusty nails. She was bewitched by the heady aroma of sweet smelling hay, the rich essence of sticky feed grains mingled with earthy odors of storage potatoes and animal scents. Even the forbidden barrels of fermenting corn whiskey hidden carefully under the eaves supposedly obscured from view, gave off an intriguing pungency. The sleighs, the lanterns, the wheelbarrows, the buckets, the ladders, all became her props, her stage, the setting for her bouts with make believe.

Sarah spent hours in the old barn, fantasizing that she was some fiery heroine or a dutiful queen and giggled to herself as she portrayed a scarlet woman. She liked best to be a sassy saloon dancer like the ones she read about in the French novels. Falling onto the nearest mound of hay, Sarah would laugh herself weak, thinking of how her God-adoring parents might react to having a Jezebel for a daughter.

When she tired, she straightened up, rid herself of any telltale signs of mischief and climbed, cat-like, down the back ladder from the loft out into a thick hammock of trees. She would make her way quickly back to the main house, stealing glances in every direction, assuring that she was not being followed. Quietly she resumed her chores.

The barn had afforded her such joy, and now it was the scene of violation. She had hardly known what had happened to her that day except to realize she had been terribly harmed. She had felt the pain, she had bled, and she had known the raw anger of invasion. For a long time Sarah dared not tell a soul of the dreadful event, fearing the godly church folk would accuse her of being possessed by the devil, because, in 1872, virginity was an honorable virtue, one a young maiden should embrace.

On that awful day Sarah had cried as she rinsed out her homespuns; she sobbed and trembled frantically as she tried to wash away the horrors of the moment. How could she expose the truth of that afternoon to anyone? Surely, she envisioned, she would be burned at the stake.

Sarah's parents were good people, fiercely dedicated to church and home but blindly intolerant to the ways of the world. They were imprisoned by their unbending religious teachings and willingly bound, by church law, to confess any moral transgression, knowing they were unconditionally protected by the security of the priest's vow of secrecy. It was simple; confess and the sin was pardoned. They also reasoned, in some warped way, that if a sin was buried, it would automatically vanish, thus immunizing the sinner against the blackening curse of malicious slander.

It puzzled Sarah that her parents were so unforgiving of human frailties, allowing no margin for error, when Christ, the very model they chose to dedicate their lives to, pray to, and revere, was the most compassionate and forgiving of all men. It made no sense to Sarah...that was just the way it was. One thing she had no doubt about, was that a young colleen's bringing disgrace upon her upstanding "pure-as-the-driven-snow" parents, was unthinkable, unforgivable.

As the weeks turned into months, Sarah became fatter. Her breasts were enlarging and she felt strange flutters in her middle. Neighbor's tongues were beginning to wag. She dared not confide in her mother, who was the self-acclaimed pillar of goodness, nor her elderly father. God spare him, his weak heart could not survive the news.

Aunt Haddie! Her mother's younger spinster sister. *She could tell Aunt Haddie!* She would understand. She always understood. Sarah fervently believed that they were kindred spirits because they both had natural curls the color of fire, sparkling eyes greener than shamrocks and an army of confounded freckles that danced, shamelessly, across the bridges of their upturned noses. They often poked fun at themselves and partook in playful bouts of self degradation.

Haddie had an attic full of old volumes and empathized with the little girl's passion for reading. Sarah chuckled when she remembered the day Aunt Haddie tried to conceal *The Canterbury Tales* in her bloomers. It was on a Sunday morning, after church services, that Haddie had slipped the rather awkward book under her long skirt, tying it tightly around her ample body with ribbon, in an effort to hold the taboo parcel securely in place. As she entered her sister's little stone cottage, the book unwittingly slipped to the floor.

Aunt Haddie, as only Aunt Haddie could, immediately flopped on top of it, dramatically feigning a fainting spell. Sarah's distraught mother scurried for her vapors. Haddie winked mischievously up at Sarah from her vantage point on the worn rag rug and impishly slipped the precious cargo into the outstretched hands of Sarah, who excitedly fled up to her room where she buried the treasure under her feather mattress. Sarah threw herself down on her bed and suffocated her uncontrollable giggles in a lumpy pillow. Dear Aunt Haddie, she had pulled it off again!

She loved Haddie and the feeling was returned a hundred fold.

Haddie Mary Kelly never had a fondness for the "uncouth ways of men folk." It did not bother her one bit that the town's women gossiped relentlessly behind her back or preached within earshot, *"One should marry and propagate the faith as the good book says"*; *"A woman living alone is hardly a healthy existence."*

Haddie treasured her freedom. She came and went as she pleased and defying the tongue-waggers, boldly took a position in a small one room book house. Young Sarah loved visiting her there.

This afternoon, instead of sneaking off to her hayloft retreat, Sarah ran all the way to the quaint bookery where Aunt Haddie spent her days. Her heart raced with wild anticipation. She tugged at the big iron handle, unlatching the rough wooden door. A familiar screeching of hinges heralded a welcome. Once inside, the pungent smell of musty papers and leather permeated her nostrils. It was like stepping into a previous century and she was immediately wreathed in the security of it's ambiance.

Upon seeing Aunt Haddie, Sarah flung herself into her welcoming arms and without pause, tearfully spilled out her traumatic secret. As Sarah had expected, Aunt Haddie was most sympathetic and nonjudgmental. Dear, loyal Aunt Haddie. She innately trusted Sarah to confide in her truthfully and never once questioned her integrity.

The older woman, with a vice on her own heavy emotions, held the whimpering child close to her heart, tightly locking her arms around Sarah, until the child's involuntary quivers calmed. Haddie was filled with compassion for the budding young girl, who had her youth so harshly stripped away by some unthinking buffoon.

They talked, they hugged, they cried, into the wee hours of the morning. It was decided that Haddie would be the one to deliver the indelicate news to her sister. "It would be easier that way," Haddie had reasoned to Sarah's relief. There was no need to exacerbate an already potentially explosive confrontation with any unnecessary drama.

It was several weeks later, when Sarah could no longer disguise her condition under layers of loose clothing that Haddie confronted her sister over mid-morning scones and coffee. Sarah had stayed in her loft bedroom and listened through a knot hole in the warped door, as Aunt Haddie calmly related the tragic episode to Sarah's mother.

The woman was stunned! She was heart-broken, disgraced, repulsed. Her initial reaction was not concern for her daughter's emotional health or the welfare of the pure new life that was forming within Sarah's womb but for her own reputation and that of her family. The welfare of the bastard infant was secondary to the immediate concern of covering up the unthinkable sin. No disgrace had ever befallen the immaculate Haggartys and by all the holy saints, one would not soil their celestial image now. And that was that!

Sarah's horrified mother sank to her knees, racked in pain. She began to wail, from the depth of her grief, as she swayed back and forth, violently pounding her chest with her fist. Then she began to mumble what sounded like gibberish. Haddie assumed it must be an invocation to the heavens for strength. Between the poundings, she blessed herself over and over again with absurd, exaggerated motions. At proper intervals, she flailed her arms, moaning dolefully, and acting out the torturous plight of the martyred. Not at all resembling the strong, unflappable pillar of holiness that she so grandly aspired to.

Sarah watched the saga unfold.

All at once, as if shot from a cannon, Sarah's mother bolted to her feet. Abandoning any semblance of a poor, persecuted soul, she adopted the stance of a militant general posed for war. And war it was! The histrionics ceased as quickly as they had begun. She stood tall, her back ramrod straight and without warning, grabbed Haddie's shoulders, shaking her wildly as she spoke. Haddie had never seen such rage in her sister's eyes and knew she was certainly no force to reason with at this particular moment.

Suddenly Sarah's mother ceased her physical attack on her sister and began rapidly pacing back and forth over the floor's uneven planks. She stopped right in front of Haddie, glared into her eyes and in a low muffled voice announced exactly what the plan was to be. Sarah would leave Ireland quickly and quietly. *Hide the problem and it will go away, as usual*, thought Haddie.

Without consulting Sarah, it was decided that the pregnant little girl would be shipped to America, placed in a nice convent school, to await the birth of her illegitimate child. It was a well known fact that there were many childless families of means in the new world, eager to adopt a poor, unfortunate one. It was, also, automatically assumed that the child would be reared in a proper environment, with good loving parents by its side.

It was settled. Sarah would leave as soon as arrangements could be made, thus alleviating any obligation on the part of the grandparents in rearing the tainted child.

When confronted with the frightening turn of events her life had suddenly taken, Sarah insisted on one stipulation. That if her child was a girl, it would be named Haddie Kelly. It was hurridly agreed to. Anything to comfort the distraught lass.

Fourteen year old Sarah Haggarty was among the thirty thousand immigrants that herded on ships bound for America, all running from the bleak conditions in Ireland and fighting to survive the raging seas of the Atlantic. Iron steamer ships had now replaced the old wooden firetraps that crossed the ocean in earlier days, drowning thousands of desperate souls, seeking refuge in the new world. Sarah spent most of the two weeks voyage doubled up with a racking case of sea sickness, shedding six pounds from her scant body before reaching Ellis Island.

The baby was born five months later, in America, in the Springtime. The child's only link to her birth mother was a hand-carved wooden pendant, made for Sarah by her father, that she left with her infant. The baby's adoptive parents were ecstatic at the sight of their beautiful new daughter, a bonnet of red ringlets blanketing her tiny head.

Little Haddie Kelly began her new life on a grand country estate, lauded over by the McFees, her adoring parents. She was fashioned in the finest laces and strolled in an ornate wicker perambulator by a very proper nanny in a black uniform and white pinafore.

Sarah regained her strength and returned to Ireland. Several years later, she married a fine gentleman farmer and over the years, to her husband's pretended distress, birthed a brood of girls. Her first legitimate daughter, at eighteen, was sent to America to better her chances for a more fruitful life, without ever being told that she had a half sister, much her senior, already settled somewhere in the great new land of opportunity.

It was not important.

There was no purpose in opening old wounds. Sarah alone had silently suffered the agony of parting many years before, in what now seemed a different life. She had prayed all of her days for the welfare of the precious child she was not allowed to see or hold. Until the hour of her death, she was imprisoned by an indescribable ache of longing that burned torturously in a silent corner of her heart. The torment of unrequited love, for an innocent little creature, so coldly whisked away from her at birth, never vanished from her soul.

But for tiny Haddie Kelly McFee, life began without flaw.

Haddie Kelly McFee
"Grams"
80 Years Later
1953
Providence, Rhode Island

Happy birthday dear, Gra-ams. Happy birthday to you.

Haddie Kelly McFee Halloran was eighty years old. Although the genteel lady was pitifully frail, ravished by a relentless assault of crippling arthritis, she was somehow able to exude the freshness of youth. She fought bravely to maintain a cheerful facade.

"Oh my," she laughed. "Am I not too old for all this mollycoddling?" Grams Halloran squirmed, embarrassed by the uncomfortableness of being fussed over.

Heather O'Shay, with gracious precision, placed the large blue glass plate, showcasing a sumptuous confection, squarely in front of her mother.

The towering cake, smothered under a mountain of sweet white fluff, boasted eight fat frosting roses, each centered with a tall thin candle symbolizing the eight decades Haddie had graced the earth. The white tapers flickered haphazardly, unkindly exaggerating deep crevices in the aging face.

Tonight Grams sat, regal and proud, at the head of the wide old mahogany table, surrounded by her small family; her daughter, Heather, her son-in-law, John, and her three grown grandsons. A contented smile fashioned her thin lips as she savored the stroke of good fortune that had been dealt her. To have lived so long! To be allowed the privilege of tasting such a meaty chunk of life's unfolding.

The elegant woman had administered much comfort over the years and was dearly loved by all who shared even a breath of time in her presence. Haddie Kelly Halloran was, in every sense of the word, a grand matriarch. She lavished them with her love and natural wit. She never preached to them. It was through her example, that she shared her wisdom. One of the most important facets of human existence, and she felt the most neglected, was the ability to see humor in almost all dimensions of life.

"Learn to laugh at yourself," she would direct.

Her family deemed it incredible, that with her twisted body and aching joints, she was able to maintain a sense of comedy, poking fun at her own arthritic fingers and toes, horrendously deformed from the painful disease.

"Make a wish dah-ling. There now, make a wish." Her daughter coddled, in a slightly maudlin tone emphasized by exaggerated hand gestures.

Commands rang out from around the room.

"Blow out the candles, Grams."

"C'mon, Grams, you can do it."

Cheers reverberated off the walls as she extinguished the tiny flames with the help of her youngest grandson. Patrick had moved his chair very close to his grandmother's right side, enabling him to speak directly into her working ear.

Grams had no visible favorites but she was inordinately drawn to Patrick, home from college this weekend for her birthday.

"You're the only one in the bunch with fire in your blood," she would josh with him in private.

Grams loved Patrick dearly and admittedly sanctioned his foolery, allowing him to get away with murder. He reminded her, unbearably, of her own young son who had been killed years ago in a grisly accident two days before his seventeenth birthday.

After Grams had made the first cut in the cake, Heather O'Shay abruptly took over the job with her usual robot-like efficiency, doling out appropriately sized portions to each.

Patrick sheepishly reached under the table and put his hand over his grandmother's gnarled fingers. He leaned toward her.

"Hey, Grams." He teased in a low monotone voice slowly escaping from the side of his mouth. "You're still a pretty sexy ol' gal." He clucked his teeth.

She shot him a spurious look of utter shock, reacting exactly as she knew he would expect her to. "Why you devilish rogue!" she whispered back, gibing him with a playful slap on his knee. They knew each other so well, they were much alike.

It seemed incongruous for a weathered old bird and a vibrant young buck to relate to each other as they did. Theirs was truly a rare blending of souls, uncolored by false pretense, nurtured by unconditional acceptance and a feeling of genuine concern for the welfare of the other.

"You know, dear boy," she whispered, in response to his impetuous remark. "Nature is a bit tricky. While she wrinkles our skin, steals our sight and plugs up our ears, she sportingly allows our spirit to remain forever young. Isn't it a marvelous trade-off?" She wanted to tell him, that in her heart she still felt like a girl of twenty but she knew he was still much too young to understand those feelings. As she slowly turned her head away from his marvelous young face, she seemed to shut out the room's activity.

After her son's traumatic death, Haddie Kelly Halloran's life had lost it's luster. For years she merely existed. She had masterfully learned to mask the agonizing memories that ripped at her very core. It was only when Patrick's young limbs grew into manhood that she succumbed to his heart and allowed him, only him, to pierce the armor of her disguise.

Patrick Sean O'Shay was her salvation. He brought the twinkle back into her fading green eyes, he made her laugh with his silliness. He revitalized her senses with strains of a poignant Gershwin rhapsody, the booming crescendo of a Tchaikovski concerto, all the great works she had once studied. He soothed her soul with the poet's tongue, he brought the wild fragrances of field flowers into her rooms. He invited her to feel again, to view the world through his own youthful vision. How she loved him.

Over the years they had shared many long comforting hours together in Gram's joint, as Patrick lovingly referred to her third floor assemblage of rooms. Grams and he were of the same mold, both artists in their own right. She a pianist. He a musician and painter, both of them were weavers of dreams through words, music, and painting.

It amused Patrick to hear Grams announce, "Creative beings are surely not of this world." She was adamantly convinced that the spirits of all artists, whether they were painters, dancers, poets, musicians, or authors, roamed just a trace above the earth—on the outer rim of society. Here, their geniuses mingled constantly being refueled by another's dream, a fertile atmosphere of visionary magic; a place where hearts and minds were nourished by the magnanimous presence of a generous God. This she truly believed.

"Grams, hey, Grams?" Patrick lightly touched her fleshless arm. "Where were you, Grams?" he asked, nudging her gently. "You left us for awhile."

She patted his hand in a loving way and without verbal explanation, was able to convey her mental absence to him, while seeming to remain in some distant place.

He understood. She often reminisced now and he patiently allowed her the solitude of her daydreams, to drift back in time long enough to savor the passages of her life. She had traveled the most rugged of roads; burying her beloved husband under the worst of circumstance, helplessly watching her securities disappear overnight, witnessing the uncanny death of her talented young son, and she had, incredulously, remained whole.

"Open your presents, Grams." The suggestion brought her back to reality.

The humble woman truly disliked being on center stage but in her wisdom, knew it was important for those who loved her to award her their show of affection and she was clement in her honest acceptance of their generosity.

Her stiffened fingers fumbled awkwardly with the ribbons and wrappings of the brightly papered packages; hand creams, candies, teas, slippers, the usual. Nothing of great value, only the symbolic worth of expressing love to a heart dearly cherished by them all. She had begged for no more clutter to wedge into her already crammed space, but it was always "just some little thing."

Haddie Kelly Halloran looked around the familiar dining room which had been a silent observer at many a celebration over the years, and marveled at the dramatic transition it had undergone. Fresh wall paper brightened the walls; dark stained moldings and chair railings had been stripped away and redressed in a light ivory; the faded gold needlepoint seats were now covered in a lovely ivory damask; sheer ivory curtains replaced the heavy, gold brocaded draperies. Even the blackened brass chandelier had been polished to a blinding brightness and hung from the embossed tin ceiling with new stately grace.

Grams was pleased that the deep red and gold Oriental rug, one she had chosen herself years ago, remained, framed by a wide border of highly polished oak flooring.

This beautiful home had been a faithful spectator to her life's bittersweet saga. It belonged to her daughter now. Grams was an honored guest in what had been her own home for so long. It was as she wished.

Years ago, Grams had decided that the three story Victorian, housing a museum of her valuable old pieces, was too much upkeep for a woman of her age to do battle with. She offered the place to her only remaining child, Heather, and her son-in-law, John O'Shay, as a grand place to raise their three sons. She suggested, honestly, that they take her off to an old age home for the remainder of her years.

The family would not hear of it.

The young O'Shays agreed to move into the stately manor on the one condition that the top floor, including the old maids quarters (her temporary home for several years, now being used for storage) would be remodeled into a living area. It was only after a lengthy, tedious debate that Grams conceded defeat.

The rooms were redesigned to hold her most sentimental belongings. The tiny kitchen was updated, modernized with the latest stove and refrigerator. The green painted wainscot was stripped and repainted a creamy hue, giving an airy feel to the modest area.

During the conversion, it was decided that an elevator would be installed so Grams could visit her family whenever she pleased. Grams thought the more appealing aspect of the convenience was that she could also retreat if she felt the need to readjust her bones.

Grams walked with a cane now, a find, that Patrick unearthed in one of his regular rummages through junk shops. She had been a trifle put-out the day he presented it to her. She held it in both hands and in obvious annoyance, mulled it over without comment. After an awkward spell, she became playfully blunt.

"Do I appear so feeble as to need a crutch, eh?" She did not allow space between her thoughts for him to defend his offering. "Well, perhaps I am becoming a bit more creaky as the days wear on."

"It's not a crutch, Grams, it's just a cane."

As if he had not spoken, she went on. "Yes, indeed, I shall use it to good advantage."

She continued to examine the elaborately carved wood, rotating the piece, slowly, in close scrutiny. Then, looking over her glasses, she flashed him a mischievous wink in dutiful surrender.

"You're right again, dear boy, and I, the old fool that I am," emphasizing her words with a slight bow, "must admit that the time has come to yield to the young." She was quick to add, pointing her index finger above her head, "In some things." They both laughed. Patrick knew, only too well, that the tiger in her blood would yield little in her fight to persevere.

She had tapped him on the leg with her new walking stick in unspoken appreciation of his genuinely sensitive gesture. It was very much like him, to think of her comfort, easing the cruel burden of old age in any way he could.

Coffee was being served now. The conversations circling the table grew louder and more animated as the subject, inevitably, drifted to the family business. Haddie Kelly continued to consciously block out the commotion and allow herself to slip back forty years to the day she and her husband moved into this charming house with twelve year old Heather. She remembered it well.

It was the third of July, 1911, every home on the street was flying the stars and stripes. She recalled feeling such pride in being an American.

The three story brick house was formally appointed with stained glass windows, large impressive black shutters and open porches; one of the better known show pieces on the boulevard.

She remembered watching, with curious concern, as the movers unloaded the long van coveting her valuables. As the two muscled men removed protective felt coverings from her lovely furniture, Haddie was nicely surprised to observe the exceptional care taken, as each piece was positioned in it's designated resting place. They worked quickly, efficiently and with scrupulous professionalism.

Haddie was amazed at how smoothly the transition was executed. The Hallorans quickly settled into their new residence, without interruption to their uncluttered lifestyle.

Over the years, a six o'clock supper hour had somehow emerged. A well established pattern of quiet exchange was initiated, often a simple rehashing of the day's events. Meals were well thought out, fresh flowers from the gardens chosen to compliment the table setting, melodic strains of violins drifted lightly into the dining area from the Victrola in the parlor, lending a soothing background conducive to pleasant interaction. All was serene.

Haddie and her husband had one of those unbelievable marriages of enviable devotion. It was a love story straight out of the pages of make-believe.

As an only child, Haddie had, herself, been reared in a loving household by gentle, well mannered parents. She knew no other form of existence. She often looked back at her fairy tale childhood and admitted it was not the best training ground for the real world. With all her explosive zest for life, she also possessed the innate softness of a naïve child and her husband, thirteen years her senior, loved her all the more for the sweet innocence she brought to the union.

Haddie performed the household duties with usual exuberance, gleaning great fun from decorating the large rooms. She spent countless hours scouring museums and antique shops, in hopes of finding that one irresistible object of art to add to an already extensive collection of valuable pieces. She shuffled the hours in her day as her whims would dictate, to satisfy whatever artistic urge begged fulfillment at the moment. Although she religiously devoted two or three early hours to hone her skills on her beloved piano, the rest of her day was never tightly planned. It was in diametric contrast to her fun-loving nature, to be bogged down with binding schedules.

She tended to the gardens when the gardener was not on duty, puttered around the kitchen concocting new recipes, only when the cook was not bothered by her presence, listened to her favorite recordings, and read as many biographies and auto-biographies of famous artists and musicians as time would permit.

Haddie Kelly Halloran's life was full. Peaceful. Her dreams had been realized. To know the delicious satisfaction of love's passion, to be honored with the privilege of motherhood, and to be granted the luxury to pursue one's own talents. To live life as one chose, to Haddie Kelly, was the ultimate success, the greatest gift of all! Her only lament was that she would not be awarded ten lives to fully explore every aspect of her talented world.

As impulsive as Haddie's nature was, her pragmatic husband was an abrupt opposite. Even during the disrupting move, he did not lose one moment of precious slated time. Never once did he succumb to outside distractions that might threaten to sabotage his daily routine. He hired service people to fix whatever it was that was broken and caretakers to manicure the lawns, leaving him the effortless task of paying bills and playing with his fortune.

Mr. Halloran left his home before dawn every morning, like clockwork, enabling him to utilize quiet pre-office hours to juggle his personal accounts before being inundated with a hoard of stimulated clients. They came, toting impressive mounds of evidence as to why each felt he or she should be exculpated from an alleged crime.

The law had always fascinated Oliver James Halloran. He thrived on a finely orchestrated, controversial debate, thoroughly savoring the drawing of swords with gyrating tongues of opposing counsel.

The snug little family of three was securely cemented with the mortar of love which afforded them the freedom of unselfishness and self-expression. They could not, in their wildest imagination, realize how the traumatic events of the next few months would strain every fiber in their unflinching devotion.

Grams stirred in her chair. The memories were all so vivid, so painful to remember. If only she could stop the images from reappearing in her mind. Over and over again they surfaced. She rearranged her bony back against the dining room chair and again, lapsed into a more familiar era, far back in time and remembered...

It happened shortly after the move into their new home, this very place which she had named Harmony House, a result of her musical background and an apt description of the flavor therein. During a Sunday morning church service, Haddie Kelly had felt herself go weak, a sort of "sinking spell" she had labeled it. Later that same day, at the picnic on the church grounds, she had been dealt an unmistakable bout of nausea. She did not need a master's degree in calculus to piece the equation together, quickly recognizing the familiar signs of pregnancy.

At first she was in denial, then in shock.

"How could this be? I have a twelve year old daughter." Haddie was stunned!

She had heard of "change of life" babies from a friend or two who had been caught in their middle years and now, unbelievably, it was happening to her. At forty years old, the initial reaction to her state of being was hardly one of profound elation. Her psyche was bombarded with a barrage of contradictions; shock, incredulity, joy, bewilderment, embarrassment, and the sheer terror of facing diaper pails, chicken pox, two o'clock feedings. She shuddered.

For weeks she wrestled with ways to present this rather staggering revelation to her unsuspecting husband and her almost teenage daughter, in the gentlest way possible. News that, at best, would cause significant upheaval in their domestic tranquility.

Haddie Kelly decided she would take them on, one at a time. Be sensitive to each one's feelings, by telling them separately, thus, offering both the privacy of his and her own reaction, whatever it might be.

She waited for the right set of circumstances to reveal her good tidings to her husband. She chose a lazy evening before retiring.

"How does one gently drop a bomb?" The thought made her stomach lurch.

She had a grand, eloquent speech prepared to make the announcement less jarring but upon coming face to face with the attentive, gray haired man before her, she suddenly became helplessly penurious with her words.

"I'm pregnant," she blurted.

At first he thought she was teasing, as was often her style, to arouse some playfulness in his usually disciplined demeanor. Assuming it appropriate, he dutifully chuckled at her joke.

"Now wouldn't THAT be something!" he burst into a hearty laugh. "Wouldn't the ol' boys have a field day with THAT one!" He guffawed at the unlikely prospect. But when he saw there was no change in her expression, he realized her words were of a solemn nature. He came closer, steadying himself by resting his hands on her shoulders. "Are you serious?" he whispered, evaluating her more closely. Her expression could not belie the blatant truth of the matter...yes, she was serious. He was going to be a father again. His reaction was spontaneous.

"Why my dear, that's splendid. Splendid! What incredible news!" He cradled her in his arms, rocking her as if she was a tiny child, for a very long while, before speaking, "I hope you are as happy as I am."

"Yes, I am." She expelled the breath that had been bursting in her lungs. Her heart could rest.

Haddie smiled to herself. She was sure his male ego was secretly gloating with the idea of producing an offspring at his age. As sure as she was that he would coyly brag of his virility to the ol'boys down at the men's club.

Her daughter's reaction was quite another matter, one she hadn't at all counted on.

"How could you!" Heather cried out, "It's awful! How will I face my friends? It's awful! Just awful! I can't believe it, it's ridiculous!" Heather left the room, in a storm of tears, leaving her mother in utter confusion.

Surely, Haddie had assumed, being a young girl with innate mothering instincts, the prospect of having a baby to nurture, would be a pleasant experience. But nothing could have been further from the truth! Heather never liked playing with dolls or pretending dress-up like the other little girls of her age. She was much more excited talking of investments with her father from the time she knew what money was. It was like a game to her, and the two delighted in their time together.

Little Oliver Henry Halloran, named after his two grandfathers, entered the world in early summer, without complications, to an overjoyed mother and ecstatic father. His sister remained non-pulsed, politely accepting her uninvited sibling into her previously unshared space. The two never bonded as brother and sister, the age difference too great.

As the young boy matured, he began showing substantial talent for the piano, thrilling his mother. She found herself spending long periods of time at his side, going over chords and interpretations of the more difficult compositions. As a result of a common talent, the two soon became tight friends, often losing themselves for hours in their own private sanctum of melodic euphoria. He became her greatest joy...she, his mentor, and music, their obsession.

As this extraordinary relationship flourished, it was not without it's detrimental side, opening wider the gap between mother and daughter.

Haddie Kelly continued to raise her daughter as conscientiously as she knew how, albeit the two were of different worlds. They were unable to develop the closeness that mothers and daughters usually share, finding it impossible to meld their personas. Their needs too extreme.

Young Heather was a pragmatist. She was, in her mother's eyes, unimaginative, too practical, annoyingly methodical in every aspect of her life. She planned her day carefully, wrote herself notes, filled each hour with rational productivity and sadly, in Haddie's eyes, was hopelessly void of any warmth or creative excitement.

Haddie, on the other hand, was spontaneous, alive, inventive, a dreamer. She was a spiritual being, her emotions were stroked by experiences that inflamed the soul, passions that filled the heart and flooded the senses. Her daughter viewed her mother as the perennial child, a trait she found intolerably tiresome.

The two adult women never understood each other, passing almost as strangers through the portals of their lives, but love endured between them, the bonding of blood could never be denied.

Heather continued to be drawn, like a magnet, to her father. She found great satisfaction in his company. He admired his daughter's skills and temperament, both a carbon copy of his own, and she, unconsciously, emulated his style in every way.

O. James Halloran was an honorable man, much admired by his peers. He had a righteous conscience and a natural aptitude for appropriate behavior toward his fellow man, treating everyone justly, without prejudice. Scrupulous work ethics had earned him a spotless reputation, gaining him notoriety as the most sought after trial attorney in Rhode Island. Yet, with all his prominence, he remained a simple man with simple needs.

Providing premium care for his wife and two children was his most prideful achievement and selflessly dedicated his life to their welfare and betterment. His small family, in turn, expressed a natural gratitude for the comforting stability his steadfast devotion rendered them.

And yet, with all his sterling qualities, he did toy with one rather ticklish indulgence. He delighted in playing the market. Over the years, goodly quantities of his earnings were invested in stocks and he had fared extremely well, with his highly diversified portfolio. His gambling spirit resulted in an undeniable addiction to the rise and fall of his companies. He charted graphs, checked papers daily and when time allowed, made phone calls to his investment brokers, experiencing tremendous rushes of gratification when his selections paid off sizable dividends.

O. James Halloran had been incredibly successful in his speculative ventures, amassing a substantial fortune from his affair with Lady Luck. As time passed, he invested heavier into the market, acquiring larger and costlier bundles of stocks which constituted a healthy portion of his estate. A few small land parcels rounded out a meager percentage of his holdings, leaving his cash flow at a minimum, as he had planned.

He had no worries. He was robust and hardy, his reputation was well established. His finances were never more solid. His loving family at his side, life couldn't be better. Onlookers, eager to emulate a text book marriage, had the perfect model.

But it was not to last long.

Tragedy would strike the flawless household like a rampaging avalanche, sending it spiraling into a series of heart wrenching disasters.

September 1929

Thunderous headlines roared across the front pages of every newspaper in the country. Without warning, the stock market had crashed, launching catastrophic explosions of despair over the entire nation.

O. James' great fortune in stock certificates was virtually worthless. He was left without enough reserve to pull himself out of debt and without adequate cash flow to maintain the family's gracious style of living. Overnight, his ivory tower had collapsed on top of him, burying him in a heap of suffocating debris. His self-esteem plummeted out of control. He was traumatized with incredulous disbelief and mortification.

He could not face his wife, his daughter, his son.

The once proud, dignified gentleman, distraught with humiliation, suffered the blackest depths of depression. His nerves were raw, razor edged and tensed to the breaking point. He was unable to face the disgrace of failure, unable to right himself.

Oliver James Halloran flung himself from his eighth floor office window, crashing to his death. Several of his colleagues, finding themselves in the same destitute condition, followed suit.

It was a cruel, relentless time.

Her husband's wake was held at home in the same formal parlor that, only a few months earlier in late June, had burst forth with the joyous sounds of wedding guests. It seemed only yesterday, that the beautifully furnished room had been aglow with love and promise in celebration of their daughter's marriage to John J. O'Shay, a young accountant with a rosy future.

A casket now replaced the bride and groom in front of the fireplace. This day there were no photographers, no champagne toasts, no violins, no bright hopes for the future. Doom draped it's suffocating blanket over all... heavy, foreboding.

Haddie, still a young woman, was left with an enormous house, a bewildering stack of bills and paperwork of which she knew nothing, two longtime maids and a young son to raise by herself. Finances had always been O. James Halloran's field of expertise and she had, all too willingly, left such matters in his capable hands.

Now she was alone, weakened by the anguish of grief, frightened, infuriated that he left her without even a word and not knowing where to turn. She simmered in a caldron of despair for what seemed an eternity and could not help herself escape the strangling forces of depression.

It was after these long periodic rounds of self-persecution that she awoke one day, mysteriously fueled by a bolt of power. An unfamiliar surge of willful determination propelled her body. She had been unaware that such a dominating force lay dormant within her. She was a survivor and over the next crushing months and years would be tempered and tested a hundred-fold.

As the true grit of her character exploded, she was able to make sound judgments for her teenage son, who now looked even more to her for reassurance and direction.

One of her first and most distasteful duties was dismissing her faithful servants. She was unable to eke out their wages from a straining purse.

The second grim urgency was to tack a For Sale sign up on each of the two lots sandwiching the main property. Her husband had purchased the land to ensure privacy on both sides of their love nest and as a good investment. The signs went up in front of the juniper bushes bordering the broad sidewalk, in hopes that a would-be buyer might take notice.

As Haddie Kelly waited for a miracle, she tried to teach a few piano students but days were bleak for everyone. When one could not afford bread, piano lessons were hardly a priority.

It wasn't long before Mr. Silas Brant, wealthy enough not to be affected by the market plunge, showed up at her door. He was a crafty, heartless creature, who made his fortune largely on the vulnerability of widows like herself. Mr. Brant, scouring the affluent areas for a good deal, was drawn to the For Sale sign on the valuable property and proceeded to inquire of the owner's pathetic set of circumstances. He was primed to take full advantage of the lady's obvious exposed need for immediate cash and boldly offered her far less than the value of the select land. He assumed she was strapped for funds and sooner or later would be forced to liquidate her properties for very little. He had played the same scenario many times over; the struggling widow with little choice but to acquiesce and yield to his insulting proposal. He was determined to lap up any choice land while the opportunity was ripe. Later, when the economy righted itself, he would make a killing on the resale.

Much to Haddie's disgust, the virulent Mr. Brant seemed exhilarated by the prospect of acquiring her assets. Vulture-like, talons bared, he was ready to swoop down on his prey at the slightest sign of vulnerability. He was a loathsome, venomous man.

For years, Mr. Brant had harbored grandiose fantasies of residing in this prestigious area of the city. Penurious to a fault, he had become obsessed with the accumulation of wealth, living a self-inflicted, miserly existence. Even his wife was unaware of the modest bounty he kept buried in a metal box in the basement. He trusted no one with his money, the government, the banks, no one and willingly forfeited the interest for the comfort of controlling his own funds.

As he aged, Silas Brant's envy spawned a host of cynical, disagreeable traits that set him apart from the average hard-working man. He became devious, uncaring of others, driven, as though whipped by the devil himself.

Why should he be deprived of a prized existence? Homes in this prestigious area were owned by a contingent of successful business and professional men; a golden citizenry of culture, affluence and position, forever attending fashionable social events, museum exhibits, benefit balls, holiday galas. Silas Brant's mission was to be a cog in the wheel of that well-oiled society of abundance.

Haddie Kelly Halloran, once again, shifted position in her chair. The very recollection of her interactions with Silias Brant made her skin crawl. She recalled the day he boldly announced he wished to buy her home. The For Sale signs were on the lots, not the entire property. He offered her an outrageously low price for the entire estate. She was enraged.

"I will have nowhere to go." Haddie explained, fighting to keep her temper in check, angered by his brazen offer. "I will not sell, I intend to hold on to my home for as long as I am able." She was adamant.

Mr. Brant was not impressed with her little charade and continued to press the issue.

"Uh, now listen here, young lady." His tone condescending.

Haddie had to bite her lip for fear of saying something she may later regret. The slick little man, clamping a grossly chewed Corona between his stained teeth, continued his proposal, edging in closer to whisper his words, making her almost retch at his putrid breath.

"Uh, how about renting out the, uh, first two floors, uh, to me an' the wife, uh, and my two good girls. Uh, you'd have a nice comfortable monthly income, uh, and still own your own, uh, place."

By offering to occupy the lady's rooms, he would have a foot in the door. Once in, he was sure he could wear her down. He was, after all, a salesman. He should easily be able to purchase the property for very little. The woman was in need. She would be a push over.

What Silas Brant had not counted on, was the iron-willed lady in mention. She was not the easy target he was counting on.

If he would come back in the morning, she would give him her decision.

Haddie had watched as he rounded the corner and she immediately removed the For Sale signs from the lots. She would give in to his proposal to rent her home. In that way, she could hold on to her property. The cash from rent and a few piano lessons would be adequate to assuage her current needs.

Her answer was without frills.

Yes. She would rent the downstairs rooms for one year; no, the lots were no longer for sale.

Haddie, with little other choice, agreed to the distasteful arrangement, holding him to a one year contract in hopes that time would be on her side and she would be able to normalize her life soon.

It was planned that she and her son would take over the now vacant third floor maid's space. The black iron fire escape steps that clung to the side of the building, would be their entrance. She could do nicely with the small kitchen facilities and tiny closets for, hopefully, the short term of necessity.

With heavy heart, Haddie left her spacious, luxuriously appointed lower floors in the hands of this unpleasant man. She insisted on keeping the master suite under lock and key as a private storage area, utilizing every inch of space to safeguard her valuables, leaving the other bedrooms for the small family of four to reside in.

It wasn't until much later, when Haddie could not longer deal with the unscrupulous ways of her tenant, forcing him to leave the premises, that she would discover several of her rare statues and paintings had mysteriously vanished from the secured room. Some pieces of priceless sentimental value, having been chosen by her late husband to commemorate special occasions; birthdays, anniversaries, Christmas. She would have had to become destitute to ever think of parting with them and now they were gone.

One ace card Haddie held in her hand, that Mr. Brant would not get his slimy fingers on, was a golden parcel of land…a prime corner in the downtown shopping district in Providence, one that her father had signed over to her when she married.

"This will be our secret," he lovingly spoke, upon presenting her with the deed to the acreage. "Haddie, my child, I ask of you…" he paused to look straight into her eyes, "…tell no one of this gift. Someday it may be your security. None of us knows what the future holds, what set of circumstances are destined to obstruct our path. You must vow, my dear, never to sell, unless the need is great" he had instructed.

"I won't P'pah," she had promised.

At the time, she did not fully understand his foresight. Her new husband, much older than she, was already a well established lawyer and would, surely, be able to provide a handsome existence for her.

She had faithfully kept the secret promise and now her thoughts wandered back to her father's sagacious words. This property would be her return ticket to "the good life" when the economy righted itself.

People would gradually bolster their income, enabling them more purchasing power. She would patiently wait it out. Someday the land should bring her a healthy return. She would continue to live as parsimoniously as possible, enabling her to stash away a tidy sum for her son's college education. She so desperately wanted him to pursue his musical genius, at Juliard, perhaps, maybe the Royal Conservatory of Music in Naples, or Vienna, wherever his heart led him, as long as he was contented, fulfilled.

Mr. Brant engaged Haddie to give his daughters piano lessons, allotting her a few extra dollars. At first, she felt increasingly uncomfortable in someone else's place. Mr. Brant began to plan his appointments around the times she arrived for lessons. He would sit, like some pompous arch duke, on the red velvet Queen Anne's sofa opposite the piano and spend the entire hour devouring her with his eyes from across the room. His ogling disgusted her!

Haddie's heart went out to the sweet little girls who were forced to persevere, by order of patriarchal decree. She kept them on out of sheer empathy, regardless of their obvious lack of talent, or maybe it was Mrs. Brant that her heart vicariously ached for. She felt such sick pity for the timorous, mousy little thing, who cowered in self-conscious submission, behind the kitchen door, as would a fearful servant under the inflated ego of her controlling master. Often, Haddie would catch a glimpse of the painfully shy woman, crouching near the slit of the barely open door, as she instructed her pupils.

Haddie stood it for several months and under threatening protests from their father, she told the girls that she was going to have the piano transferred to her place on the third floor. They reacted with perplexing pleasure. Lessons would continue as scheduled.

She found movers, willing to work for lean wages, to deliver the Chickering upright to her studio. She would somehow find a way to wedge it in. The shiny black instrument, with it's carved legs and ornate windows, had been a gift from her parents on her tenth birthday. It was her most prized possession. She regarded the high-back, swivel stool as her very own throne.

Unable to maneuver the cumbersome instrument up the particularly narrow staircase, to the top floor apartment, a system of pulleys was concocted. The heavy freight would be hoisted from the outside of the building and guided through a set of long doors that opened onto a parapet.

Curious neighbors began to assemble, fascinated by the operation. After hours of preparation, the ropes hugging the piano were checked for the last time and the upward journey began. Inch by inch it strained toward the sky, slowly, with measured caution. The onlookers, lost in the tenseness of the moment, dared not twitch a muscle, for fear of jinxing the haul.

Success was within inches from it's destination, when one of the over-extended support straps snapped and the massive tonnage plummeted wildly to the ground.

The terrorized crowd expelled a gasp of horror! They froze, paralyzed with disbelief, silent in their helplessness.

Haddie's young son, mesmerized by the workings of the plan, had been standing below totally absorbed in the mechanics of the lift, when the unleashed cargo lunged earthward, instantly crushing his adolescent bones.

With the vivid memory of her husband's tragic suicide still smoldering in her heart, Haddie was dealt yet another ghastly parting.

Her dearest, dearest son...her life. How she had embraced his being, not only as a mother does a child, but also as a fellow artist bursting with the same idealistic fervor and rhapsodic zeal as she. He was her heart of hearts, her true joy. They were fashioned from the same tapestry, savoring the simplest of earth's gifts, needing little more than the power of their music. Something happened to Haddie on that horrible day. She became unfeeling, a wax statue. She treated the death of her son as though it had never occurred.

Haddie was stalwart throughout the entire funeral preparations, valiant in the performance of her duties.

Placid...calm. She was in a place, far beyond the grave, where panic stuns the senses into a stupefied state of nothingness. She was powerless to react to the cries of despair that howled in the deepest chambers of her heart, resounding off it's darkened walls with excruciating pain, begging to be freed. She was incapable of granting herself license to weaken. She could not permit the restorative water of tears to flow.

Her son was gone, her husband gone, her daughter married.

Haddie Kelly Halloran could no longer cope with the Brants occupying her home. Promptly, after their lease was up, Haddie confronted her irksome tenant with departure. He reacted with annoyance. After a last ditch effort to scurrilously berate her, accusing her of being a foolish widow he saw no further purpose wasting precious time in pursuit of a lost cause. The renters departed amidst acid protests. Their paths never crossed again.

Slowly, she re-inhabited her original rooms. Masterfully, she was able to block that shattering black Monday from her mind. She refused to acknowledge the absence of her child, treating the horrendous episode as though it happened to someone else, in a far off part of the universe.

Haddie had deluded herself that her son was alive, joyously performing the challenging movements he had become so proficient at. Somewhere, someone was being impassioned by his profound musical artistry. Dissociation from reality was her sole avenue of survival.

"Hey, Grams." Patrick shook the old lady's arm. "Hey, Grams, the party's over."

She turned to him with a far away look. He noticed the glint of a tear in his grandmother's eye and knew she had been reflecting again on the stages of her life. It always saddened him to see the elderly lady melancholic, but recognized her bouts with the past to be a soothing elixir, a natural part of the aging process.

"C'mon, Grams." Patrick was behind her chair. "Let's turn in. It's been a long day."

After warm exchanges with all present, she and her grandson walked slowly to her private elevator, off the main hall. Her limbs had lost their suppleness and tonight she leaned more heavily then usual, on Patrick's arm. As he pressed the button to engage the small lift, she motioned to him with a lazy wag of her finger, indicating she was not up to their normal late night talk.

"Not tonight, Patrick, dear, I'm tuckered out."

He, as always, respected her plea for privacy.

Patrick left the premises with many mixed thoughts. It was almost midnight before he reached the college campus in Kingston. Tomorrow would be a new day, he would see Angie.

The O'Shays

Patrick's father, John J. O'Shay, enjoyed the fruits of a successful accounting firm, as did his prominent father before him. Patrick's two older brothers dutifully followed in the family tradition, pleasing the "ol' man" by emulating his choice of profession. The pair had made their parents proud by excelling in scholastic pursuits and harvesting cum laude degrees from the highly acclaimed Brown University. They donned solely Brooks Brothers button downs and hobnobbed, by design, at the most prestigious night spots in Providence. Good for business was the private tongue-in-cheek justification for penning large amounts in the company ledger under entertainment.

The O'Shays were blissfully inundated with work, and awake or sleeping, thought of nothing but the business, a family enterprise thriving on the all-consuming pressures of being the best. They were good at what they did and posted fees accordingly.

Heather Halloran O'Shay, Patrick's young looking, fashionable mother, wallowed in the importance of her self-assigned role as head of the firm's public relations. She took the job most seriously, albeit forced to admit, found it at times a trifle harrowing to juggle social gatherings, receptions, trips, business lunches and sundry appointments, in an orderly manner, as to avoid costly conflicts.

Heather O'Shay had no real friends but bragged of hundreds. She instinctively knew all the right contacts in the corporate jungle and saw to it that they were wined and dined royally by the firm of O'Shay and Sons. Mrs. O'Shay was acutely savvy when it came to birthing an impressive guest list, inviting only moneyed names to company functions. These gatherings were considered business affairs and indulged in for the sole purpose of romancing new contacts. Her reputation as the perfect hostess was touted from every corner of the city, a label she wore with gracious acceptance. Heather's personal goal was to lure a few new names each month into the already serried web of illustrious O'Shay clientele.

Patrick, the youngest of the three sons, never felt a part of this structured world of finance. His family had little tolerance for his utter disdain for the accounting world. Numbers, in any form, were alien to him; mathematics being his Waterloo throughout his academic life. Because he managed to maintain above average marks in the majority of his other high school subjects, he was able to gain passage by the skin of his teeth into the state college.

Patrick thought his family resembled the hyperactive little ants in the ant farm he had when he was seven years old. All going every which way at break neck speed, crawling all over each other in a wild frenzy, unaware of whom they were stepping on...driven to get the job done.

Even as a young boy, Patrick had been repelled by the social urgencies that his family was so ruled by. He abhorred the snobbish falsity of an over-crowded cocktail party. It was an effort for him to exchange witless prattle with overdressed strangers, who neither listened to nor valued anything he had to say.

Patrick had always been out of step with his brothers, and finally as an adult realized it really didn't matter. When a youngster, he had been the butt of everyone's joke, religiously told he would never amount to a hill of beans. Through those adolescent years, his behavior was grossly misinterpreted and his poetic soul, inadvertently, trampled on by his naïve siblings.

Even his father, who Patrick admired and silently begged acceptance from, labeled him lazy when he sought quiet space to create his poetry or lift a melody from his guitar.

"Where, in hell, is that sissy stuff going to get you, son?"

John O'Shay could not stomach watching his young son spend, what he considered worthless hours, lounging in a hammock under the oaks.

"Don't you understand?" the older man criticized. "You are squandering your good brain on rhyming a bunch of damn words!" He would shake his graying head in stark disbelief. "Good God, son, how many people do you know who have made their fortune writing poetry or painting pretty pictures? You need to focus your sights on something more substantial. Medicine, law, accounting. Hell! Got a spot right here in the firm just waiting for you. Need to give it some serious thought."

Patrick could feel his father's frustrated disappointment and gleaned that the pursuit of his own innate talents, hardly worthy of praise.

If it had not been for dear Grams, whose honest love had taught him to just slam the door on negative remarks, he would not have survived. She theorized, that it would be beyond the bounds of reason, to assume that those, not possessed with that unexplainable surge within their souls to create, could ever be expected to relate to those who do. It made sense.

Patrick was a romantic and there was no need in the O'Shay accounting firm for dreamers. He knew that he could never entomb himself in such a sterile place. It made his skin crawl. His soul yearned for constant refueling from the glorious gifts of the earth...the sea. He was obsessed, with an overwhelming hunger to consume the wonders of nature and experience first hand, all he could of the planet's offerings.

Grams was right. They, whose very existence depended on antiseptic rows of cold steel cabinets and miles of monotonous numbers, could never fathom his burning need to escape such a smothering atmosphere.

It was impossible, they were of unmatched worlds.

Roommates

Patrick O'Shay was not quite nineteen when he entered Rhode Island College, a small country school, nestled in the sleepy New England town of Kingston. Many of the area's proud inhabitants resided in century old homes flaunting Historical Society plaques boasting their date of birth.

The great majority of first semester freshman vacated the dorms every Friday, after last class, to trek home, all eager for a reassuring hug from their hometown honey or a hearty dose of mom's familiar cooking. Sunday evening witnessed droves of returning students, eager to touch base with their new friends.

The end of the first college year brought remarkable changes. Now, very few students felt the need to leave the campus on weekends. Photos of high school sweethearts were mysteriously absent from old frames and quietly replaced with fresh faces. Over and over, each year, the same drama played out.

Patrick determined early on, that weekends on campus offered him far more satisfaction and time for his creativity. Going home for the few hurried, insipid moments his family could politely eke out for him, away from their over-loaded schedules, was hardly worth the drive.

A perfect crisp, sunny September day welcomed the incoming freshman to the college campus in Kingston. Landscaped grounds, dotted with ivy covered stone buildings, reeked of stability and tradition. An open quadrangle, crisscrossed with ribbons of sidewalk, was fringed with ancient trees that had sheltered many a flirtatious couple from the eagle eyes of a dutiful housemother.

Patrick stood in the winding line of perplexed looking teens, waiting his turn. He was handed a freshman rule book, a green beanie cap and a map that directed him to "Hut City." This affectionate appellation referred to the rows of elongated metal igloos, surplus barracks from the Quonset Navy Base being used as temporary living quarters to accommodate the influx of returning Korean war veterans.

Patrick located his assigned quarters. His bunkmate had already unpacked and settled in.

"Frankie Zaffini." A strapping lad, with an easy smile, extended a hand.

"Hey, Patrick O'Shay here."

"Sorry, you just missed my folks," Frankie spoke.

Patrick couldn't image his own parents leaving the business for a day to see their son off to school.

Even though the two young men were of dissimilar ethnic and financial backgrounds, (Patrick, blue eyed, light skinned Irish...Frankie, dark-eyed, olive skinned Italian) they smoothly fell into the comfortableness of old friends, both attacking life with the ferocity of two boxers facing a championship bout. The two were forever scheming, to out-wit the other with some better-than-the-last-one—gotcha! This nonsensical horseplay was a propitious component of their trust, in which they would come to depend, way beyond the maturity of their years. They were a good match.

Frankie was a listener, Patrick a talker. Frankie allowed Patrick to vent his unending quest for understanding of the world he lived in. He sought answers. Frankie, on the other hand, took each day in order, resigned to the fact that the days unfolded the way God meant them to, one after the other. You took it as it came. No questions.

"Life plays by some pretty screwy rules," Patrick would agitate, a topic he and Frankie regularly kicked around. Patrick, ceaseless in his probing for understanding, struggled desperately to justify the unfairness of human existence.

Here he was, with a father successful enough to send an army to Ivy League colleges and his own son, finding it strangling to cope with the demands of academia. And then there were guys like Frankie, with a hard working father, who could not afford to send all of his eight children on to higher education. Frankie struggled every hour to juggle part-time work with studies, determined to stay in school.

The consistency of injustice festered in Patrick's soul, playing havoc with his psyche. What was it all about? Would he ever know?

Patrick was comfortable in his honesty with his friend and relaxed in airing his frustrations during great talk sessions, involving common issues.

Frankie was one of six brothers and two sisters. His oldest brother, a priest, his youngest sister, a nun. Patrick thought it a sinful waste, for young budding adults to join a holy order, before they were old enough to know what life was all about; or bury themselves behind the walls of a convent, never to be tested or taught by the apprenticeship of human experience, before they were shrouded in the strict teachings of an ancient religion. He didn't get it.

"Hey, Frankie, I don't understand. Why do you think our church doesn't want priests and nuns to marry? All other religions think marriage is o.k. Seems to be a normal thing."

"Eh! How am I suppose to know that?" Frankie used his hands in emphasis.

"Have you ever thought of becoming a priest?"

"Me? Naw, I never had the calling. Either ya have it, or ya don't. My brother said he always knew that's what he wanted to do. Mama says it's all by God's design. He's got a master plan or somethin' an' we gotta carry out His will, while we're down here."

Frankie accepted the inflexible faith of his parents, with ease and strength. *Just like Grams*, Patrick thought.

"But don't you think God would be insulted to have man, His genius creation, turn against His blueprint to 'propagate the faith'?" Patrick searched for answers. "What do you make of this celibacy thing?" Patrick was relentless, knowing that he could never opt for such a restrictive life.

Frankie laughed. "Never thought much about it." He stopped polishing his one pair of Sunday shoes and looked at Patrick. "I guess if you have the calling, it's all a parta what ya gotta do."

He threw his arms up in mock despair, one hand shod with a shiny black loafer. "Eh! Whatta I know?"

"It doesn't make sense," Patrick baited.

"Hey, Pat! Write a letter to the Pope!"

They would change the subject from religion to politics, to girls, to family, to books. They were just as relaxed with each other, within the heat of a good argument, or in total silence; listening to music or lost in their studies; wrestling on the grassed quadrangle or shooting hoops in the gym, all the factors imperative to satiate the voracious appetites of the young.

Patrick accepted Frankie's invitation to visit his home in Providence, on "the Hill," to meet his parents and his beloved Tomasina. Frankie would marry his "forever" girlfriend, as soon as he was out of school and had a job. Since they were children, it was taken for granted, that the two would wed as decreed by two sets of loving parents, who approved of their similar Italian heritage.

Patrick was immediately welcomed into the large, loving Zaffini family. He went home with Frankie, as often as possible, and each time, came away with a rejuvenation of his spirit. The extraordinary celebration of life, that lived within the hearts of this vivacious family, cloaked Patrick with a sense of worth.

Mr. Sams

With the completion of freshman year, Frankie went back to Providence to work in the family trattoria for the summer. Patrick stayed on campus and registered for the three month art program. He was one of the eight, hand-picked, students granted a space in the coveted water-color class, taught by Professor Sams.

Many fledglings, not savvy to Mr. Sams' reputation, signed up for his art workshops to glean easy credits. To their dismay, the so-called "cake course" covered a formidable amount of material. Hours of serious work were required, just to complete the studies. Most would never see that illusive "A." The popular instructor reserved that grade for a thimble full of deserving talents.

Mr. Sams was dedicated solely to his profession. He never married. He had no ties. Living a frugal existence, seemed to suit him just fine. His students were his family...art, his love.

The aging professor was a humble man. He required little to fulfill his worldly needs and presented himself much resembling a hamper of rumpled clothes.   What little hair he had left, formed a low ruff for a balding dome. His beard, thick and white. In his clenched teeth, always an unlit pipe. That was his signature.

But when it came to his professional goals, Mr. Sams pushed himself to the breaking point. He was well-liked and admired by colleagues and students alike.

As the summer progressed, Patrick and the professor became fast friends. The older man opened his home studio to his young protégé.

Here they had license to interact for hours over the world of art, experimenting with new ideas and techniques.

After the intense morning sessions in the college art program, Patrick spent the afternoons outdoors. He was bewitched by the peaceful, untouched ambience of the town of Kingston and spent the summer capturing on paper, its raw natural beauty through his poems and paintings.

He wandered down winding back roads, onto fields, across streams, over ancient stone walls and into grassy pastures. He explored tilting barns, meandered through apple orchards, raced between rows of tasseled corn stalks, dodged among knee high doilies of Queen Anne's Lace, always searching for the right lighting, the perfect angle.

Patrick luxuriated in the intoxicating perfume of purple lilacs spilling over a split rail fence. He sketched trellises masterfully woven with flowering vines of honeysuckle that invited him to pluck their fragile yellow blossoms. He smiled as he held the ambrosial drop of honey on the tip of his tongue.

His fingers itched to record every minute architectural detail of a bygone era. He made articulate pencil studies of chimneys fashioned from uneven, molded bricks that had baked in the sun for generations. Green tinted windows with tiny, imperfect panes, hand-hammered copper weathervanes, roof lines with a conglomeration of puzzling gables. Houses that seemed to stretch on forever, with a rambling collection of makeshift additions, intrigued him the most.

Patrick set his easel down wherever his senses led him, often losing all sense of time and reality.

Each New England season held its glory for Patrick, but he was most euphoric celebrating the deliciousness of early summer, a time when the earth came to life. He felt an overwhelming pounding in his chest just to be a part of the magnificent unfolding of the universe.

He wanted to sing, to write, to sketch, to race with the wind, to plunge into the pounding Atlantic surf!

He wanted to taste it all!

Summer's lazy freedom abruptly ended. Fall Semester began with the expected high-intensity chaos of returning students. Frankie and Patrick reconnected and things were back to normal. But not for long.

Only a few weeks into their sophomore year, Frankie's father suffered a debilitating stroke. The young son was called home to help his mother in the trattoria and alleviate the burden of her large family. Frankie was the first among his siblings to attend college and the news was devastating, but his allegiance was to the family. They came first. He had entered the four year program, dedicated to earning a degree. It was a tough blow for Frankie, and Patrick shared the sadness of his good friend's fate.

Little did he know, that he too, was soon to face a life-changing trial of his own.

It was January, just after his return from holiday break. Patrick dragged himself out of bed. His head ached, his body racked with chills and fever. He struggled to wrap himself in a couple of sweaters and a coat and plodded through falling snow to the college infirmary. The small, antiseptic rooms were a frenzy of activity during winter months.

Patrick, in turn, asked the nurse for some stuff for his nose. His self-diagnosis brought him to the conclusion that he had caught the latest flu bug, rampantly infecting the entire campus. Nothing to worry about. Just a nuisance.

After a series, of what he assumed were routine precautionary tests, Patrick was ordered to the local hospital for more work. At first he refused to go.

It was there, that a kindly doctor with somber eyes, informed Patrick that his worst fears had been realized.

Patrick had gone totally berserk in the doctor's office. He could not believe the diagnosis. How could he accept such lunacy?

Dealt with an incurable illness at such a young age was in itself brutal, but to single out one so brimming with promise was incomprehensible!

Patrick relished life and could not justify the logic of a supreme being who would sculpture a gifted creature, like himself, and not allow him the time to develop his skills. His mind was sharp, prolific...and now diseased?

How could this be?

He was only twenty years old.

"WHERE IS YOUR GOD, GRAMS?" he yelled out into the stark room. "WHERE IS HE NOW?"

Surely, this was some kind of cruel joke. But there was no mistaking the x-rays. The doctor said the growth was small and as it grew it would begin to crowd the brain, causing increased pressure. Patrick may experience headaches, nausea...possible weakening in his limbs...altered vision...poor coordination. There would be times of pain...there would be deceiving lulls of normality... it is hard to predict the behavior of the disease.

When the pain became unbearable, he was to call the doctor. That the tumor in his brain was real, inoperable, and would slowly, methodically herald the end of his young life, were the only words the young man heard.

Frankie was not there to vent with. He would not call and burden him with his pain; his friend had his own purgatory to deal with. He would spare aging Grams the anguish of losing her dearest heart. And to introduce the turmoil of a huge dilemma into the precision run lives of his parents was not an option.

He would go it alone.

Parting

The bulk of the Christmas holiday was spent with Grams and visiting Frankie on the other side of the city. During one of the brief meetings with his family, Patrick presented them with his decision to leave college at the end of the year. There was no fanfare, no debate. The blasé reaction of his parents was predictable. They had given up on him, long ago, reluctantly accepting him as is. It was far less fatiguing than the constant prodding to program him into their system. His lifestyle was his choice.

Patrick returned to classes in January without much enthusiasm. He felt obligated to finish out the already paid for term. He forced himself to ignore the secret burden of looming death. It was the only way he could cope. He had never been a quitter, Grams taught him that.

He attacked each day, as if it were his last, and he once again, became exhilarated.

Mr. Sams, knowing how much the young man missed his close friend, made him an offer. To share his rented, century-old home for the last half of the year. Patrick jumped at the opportunity.

Willingly, he worked for Mr. Sams, shoveling snow and cutting wood in the winter; mowing the lawn, raking leaves and switching screens for storm windows, as the warmer months approached. It was a gracious trade-off for room and board.

He took the spare room off the kitchen and was welcome to use the professor's art shed for any of his projects.

Patrick found the aura of the cozy bungalow, blanketed with the warmth of its owner. Ceilings were low, doorways skimpy, floor boards worn and uneven. Furnishings had no rhyme or reason, all haphazardly mingling to offer a harmonious feeling of comfort. The place was alive with a potpourri of scents; old woods, fresh oil paints, shellac, coffee, mothballs, pipe tobacco, fireplace ashes.

The older man needed the young back to maintain the in-need-of-help structure, while the younger was eager to learn the technical skills of his mentor. They both welcomed the friendship. Mr. Sams became the male figure that the boy longed for to approve of his artistic pursuits and foster a belief in himself. Both gained greatly from the union.

The shared haven lasted only three months. It was the professor, who took a turn for the worse. He battled a few sniffles and in days, full blown pneumonia developed. Without a trial period long enough to deal with his sickness, Mr. Sams' life was stolen from him. During a violent coughing spell, he was void of adequate strength to recover, and in the matter of moments was gone.

Patrick who had been the old man's strength, held the near weightless bones cradled in his trembling arms until he was able to exorcize the emotional explosion of disbelief.

After Mr. Sams died, the owners of the quaint little bungalow decided to sell their highly sought after parcel. It was quickly gobbled up by an English professor and his wife, who graciously allowed Patrick to remain in his room until he finished the last few weeks of the scholastic year.

Patrick welcomed the month of May with open arms. No longer would he be forced to agonize over the drone of classes or face the intensity of final exams. His soul had never been overjoyed by organic chemistry, nor was he ever touched in any tender way by dissecting putrid rats in a Bio lab. That was all behind him now. He would celebrate the glorious freedom he was feeling at this moment for as long as he was able.

With Mr. Sams gone, the void in his life without Frankie became more pronounced. He painfully wished his college friend was available as a sounding board or for a spur-of-the-moment jaunt down-the-line for a late night pizza.

In spite of the distance in miles between the two young men, Patrick and Frankie kept in touch as often as time permitted through visits and phone calls. Frankie worked during the day at the family trattoria and went to school at night to achieve his college degree. Patrick applauded his friend's determination to persevere. Frankie had made up his mind that he was going to be a teacher and coach and nothing could deter his mission. Patrick rejoiced for the generation of young hearts whose lives would be touched by this strong, kind, unselfish man.

Things were different now; Patrick's life had become more unpredictable. Sporadic bouts with raging headaches began to surface and any kind of rigid concentration seemed impossible. He had made the right decision to leave campus when he did.

Days were racing by out of control and Patrick had never been so aware of time passing.

Time, precious time.

He decided that he would not seek out any new friendships. His time with Mr. Sams had filled the gap of Frankie's absence and now, to fritter away even an instant of the few apportioned months or years he had left, would be insanity.

He would look for a place to work and reside, perhaps checkout one of the grand old mansions he loved to sketch along the ocean in Narragansett.

Tonight he'd call Angie for a movie.

The Rose Garden

Molly had watched, skeptically curious, from an upstairs bedroom in the main house, as the unfamiliar figure helped himself to an armload of American Beauties. Now, as she cautiously approached him, she noticed with heightened annoyance that he had discriminately chosen to pilfer only the largest, most perfect blossoms. His boldness infuriated her and she started toward him with accelerated speed.

With arms flailing wildly, she came after him, ceasing her tirade only long enough to ring her weathered hands in a newly laundered apron. Wisps of fine gray hair spilled randomly from under the starched white bonnet, undeniably announcing her role as a domestic.

"Wha tin the nem o' Sent Paddy are yar doin' in thar?" the old woman breathlessly shouted. Molly McGeehy verbally accosted the young stranger, who assumed he was well camouflaged among the towering hedges that boarded the estate's rose gardens. "Remove yarself et once, go on now, let me git a look at ya." The elderly maid was visibly shaken by the presence of the uninvited guest.

Startled by the abrupt intrusion into his tranquil mood, Patrick Sean O'Shay jerked straight up. He took immediate inventory of his surroundings in an attempt to locate the source of disruption. He could not believe his eyes, for standing before him was a tiny lady no taller than a leprechaun. Where had she come from? When Patrick had squeezed through the tall, thick hedges, he had assumed the big vacation house on the ocean was still vacant. He was unaware that the servant staff had arrived early to begin preparing the estate for its summer inhabitants.

For an instant, he was overpowered with the strange sensation of having touched this little lady's life before. The warmth of instant recognition bathed his being and he found himself puzzled at the peculiar effect she had on him.

He stood, mesmerized for a moment, studying his sprightly four foot, ten inch assailant, with measured interest, as she stormed closer toward him, continuing to loudly dishonor his character. She was, indeed, a feisty one!

Patrick continued to study the lined face, somewhat amazed by her courage. Her voice became higher and higher pitched, as she persisted in her animated scolding.

"Go on now, shoo! shoo!" waving him off with the back of her hand.

Molly was now threatening to sic Poochy after him, if he was not gone from the premises immediately.

Patrick, a well muscled, five foot eleven, was not terribly daunted by the vision of being viciously attacked by Poochy, the fluffy white puppy of about eight months, playfully nipping at his heels. The frisky little whelp, energetically wagging his tail at the prospect of a new playmate, hardly appeared to have savage combat on his mind. Patrick found the whole scenario rather comical but remained expressionless.

Molly had no way of knowing what she had taken on in confronting this rugged young man. How could she know that Patrick was a born charmer and no match for an inexperienced spinstress. Although, to his credit, and in spite of his inherent appeal, he had remained remarkably unspoiled.

In spite of her feigned rage, it did not take Molly McGeehy more than a close glance into those "laughin' blues" to find herself stricken with the inevitable fate of being a wee bit bewitched by the magic of this beguiling thief.

She had a forgiving heart and could feel herself softening in his presence, but was honor bound to rid her Lady's beloved rose garden of its bold intruder. She gathered her wits and continued her aggressive pursuit with a barrage of idle threats. Again, mustering up her sternest voice, she asked what in hell's fire did he think he was doing in there?

"Borrowing a few of your roses, Ma'am" Patrick deliberately flustered her, using blatant honesty, while playfully weakening her defenses with his most seductive grin.

"Well now, ain't ya' a cocky bloke!" evaluated Molly. She instantly reassessed her observation, rationalizing that he could hardly be so terrible a lad, having such a forthright manner about him, now, could he?

"Borrowin' tis it!" Molly mimicked. "Well, yar should be 'shamed o' yarself! An' on a holy Sund'y." She fought hard to maintain her authoritative posture, hoping to inflict a lofty impression on the self-confident vagrant.

"Yes, Ma'am, I did a terrible thing." Patrick played his part skillfully. With mock remorse, he hung his head, keeping watch on her reaction through half lowered lids. He was an adept performer and she was coming unglued under his spell. Patrick slowly lifted his head and with all the visible humility he could muster, gazed at Molly, who by now was completely befuddled by his sudden act of contrition.

He slowly approached her in a manner most disarming. The poor old servantess involuntarily stepped backwards. She looked up at him in questioning astonishment.

"I'd like to take on some temporary work here in payment for the damages" he offered in a humble tone, one arm outstretched in surrender, the other guarding the magnificent bouquet.

"Wal, would yar now" Molly stalled "'nd jest what was it yar had in yar mind t' be doin'?" she quizzed, hands perched on her hips.

"It seems to me you could use some help around here" commented Patrick tongue-in-cheek, toeing a clump of hearty weeds that had bravely chosen the pathway to boast their tenacity. The grounds were left casually groomed in the winter months when the home was unoccupied. "I could hire on a few days a week as a gardener, handyman, wherever I'm needed" he shrugged his shoulders. There was that devastating half-cocked smile again.

"Just one condition." He toyed with her, holding up his index finger and giving his head a slight tilt. "At the end of each week, one dozen roses be included as part of my pay."

Patrick did not deem it necessary to tell Molly that the flowers were for his friend Angie, a tantalizing little barmaid he had befriended in Narragansett at one of the "in town" taverns. Angie was all too willing to ply him with her flirtatious skills, laced periodically with a bit of mindless conversation.

"So yar wantin' wark, now, ah yar?" Molly queried. The audacity of him! She was dumfounded at what she misinterpreted as unabashed arrogance. Imagine, offering to make a deal, after deliberately stealing the flowers.

She was intrigued by his offer and tactfully agreed that some sort of retribution for "borrowing" was certainly in order.

"I'd be willin' ta bring yar proposal to the attention o' the' "missus" 'n if yar'd be up ta comin' 'round a week from t'morro' t' th' service door," she waved haphazardly in the direction of the gracious old home, "I'd be able to give yar th' word."

"Thank you, Ma'am."

Patrick mischievously chucked Molly under the chin and commenced to walk backwards, slowly retreating from the scene. He held her eyes in his, bathing the older woman with a soft hypnotic gaze, leaving her old heart pumping much faster than it had in years.

"Scoundrel!" she accused, when he was out of earshot, secretly wishing that she was forty years younger. With a resigned sigh, she scooped up Poochy, in her pudgy arms, and languidly retraced her steps through the fragrant gardens that returned her to the cottage.

Before going in to rejoin the others in readying the old mansion for the arrival of its New York owners, Molly meandered back to the small kitchen porch that faced the carriage house. She slowly sunk into a badly warped, wicker rocker, lodging her fleshy buttocks into the worn, concave seat. Poochy, never one to miss an opportunity to rock, jumped up onto Molly's inviting lap and wiggled himself cozily into the folds of her apron. Molly had been entrusted with the care of Poochy, until his mistress arrived at the end of the week, so he could get acquainted with his new surroundings before the summer festivities began. They were fast becoming tight buddies, relishing their time together.

As Molly closed her eyes, mesmerized by the rocker's lazy motion, nostalgia gripped her heart. She was transported back in time to another era and another vibrant young man. Patrick Sean O'Shay had brought back memories of her own green years, when she had fallen in love with the carriage boy. A smile rearranged her lined face as she remembered her dear Roberto, her "Roman God." Molly smiled, recalling how she and Roberto would meet after work, or on days off, and covertly sneak off to romp light-heartedly over these very acres, years before any of the rose gardens were designed.

Roberto was the brother of Angelo, the gardener. They had been hired on about the same time she was, so many, many years ago. Angelo, too, had remained single all these years. They had become the dearest of friends and grown old together, with the silent memory of Roberto as the glue of their devotion.

Sweet sadness befell her. Her hand involuntarily reached for the silver ring pinned to her under linen. No one knew of the tiny silver wreath— not even the "Missus." It was her private bittersweet memory and to share it would lessen its dearness. Roberto had pounded the circle out of a silver coin and pains-takingly etched their initials in it with the tip of a nail. It was a crude job, but to Molly it was more precious than the most prized jewel. They would pretend marriage ceremonies with it, planning that someday, when Roberto could afford to support her, they would wed.

Roberto had loved to gather lavish bouquets of whatever wild flowers were showing off their blooms at the moment. He knew her favorite was Queen Anne's Lace and made sure those were among his offering. Molly would laugh as she watched him pluck the flowers so swiftly from the earth that often clumps of dangling roots came up along with the flowers. He would invite her to sit on her "throne" a mammoth flat rock in the corner of the meadow and await his return. Years later, when Angelo planned the rose gardens, he used her royal throne as a fitting cornerstone.

When his arms could not hold another blossom, Roberto would run to her and with a low bow, present her with the huge harvest.

Amidst her giggling, he lyrically proposed to her in grand, flowery speech, like a proper gentleman. He would sing to her in his booming tenor voice and she would try, in vain, to hush him, for fear someone would come running, thinking she was being assaulted. They stole kisses with exaggerated passion, stopping as quickly as they had begun, afraid of being discovered.

Lazy summer days were theirs, spent in search of four leaf clovers or white butterflies or lying on their backs intrigued by the ever changing cloud formations that would constantly amuse them with new configurations. Such a simple, uncomplicated time, so sweet and innocent. *Not a'tall like the youn'uns t'day juttin' 'bout in cars, doin' Lord knows what,* thought Molly, "s' bold 'nd forward."

All Molly had left of those gentle days in the sun was a small picture of her beloved proudly posed on the seat of a black lacquered carriage, a yellowing stack of handwritten poems, the fragile remains of a few stems of Queen Anne's Lace and a ring, too inelegant to wear. They were her link to the past, they were all she needed. These memories of her dear Roberto had nourished her being over the past forty-five or so years.

Molly shook her head. His death had been untimely...so senseless.

It was July 1st, a date emblazoned in her memory. Roberto was twenty-one years old. He, and three of the stable boys, had guided four horses out to the back fields for another practice run before the fourth of July parade. He had wanted to hitch them up one last time, to be sure they were comfortable being part of a team. While maneuvering the huge animals through their paces, two abreast, one of the front prancers stepped into a narrow hole in the turf, twisting an ankle and plummeted to the ground. As the horse lurched toward the earth, the other three animals, all tethered together by their harnesses, spilled helplessly down on top of each other. It was bedlam! The weighty beasts thrashed about, writhing and wailing in wild terror, becoming more and more entangled in a sea of twisted reins. They were helpless in their exhaustive efforts to right themselves, a pitiful sight. It had all happened so quickly that Roberto and the others were stunned!

Roberto, a master equestrian, thinking only to save the valuable animals, jumped onto the back of one of the victims in a futile attempt to untangle the maze of leather strips. In his struggle, he lost his footing on the slick coated beast and was hurled into a frenzied bed of strangling horses. His head caught the powerful blow from a hammering hoof and he died instantly.

Molly had mourned for months, feeling like a grieving widow. Laughter had left her life and she was sure she was doomed to 'an existence of melancholy.

The depth of love she had felt for Roberto could, surely, be offered only once in one's lifetime and she resigned herself to its loving, romantic memory, becoming sweeter as the years passed. Although she was only twenty years old when the tragedy struck, and several suitors followed, her heart never betrayed the solemn vows exchanged at the alter of her youth. She regretted nothing.

Poochy reared his head to scratch his ear and stirred Molly out of her daydream. With wistful sentiment bursting in her heart she slowly opened her eyes. "Ol'right, lit'el one, let's go round a bit, eh?" She stopped rocking and gently shoved Poochy off her lap. Getting up slowly, Molly decided to stroll around the cottage awhile before going in.

As she walked, she gazed lovingly up at the intriguing gables and masterful chimneys of the regal old New England lady, towering above her. It always humored Molly to think that these huge summer mansions were called "cottages," regardless of their enormous proportions. The sacred parcels of prime waterfront property, anchored securely to the great Atlantic Ocean, had become not only excessively valuable, but rarely available. They had been occupied by the same blood line for generations and to find a crack in the lineage, was short of miraculous.

As she wandered slowly around the rambling old homestead, she basked in the feeling of belonging. She loved the old frame structure, wrapped snugly in its blanket of weathered shakes. Time had turned the siding into a myriad of tawny browns and grays, resembling the coat of a calico cat. Molly thanked God for allowing her the time to share in its glory. This had been home to her for as many summers as she could recall and the Huntingwells were her family. She had served them well, with pride and love, for years beginning with the master's mother. Molly was only eighteen years old when she first came from Ireland to America. Where had the years gone? It had been her first real job and she dearly loved the "old" Mrs. Huntingwell. They seemed to take to each other immediately and Molly was quickly appointed as the madam's personal maid, a position she held until Mrs. Huntingwell's death. She now performed the same role, also with great love and respect, for the new lady of the house, Prunella Catherine Huntingwell, who was, without question, in every sense of the word, a lady.

Molly had strolled quite a way under a lilac-laden arbor that guided her lazily to the ocean side of the cottage. As she rounded the corner, a warm puff of salty sea breeze gently kissed her cheeks, a familiar experience, and one most welcomed after a long harsh New York winter.

Miles of an extraordinary wide veranda came into view. This was one of Molly's most longed-for places in the whole world. Of course, "the help" was not privy to the front part of the mansion "during the season" but this week, before anyone arrived, the staff took well earned advantage of the restful setting.

In season, the veranda was fully appointed with a multitude of white wicker chairs and lounges, upholstered with over-stuffed, green and white striped canvas cushions. There was a ping-pong table at one end and a fully stocked bar at the other. Assorted large brass planters spilled over with a variety of unusual ferns and several card tables were set, at random, to accommodate the bridge enthusiasts. A good deal of socializing was enjoyed here and one could only imagine how many business deals might have been cemented over a cool gin and tonic.

Impressively wide steps of chiseled stone poured out onto the grand expanse of immaculately manicured grounds. The velvet lawn was impeccable, thanks to Angelo, who pridefully tended the greens, as one would a loving child. He was a quiet man and felt awkward when shyly accepting excessive compliments for his tireless endeavors. This pampered lawn would soon be host to friendly bouts of croquet, lawn bowling and ring toss. A badminton net would be erected, farther away on the property, for instant play. Participating would be for the more energetic souls, who might have spent a good deal of the morning in bed, "resting up" for the afternoon activities.

Shuffleboard courts were within viewing distance of the veranda so they could be witnessed by late afternoon guests, upon returning from a vigorous swim at the Dunes Club, a grass court tennis match or a competitive round of golf at the Point Judith County Club.

Molly looked up at the most popular focal point of conversation for all Sweetmeadow guests; a powerful telescope mounted, on the wide railing of the porch. It was strategically placed for the sole pleasure of the "out-of-towners" some of whom had rare opportunity to peruse the ocean. Sightseers were always in awe of the immensity of the blue-green Atlantic and the glory of its endless horizon. Huge cargo ships, resembling tiny toy boats in the distance, would grace the waters to the delight of the viewer. Flocks of sea birds lazily drifted into the lens, flaunting their precision maneuvers. Through the scope, one could drink in the full glory of a spectacular sunrise or glimpse into the private world of the shell seekers, who precariously scaled the mammoth rock formations, sandwiched between the regal lawn and the vast ocean. It was carefully planned, by Mrs. Huntingwell, that every taste be accommodated. No one ever left Sweetmeadow with empty memories. If a good time was not had, one could only blame one's self.

Molly viewed the sprawling grounds and never ceased to be astounded at the display of wealth all about her. Imported works of sculpture mounted on marble pedestals, giant mosaic urns, the imposing reflecting pool, set in the center of a parterres enhanced by three frolicking maidens, whose larger-than-life breasts exuded steady streams of water into a scalloped basin. Molly found herself wanting to clothe the bevy of naked ladies that graced the huge shell.

Year after year, the servant staff, (all except Nigel, the butler, who remained to help with last minute details in the city) had driven down the east coast, from New York to Rhode Island, one week early to "open the cottage" in Narragansett. Upon arrival, they went to work immediately, like an army of ants. Protective sheets were removed from antique furniture, pantries refilled, bars restocked, windows unstuck, brass polished, wooden floors waxed, beds made, porch furniture taken down from the storage attic, green shutters repainted, plumbing checked out, hedges clipped, lawns mowed. They saw to it that the hand-cut crystal vases, adorning every room, were filled with fresh flowers, for the guest's arrival. But most importantly, the correct toiletries must be placed in the proper baths. The "missus" favored violet scented soaps brought from England, the master was partial to 4711 cologne. The rose wallpapered guest room was scheduled to be occupied by Mrs. Townsend, who used nothing but lily-of-the-valley bath oil and the yellow room was to be host to the Smythes, who were allergic to everything and needed plain, unperfumed soaps. And on and on it went.

It was the same ritual, summer after summer and the whole process was amazingly well executed. The staff remained virtually unchanged for years, with very few exceptions. They were treated well and in turn, bore a passionate allegiance to their mentors.

Molly, slowly, mounted the stone steps leading onto the lovely "piazza" as Angelo called it. At the top, she paused to take an inventory of the premises. Her eyes swept the perimeter of the property that had, purposely, been left in its natural wild state for the sole purpose of shielding the impressive residence from public scrutiny. Guests were welcomed by a tall scrolled iron gate, a well trained security guard, and a pair of not-too-friendly looking Dobermans.

Molly inhaled a deep, satisfying breath of clean ocean air. "'Nough lollygagging," she assessed. In just a few days, this quiet haven would be teaming with a myriad of chattering guests and bursting with activity. She suddenly felt the need to try to move her bones a bit more energetically. After a moment of wrestling with the heavy keys, she found the correct one to gain entrance through the large paneled walnut door. Poochy, seeming to know he was not allowed on the Persian rugs in the main hall, whimpered to be picked up.

Once inside, Molly's thoughts automatically switched back to the chores she had set out to accomplish, before her disrupting encounter with the intriguing rose thief. With the thoughts of Patrick on her mind, she poked up the stairs and slowly went about unlatching the tall windows. A few did not budge and would need stronger hands to loosen. The fresh sea air burst through the large rooms, ridding the stuffiness from a long winter's sleep. As she hiked up the last willing window in the master's bedroom overlooking the rose gardens, she paused to reflect on the intriguing stranger.

Was it her imagination, or were the roses a bit more fragrant than usual this year?

No Strings

Patrick bolted through the scuffed-up barroom doors, like some high-spirited thoroughbred exploding from the starting gate. He barged directly into a noisy, smoke filled room and firmly planted his feet on the sticky, uneven floor boards. His eyes shot around the stuffy, over-crowded saloon, frantically scanning the mass of animated faces for Angie. He needn't have bothered, for she had immediately spotted him and was up on her tiptoes, vigorously waving a hand over the sea of bobbing heads, in an effort to catch his attention.

Angie kept her eyes riveted in his direction as she started to maneuver her way through the jostling bodies. Her heart raced with longing, as it always did, when she hadn't seen him for a few days, and she could feel a spontaneous rush rumble through her veins.

"Keep cool girl, keep cool" she scolded herself, hating the uncontrollable effect he had on her. The fever of emotion watered her eyes and a hot flush of desire reddened her cheeks, blatantly announcing her inner stirrings. When they were apart, Angie vowed to keep better check on her heart strings, disciplining herself to feel nothing, but each time she saw him, all of her strictest oaths dissipated into vapors of good intentions.

Patrick caught sight of her being rhythmically tossed through the throng in every direction. He saluted her with a wave of the battered roses that had suffered a bit of a whiplash en route. He watched humorously, as several unsuspecting "Happy Hour" regulars, who had been imbibing just long enough, did not question why their heads were being ingratiated with a shower of rose petals.

As Patrick fidgeted impatiently, watching Angie battle her way through the human maze, he wondered why anyone would willfully migrate to this seedy little bar. His nostrils were battered with the pungent smell of ale, mingled with a nauseating odor of rancid popcorn oil and a floor strewn with peanut shells, jarring Patrick's sense of the aesthetic. He could hardly force himself to breath in the acrid fumes. The few tiny tables were totally obscured from view by the packed-in-like-sardines patrons.

No one seemed to be sharing any kind of meaningful conversation, the hottest topics of the day being the results of the latest athletic battles. It was a mystery to Patrick why all these seemingly intelligent minds, so willingly entombed themselves in a dark stifling cubicle, only to retreat into a semi-comatose state of consciousness for extended periods of time. He flippantly concluded, that in some maniacal way, this "standing room only" round-up, might offer the participant an unexplainable sense of belonging to the pack, a strange kind of camaraderie, regardless of the stagnant quality of interaction. The whole concept baffled him.

Today the pub was overrun with lazy, sunburned collegians, who had spent the better part of the day basking on the beach, interspersed with a few scattered locals, who kept pretty much to themselves. Occasionally, a fight would ensue between some possessive fraternity jock and a local "townie" hot-shot, bravado enough to flex his muscles for the attentions of the already attached coed.

Most of the tavern's clientele were from the newly accredited University of Rhode Island, juniors and seniors of drinking age, or service men just back from the Korean War, who were taking Uncle Sam up on his offer for a college education under the G.I. Bill. All were enrolled in the summer sessions for one of two reasons. Either to procure extra credits for early graduation or to make up courses they had failed during the regular academic semester. Angie finally broke free from the swarming mob, to join Patrick in a tiny airless corner of the room. She noticed his face, shiny with sweat and sporting that wonderful crooked grin that invariably turned her knees to jelly. Patrick didn't give her the usual hug. Instead, without a word, he grabbed her hand and led her out through the swinging doors, onto a wide open porch that was virtually empty, except for another couple at the opposite end, too absorbed in their own interaction, to notice their intruders.

"Hi love!" Using the term lightly, Patrick gave the shapely bar maid the expected powerful hug and playfully swung her around in his rugged arms. It secretly puffed up his ego, to know, that no matter how busy she was or who she was with, she always had a few moments reserved for him alone. As he twirled her about, pressing the warm curves of her body snugly into his own, he was filled with the instant pleasure of familiarity. How comfortable he was with her. She had generously accepted him on his terms, as is, unconditionally, and for that, he was humbly grateful.

Angie knew that Patrick loved her, in his own inimitable fashion, but she was, also, acutely aware that he was not "in love" with her and often wondered if he ever would be. Theirs was a union built on frivolity...light-hearted, joyful and in no way, serious or binding. Patrick had set the ground rules from the very beginning and she, in a moment of unthinking weakness, had carelessly agreed to them. As the weeks formed months, a deeper longing gnawed at her. Angie knew, that her platonic friend had metamorphosed into the one great love of her life and, she feared, would always remain as such. Dear Patrick had unintentionally woven the threads of his being...inextricable ...into the most delicate fibers of her soul.

"DAMN him and his charm." Angie, in silent frustration, berated her own spineless decision to ever enter into such an obstruent relationship. She had tried, endlessly, to fight against staying entrapped in this "no win" situation and questioned how she could have agreed to such a childish arrangement. It angered her, to admit to herself, how helplessly addicted she was to Patrick's unreined independence. He was so annoyingly private!

"No use trying to make any sense of it." Angie relaxed knowing that she wanted him too dearly in her life to risk losing him by some foolish display of romantic adoration. That would suffocate his freedom and drive a wedge between them. She took great care to insulate herself from self-betrayal, resolutely disguising her passion behind a mask of insouciance. She knew that a free spirited kind of relationship with a woman, was all he sought. No strings, no heavy promises, no commitment.

Angie was always pleased with the roses and never failed to make a great fuss over them. Normally, she would spend an inordinate amount of time arranging and rearranging each stem. She kept an ever-ready pewter pitcher, expressly for that purpose, behind the bar, but for now, she demurely offered him a smile of appreciation.

Holding her at arms length, carefully trying not to bore her with too much detail, Patrick laughingly related how he had been "arrested by a frisky, little gray haired lady in the gardens of the old mansion." Angie always enjoyed his yarns, but upon hearing of his latest entanglement, buried her head in his chest and laughed hysterically. She looked up at his sheepish grin and knew he was enjoying her spontaneous reaction.

"After all my warnings," she boastfully teased, "you have finally been caught, red handed with the goods." She backed away with an air of feigned authority. "Now aren't you the naughty, naughty boy" she snickered in fun, shaking a wagging finger close to his face and admonishing him, like a nanny would her tiny child.

Patrick picked up her silly mood and shook a warning finger right back at her, then tossed his unruly head of hair back with abandon and willingly shared a good laugh.

He was such a cut-up and how she loved him! She would have given her birthright for a tiny drop of returned love, real love, just a drop.

It was all so ludicrous, for what Angie did not know was the unpalatable truth. That Patrick Sean O'Shay, the love of her world, was sentenced to a short life of imprisonment, of pain, of early death. But revealing his illness to Angie, or anyone else, would serve no purpose.

Hitch-hiker

Monday morning.

Early, very early...fog, dangerously dense...air heavy, wet. "Thick as pea soup" the old timers would say.

Patrick stood witness, as the willful dawn ruptured the veil of darkness to begin a new day. He had waited for over an hour.

It had been pitch black, when he was jolted from under his covers, by the piercing revelry of his bedside clock. There was no way that Patrick was going to chance being late for his job interview, at Sweetmeadow Estate. He had consciously metered out a substantial block of time to shave and shower. He had donned a pair of crisp suntans and had checked his white bucks for scuffs before taking to the road.

Patrick allowed plenty of leeway for any unforeseen mishaps that might alter his plans for a prompt arrival at the mansion. His scheduled meeting with Mrs. Huntingwell was not until 10:00 a.m. He had to rely on the luck of hitch-hiking and from past experience, Patrick knew all too well, how chanceful the prospect of a good ride was.

At the crossroads, Patrick leaned against the town's gazebo. His senses were keenly alerted to any signs of oncoming traffic and he was ready to thrust out a thumb toward the first good Samaritan, willing to risk taking on a stranger in this soupy atmosphere. Visibility was poor, almost non-existent. Patrick's form melded into the distorted shapes and silhouettes of his surroundings. It would be short of a miracle to be seen by a motorist in these opaque conditions.

"Thumbing" was a common practice among the college crowd in the protected academic community. The conscientious faculty frowned upon the practice of hitch-hiking and diligently warned of its' abhorrent dangers.

After what seemed an endless wait, Patrick's ears became sensitive to the reality of a mysterious vehicle, spewing forth an indescribable concoction of noises. He was aware of its presence, long before his eyes were able to discern its shape.

Straining his vision, Patrick squinted through the fog patches for any familiar signs of recognition. He remained baffled by the cacophony of jarring sounds that spat out into the still air, offending the morning quietude, with a bombardment of outbursts.

"Good God!" Patrick winced.

He was more than intrigued. Hands on hips, legs apart, he remained motionless, mesmerized by his own bewilderment.

From a distant hill, two weak beams of light tunneled through the mist, sending their wobbly rays ahead, as if to herald the approach of some strange, foreboding creature.

Seconds later, the bazaar looking apparition became slightly visible. It shrugged on at a snails' pace...a wounded, yellow-eyed monster...laboring through a wall of grayish-white vapors, while ceremoniously escorted by erratic clouds of fog taking on the aura of swirling ancient ghosts.

Onward it struggled. Slowly, slowly. Closer, closer, deliberately maneuvering straight at him, seeming to target him straight on.

"What the hell!"

Patrick, who moments before had hoped for an opportunity to arrive in Narragansett on time for his interview, was now focused on pure survival. With caution, he stepped off the slippery road onto the dirt shoulder, to avoid being bulldozed down by whatever this thing was that was obviously bent on obliterating him.

Tilting from side to side, on four skinny wheels, the vehicle rumbled to a stop several yards beyond him, shivering and choking, in a valiant effort to stay alive.

Patrick walked tentatively toward the quivering heap. He smiled to himself, when on closer inspection, judged it to be some sort of homemade truck, virtually held together with a thick frayed rope and some rusty chains.

As he approached the passenger side, he noticed through the door's missing window, a naked cushion of corroded springs, evidence that an upholstered seat once graced the space. Patrick crooked his neck low enough to peer through the door's glassless frame, in a curious effort to peruse the driver. What kind of being would dare to get behind the wheel of this clunk and have the raw courage to challenge its might?

Patrick met with a pair of friendly blue eyes, nested in a bewhiskered, leather face, the familiar look of a local fisherman. The amiable man, a plug of tobacco distorting his weathered cheek, honored him with a broad, juicy grin. As the man leaned toward him, to extend his noble invitation, Patrick reeled from the stench.

"Hop 'board, Mate." With an extended thumb, he motioned to the back of the truck.

The discordant sounds, emanating from under the vibrating tin hood, were deafening, almost drowning out his words.

"How far down are you going?" Patrick inquired, shouting to be heard above the clamor.

"'T' Salt Pond. Gonna tread bottom for some 'haugs', eh yuh," the old gent offered.

Patrick was quite familiar with the large, thick-shelled clams that dwelled in the soft, mucky bottom of the salt water pond. The quahaugs or "haughs" were harvested by the local families and fishermen. The simplest way of finding them, was at low tide, feeling the mud-crusted creatures with your feet.

Patrick had a split second visual recall of his first 'Haug hunt'...the art of quahauging. Frankie had invited him to spend a summer weekend with him and his family, at their fishing shack.

After an energetic morning of bending and scooping, the shells were brushed and the catch turned over to Frankie's mama. A blue spattered enamel pot was in readiness, the water ferociously boiling. With her long-handled wooden spoon, she quickly transferred the tightly closed quahaugs into the gigantic vessel, taking great caution to steam only until the shells opened, not to overcook and render the meat tough. The sweet, salty steam that escaped from the kettle wafted through the kitchen, tantalizing appetites. Every drop of the precious liquid was used to enhance Mama Zaffino's "sugo" or put away for another day's chowder.

The boys were delegated to remove the sweet meat from the hot, open shells, into a large ceramic bowl. Then Mama Zaffino would scoop up a handful of the plump morsels and with a tiny pair of scissors in her free hand, deftly snip the flesh into irregular chunks.

Patrick and Frankie watched, salivating, as she ceremoniously dropped the tender jewels into a lazy, simmering concoction of fresh tomatoes, fresh garlic, olive oil, a whisper of oregano and just enough salty broth to enhance the flavor of her sauce.

Mama Zaff' made sure all were properly seated before she presented them with the glorious platter of fat, homemade fettuccini, regally robed in her famous quahaug sauce.

She held a hefty chunk of reggiano parmegiano, covered on one end with a linen napkin and swiftly grated a generous portion of the sharp tasting cheese over an incredible mountain of piping hot pasta. The flavors of seafood, tomato, and garlic all mingled to produce the most enticing aroma Patrick had ever experienced.

Mama would disappear into the kitchen, long enough to remove her apron and return to the table with infectious exuberance. Her happiest time, was feeding the family...her way of offering them her silent love. Patrick remembered smiling, as Mama proclaimed, in her broken English, that it was only a simple "peasant disha" But for those who partook of its richness, it was a dish fit for a king.

Patrick was snapped back to the reality of the moment, by the old man's raspy voice hanging in the heavy air, still insisting on the spaciousness of the open area in the back of the make-shift truck.

"Eh yuh. Plenty o'room, eh yuh, sure is" motioning again, with a blackened thumb, to the rear.

Patrick was able to take a quick inventory of the vehicle's contents as the rickety jalopy chugged by him moments before. Now, he took a few steps back for closer inspection.

The cavity was crammed with an uncanny mass of fishing gear, dented pails, nets in all stages of repair, traps, rusty hinged boxes, coils of rope, a gaff, a tattered slicker, shovels, poles, hip boots and a canvas tarp that was tossed haphazardly over the remaining junk.

Before Patrick could rebut the claim of plenty o'room, the old salt persisted once again.

"Hop 'board, mate" he invited as before. "Eh yuh, room 'nuff for a mess o' whales." He tossed his hatted head back, with a self-indulgent chuckle, and continued on, as if talking to himself.

"Eh yuh, move the stuff 'round, fit yerself in, eh yuh, plenty o'room, won't hurt none."

Patrick, for fear of not having another opportunity come his way in this foreboding weather, opted to chance a trip with the two old wrecks.

He grabbed on to the rough splintery boards that fenced in the paraphernalia, flung a leg over the side and tried settling himself, among the grubby rubble, in the least damaging way.

The ol' tub lurched forward. Patrick struggled for balance, as he acknowledged the wave of the man's hand, indicating that all was well up front.

They plodded on for about five minutes, going at an excruciatingly slow speed, almost dying to a stall.

Patrick's hair felt damp. His clothes were wrinkling in the moist air, but he assessed that it was better than walking the six or seven miles.

Thoughts of whether the clunker would make the distance, were intensified, by a new sound that had developed up front.

"Ka-ping, ka-ping, ka-ping."

Patrick peered over the side, in the direction of the disturbance.

"Damnation!" he heard the old man grumble, as he spit a jaw full of amber sputum into the chipped Ball jar that was wedged between a pile of stuff on the floor.

Patrick had been in the process of rearranging his legs, when the old gent applied the breaks to halt his charge, forcing Patrick to cling onto the wobbly side rails, bracing himself.

"Ka-ping, ping, ping, ping."

Silence.

Patrick waited, not daring to ask what was going on. Obviously, the proud chariot had come unglued. He had a fleeting bout with nausea, envisioning arriving three hours late for his interview.

Nice first impression, he thought.

Oh, if Angie could see him now, wouldn't she have a good laugh.

"Dang belt a'gin, eh-yuh, that's it. Jus' fixed er up, too, this mornin' for I come out." He forced open the jammed door with one wham of his elbow. Patrick winced at the screech of rusted hardware.

The fisherman slid off his torn leather seat. Both feet seemed to reach the dirt at the same time. He shuffled toward the smoking hood and lifted up the side closest to him. More piercing shrieks, worse than the first, as the old hinges were forced to move. He peered into the grimy cavity.

"Garl dang it, ol' girl! Now, what in hell's fire ya acting up for?" he spoke to the dying wreck as if berating an uncooperative mistress.

Wagging his head in disgust, he shot another long stream of tobacco juice from between his teeth, calculating it to land an inch from his boots. Patrick, who had leaned his body dangerously over the side, in a vain attempt to assess the damage, narrowly escaped a dousing.

Still shaking his head, the old gent tugged at a dirty rag that hung from the back pocket of his sagging overalls. He proceeded to mop the drops of liquid that escaped the original projectile and adhered to his beard.

"Snapped 'er belt, ey-yuh. That's what she done, ey-yuh." He spoke to the ground, never looking at Patrick. Then sheepishly raised his eyes to the truck, a frown formed on this face.

"Can't ya see we got company ol' girl? That ain't a right proper thing to do now, ey?" As if hoping the clunker would reply, he went on talking, never making eye contact with his guest.

"Just like a woman, this one. Got a mind o' her own, ey-yuh. Does 'xactly as she please, runs good for a while and when it suits 'er, she sure in hell quits. Eh-yuh."

The fisherman raised his hat and scratched his mottled gray hair, in hopes of unleashing some wisdom in dealing with the embarrassing circumstance.

He fiddled with the fan belt until it came loose in his large hand. Clutching the frayed strip and still avoiding direct eye contact with his passenger, he held it high in the air.

"There's 'er problem, eh-yuh, just plumb wore out! Eh-yuh."

Patrick, not particularly savvy to the workings of an engine, inquired "Can you fix it?"

"Aw, garl dang, Mate," holding up the split leather, "see this here? Can't do nothing 'bout that. Got to get 'er to the shop, ey-yuh. That's what I got to do."

Patrick decided to peruse the severity of the damage himself and jumped over the wobbly side of the truck. Inadvertently, he hooked his suntans on a corroded gaff. He heard the tear before he could react.

"DAMN!"

Now he had a two inch tear in the side of his pants. Great! He couldn't concern himself...his most urgent dilemma was getting to his interview on time.

The fisherman felt that he had let his "Mate" down and made the ludicrous decision to continue on the way.

"Hop 'board, Mate, we'll git there, don't y' fret none. Eh-yuh, we'll git there." Choices were non existent. There were no other cars on the road.

On the clunk chugged...clattering...jostling the two occupants from side to side on its four skinny wheels. Through thick fog patches, with zero visibility, on into clearings with open sky. Every few miles the old heap rumbled to a stop.

"Gotta cool 'er down b'fore she can go on, eh-yuh."

Prunella Catherine Huntingwell

The lovely lady stirred, ever so slightly, caressed by white satin sheets, her face half buried in a mound of plump down pillows.

Puffs of early morning air billowed filmy sheers veiling the two large windows, opened just a breath allowing rhythmic sounds of the ocean to lull the senses. Cool, flirtatious breezes wafted over her stillness, lightly kissing any exposed skin, tantalizing her to awaken. Summer mornings by the sea were pure delight.

Prunella Catherine Huntingwell's boudoir was a testimony to her passion for crystal and lace, having garnered a treasure trove of rare pieces, during frequent visits abroad.

The sprawling, all white room was serene, comfortable, inviting and in every detail feminine without the frills. The single interruption, in the hypnotic flow of glacial whiteness, was a tall cut-crystal vase overflowing with roses. Every other day, Angelo cut fresh stems to fill the vessel with near perfect blooms. Today, a massive gathering of the palest pink petals displayed their glory, bathing Prunella Huntingwell in perfume scented air.

Knock, knock, knock.

"Yes?" sleep fighting to keep her hostage.

"Am I too early, Missy?"

"No, no."

Mrs. Huntingwell had slept much later than usual. Rolling over in slow motion onto her back, she raised her alabaster arms up over her head, stretching with measured caution.

"Come in, Molly."

"Mornin' Missus Huntingwell, I'm not disturbin' yeh, 'm I?"

"No, no. I need to get up. There are so many things I must do before the first guests arrive." She stifled a yawn.

"'N' don' ferget the inte'view," Molly reminded.

"Oh, yes. Molly, the interview. The young man."

The handle of a deep wicker basket lined with pink floral chintz was looped over Molly's arm. It was piled high, with an enviable array of luscious lacy things, that had been lovingly laundered by hand, the tiniest ribbons rolled to avoid creases. Piled high in the crook of the other arm, was a stack of white on white monogrammed towels, edged with heavy borders of lace. Over her wrist was hooked a quilted satin hanger, displaying a white silk nightie with ultra thin straps, an insert of Belgian lace, a rolled silk rose at the base of the v-neck. Sumptuous lingerie was one of Prunella Huntingwell's addictions.

The younger domestics delighted in peering over Molly's shoulders, as she meticulously rinsed out one heavenly creation after another.

"Oh-h-h-h, look at that one!"

"How beautiful!"

"Hey!" snatching a shimmering piece from the still-to-iron pile, Tillie held it in front of her. "Is it me?" She swayed her hips, to the amusement of the others.

"Get on wi'yeh, go on now," Molly would scold in a teasing lilt. The older domestic knew that none of these young hearts would ever know such riches. They were fantasizing, as girls do, in hopes that one day their favorite piece would find it's way into the hand-me-down basket, when Mrs. Huntingwell might tire of it. Until then, they could only dream.

Prunella collected exquisite undergarments and linens, as one would valuable works of art or rare china. It was her most extravagant indulgence and she fell willing prey to its demon. Valuing the intricate designs and workmanship of the European laces, she often walked miles on her visits abroad, in hopes of discovering new sources to add to her list. Hours were spent in off-beat boutiques and fabric houses, often on her knees, rummaging through dusty lidded boxes of lace scrapes or bending over huge bins of odd yardage that might be fashioned into a simple blouse or bureau scarf. Mrs. Huntingwell had an uncanny talent for assembling just the right combination of fabric and design to produce a stunning dramatic effect, in both her home and on her person.

As Molly quietly moved around the room, completing her task of settling each item precisely in it's right place, Mrs. Huntingwell stirred in her bed.

"What time is it, Molly?"

"Lil' pas' nine, Missus."

"Oh dear." Prunella Huntingwell stretched her limbs, aware of not over-extending her muscles. Still on her back, she tossed the comforter aside and began her usual routine of soft exercise; raising and lowering each slim, sunless limb several times, hugging her drawn-up knees and rolling from side to side, flexing her feet, rotating her neck in calculated motion, all done before abandoning her gleaming white iron bed. She commenced her daily regimen of impeccable grooming with a short, tepid shower. A luxury bath would be savored later in the afternoon.

Her days unfolded gently, slowly, always in an orderly fashion. She did not choose to erupt into aliveness quite as robustly as did her husband, nor did she seek any assistance from her personal maid in her morning toilette. After serving "th' Missus" for so many years, Molly more than understood her lady's need for privacy. Mrs. Huntingwell's rooms were never entered before 9:00 a.m. and never without knocking. Chores were carefully scheduled, when the quarters were empty.

Molly pampered her lady almost to a point of maudlinness, and at times, to the nausea of the household staffers. She did her job as she saw fit, as satisfied her own sense of pride and never allowed herself to be intimidated by insensitive innuendoes.

As Mrs. Huntingwell changed an outfit, Molly checked to see what was needed. She washed, pressed, tightened buttons, before hanging the garment back in it's appointed slot in the spacious wardrobe.

Shoes were gone over after each wearing, brushed, polished, heels checked for dirt, before replaced in original boxes or flannel drawstring bags, to await their next outing.

On formal occasions, all Mrs. Huntingwell needed to do, was let Molly know which outfit she had chosen to wear and Molly knew the appropriate accessories to ready.

Every day, at precisely five-thirty, Mrs. Huntingwell politely excused herself to retire to the serenity of her rooms. Here she found the solace she hungered for, the elixir for maintaining her overall well-being. The sweet expectancy of knowing her bath would be drawn...the beckoning fragrance of violet-scented water.

Dear Molly, not a detail was ever overlooked. Bath oils sat on a low marble-top table next to the deep, footed tub. A lace bath cap hung over shiny brass faucets. A tiny, antique book of poems rested atop fluffy thick white towels. Robe, slippers, all in place, all within reach.

Nothing was too indulgent for her lady.

Molly loved the younger woman, as a mother would a daughter. It was the closest link to a filial relationship that she would ever know. She was not only Prunella's personal maid, but her confessor, psychologist, friend. Mrs. Huntingwell always knew if she sought an honest opinion, she could count on Molly's pure heart to be truthful.

Prunella's mother had met with an untimely death, and her father soon after, when she was a young girl. As an only child, she was sent to live with her mother's high brow spinster sister, Josephine, who was "given to sinking spells" and suffered with sporadic bouts of hysteria, thus accruing many hours of relief in bed, the comfort of her cozies, as she referred to her quilts.

Aunt Jo spared none of her fortune in assuring that her young charge was to continue being reared as a proper lady, a cause her dear mother had so diligently dedicated herself to. An army of tutors was hired. Artists, teachers, governesses, of all sizes and temperaments, devoted to the same end result; that Prunella Catherine was to be perfectly versed in the "rules" and privileges of the upper class. She had been schooled to run a home graciously, deal fairly with the affairs of servants, be cultured and knowledgeable about the arts, well informed of current events and ingratiating to all in her path.

Prunella learned to be smart, clever, a paragon of self-discipline. She had been well bred to be exactly what she was...a woman of position, a wealthy man's wife. It was her lot and she was content in a lifestyle free from hardship.

The benefits of being Mrs. Thaddeus Huntingwell, the third, were many.

Thaddeus Huntingwell III

Summer mornings at Sweetmeadow Cottage found Thaddeus Huntingwell, the third, turning out of bed before dawn and doing battle with a self inflicted, cold shower.

"Awakens the senses" he would defend. "Energizes the body!" A fact he fiercely believed.

Before entering the black marble stall with it's gleaming gold fixtures, Thaddeus gave the bell tassel a tug, alerting Nigel, his long time valet, that he was about to commence his daily ritual. Within moments, the loyal attendant appeared at the door of his master's quarters.

"Morning, Nigel," a chipper greeting.

"Good morning, Sir," the reply came back in measured English diction. Nigel nodded with respect and polite refinement.

The sophisticated looking valet/butler was tastefully clothed in a pair of crisp tan slacks and matching short sleeve shirt—attire that the lady of the house thought more appropriate in warm summer months. A heavy morning coat with ascot was worn in the city.

As Thad prepared himself for the frigid dowsing, he turned to Nigel.

"Six minutes, ol' boy." Thad used the common term in a most uncommon spirit, for master and servant enjoyed a deep, unspoken allegiance of friendship. They understood each other without verbal exchange. Yet, each was manacled to his own station in life; each so separate, yet, inextricably bound by years of close interaction. Their's was a silent tethering of the souls.

"Yes, Sir, six minutes."

Nigel stood erect, heels together, back straight, head up, the perfect presentation of a well trained man-servant. He slowly brought his wrist to viewing range of his watch, using thumb and index finger as a steadying device to assist in the accuracy of the read.

Thaddeus braced himself for the first shocking thrust of cold water that would ruthlessly assault his warm limbs.

"Ready?"

"Yes, Sir."

"Yeow! Whoa! Yah! That's cold!"

"Yes, Sir."

As Nigel listened to the all too familiar sputterings, he shook his head in wonder. Why would a mature, highly educated, sane person willfully choose to persecute himself with the same torturous ordeal every morning of his life? But as a proper servant should, he kept his opinion to himself, unless of course, he was asked.

Nigel stood perfectly still. His eyes riveted on the face of his gold Hamilton, a gift from his boss. With exactly two minutes to go, he quickly left the room, went to the hall and rapped commandingly on the small door of the dumb waiter, the usual four times. This relayed the familiar signal to Cook in the kitchen below, alerting her to send the Master's towel up immediately. Direct from it's resting place on the corner of the wood stove, the thick luxuriant bundle was presented on a copper platter, tightly rolled, to retain as much heat as possible.

Mr. Huntingwell stepped out of the cold shower, onto a thick bath mat and flung the warm terry over his shivering body.

"Ah, feels good. Feels good."

As Thaddeus dried himself off, Nigel continued with his duties. He arranged the chosen clothes, in order of adornment. Each item was presented on brass hooks, mounted on the door of a massive oak armoire.

"I'm a new man."

"Yes, Sir." Nigel busied himself as he spoke.

"Nothing like a hot towel to soothe the body." Thad commented, using the plush terry for a brisk rubdown.

Nigel smiled to himself. He had heard the same acclamation, at approximately the same time, for the past ten years.

Thad draped the used towel over Nigel's outstretched arm and reached for his cotton boxer shorts, neatly hung for his convenience, over the glass knob on the bathroom door. He tossed a small towel over his shoulder and commenced to lather up his young looking, tanned face, topping off the leisurely shave with a light swash of after shave.

He donned a pair of casual tan shorts, a pale blue open neck shirt and slipped soxless feet into a pair of well worn canvas deck shoes. He arrived downstairs minutes before yesterday's Providence Journal predicted the sun would rise.

Mr. Huntingwell opened the heavy French doors that lead onto the veranda and stepped out into the cool, fresh morning. He walked across the wide porch, leaned his hands on the railing and inhaled deeply, fully expanding his lungs with salty sea air, and digested the extraordinary view before him. The ocean's power had an incredible effect on him and he marveled at how young he felt at fifty.

"Can still beat the pants off the young pups half my age." he boasted to himself. He was referring to his prowess on the squash court, still proud of his rather formidable athletic skills.

From his position, Thaddeus surveyed a cloud formation that might obscure his view of the sunrise. He never failed to notice if the fog was rolling in off the ocean, threatening to delay his tee-off time. He was always in high spirits when the early hours were clear, a rarity for this leg of coastline.

After a few moments, Thaddeus re-entered the wide hall, lavish with elaborate framed mirrors and pictures. He walked across a thick Persian rug and on through the formal dining room, to the breakfast alcove. En route, he passed swinging doors that lead to the kitchen where a slightly rigid, white aproned servantess stood. She was holding a small, doily lined, silver tray, sporting a black monogrammed mug. The vessel was brimming with piping hot, sugarless café au lait and sprinkled with a few grains of cinnamon.

Thaddeus, as was his practice, took the mug in his hand, lifting it to his nostrils to inhale the vapors. He carefully scrutinized the brew, as if for flaws and playfully flashed the anxious domestic an approving smile.

"Ah-h-h-h" he winked. "Just the right color. Good girl, Tillie."

In the breakfast alcove, his oak swivel chair welcomed him as an old friend. Its ornate, hand-carved wood was a perpetual conversation piece among the staff, who often argued in good humor, which lucky one would be awarded the unparalleled honor of buffing the "master's throne."

Thad settled himself languidly in the grand old chair, mellowed by generations of use. The handsome antique was set at a perfect viewing angle, facing the curved bay window, enabling him to bask in the full regalia of the ocean. On a clear day, he would watch as the giant orange fireball emerged from the bowels of the earth, spilling a stream of liquid gold onto the cool ocean, spewing millions of sparkling jewels out over blue-green waters.

Rays of early light filtered through stained glass panels, turning the cozy, wood paneled nook into a kaleidoscope of rich, mellow colors.

The sun was up, his day had begun.

Abruptly, as if programmed by some hidden mechanical device, he spun his chair around, away from the expansive view, perched his reading glasses precariously on the tip of his nose, picked up the Wall Street Journal and set out to systematically devour it's contents.

Thad had already mentally left his glorious surroundings, entering into his world of finance and for the next twenty five minutes, totally immersing himself in the columns of stock market quotes.

Robot-like, he consumed the warm berry croissant, silently set before him, without his eyes ever once leaving the page.

Almost to the minute, he folded the paper and emptied the last drop of lukewarm coffee.

"More coffee, Sir?"

"No thanks, Tillie."

Thad meandered back out onto the long porch, going directly to his favorite lounge chair. Cook always had a cantaloupe melon half set on the side arm, ready for him. Always the same, presented on a bed of crushed ice and twinged with a tiny splash of cognac. The melon ended his interlude of leisure.

To Cook's torment, Mr. Huntingwell savored only four or five bites of the very ripest, sweet center flesh, leaving almost the entire fruit to be discarded.

"Isn't it a shameful waste!" she would grump, when the maid returned to the kitchen with the luscious fruit almost intact.

Thaddeus lingered on awhile, content in his private thoughts. He loved this old house. It was his escape, his balance, his sanity. These unhurried summer mornings in Narragansett were a far cry from the demanding pressures of his intense week on Wall Street. New York was home to him and Prunella for the past ten years, where they resided in a posh Park Avenue apartment. They had the best of both worlds. They were without care.

He reveled in his noble position as president of his own brokerage firm and took immense pride in the respect he had earned from his peers.

Thaddeus Huntingwell, the third, warmed in the glow of his success.

Strange Union

"Darling, there is something I have been meaning to tell you." Thad whispered, breathing with mock sensuality straight out of a B-rated movie. "I am afraid I have been helplessly seduced by Cook's sensuous little buns."

Thaddeus T. Huntingwell was a self-restrained, proper, sort of a man and his rare attempt at levity was, inevitably, doomed to fall short of the mark of entertainment.

His well bred wife would cringe when he randomly chose an unsuspecting guest upon whom to vent his faulty humor. Fortunately, this morning, they were alone in the upstairs library that connected their separate rooms.

"Really, Thad." turning her back, not allowing him to see her squirm. "That is hardly in good taste."

"You're right, as usual, my dear," he accepted with a slight twinge of discomfort. He went to the tall second floor windows and looked out at the new day, trying to dismiss his failed stab at comedy.

"Ah...looks like a good one."

Prunella, still with her back turned away from her husband, tried in vain to stifle her giggle.

"What is it?" Thad pried, "surely, I..." pointing a finger at his chest, "...couldn't have said something funny." A tiny flavor of reproach crept into his voice.

Turning now to look into his eyes. "Cook's little buns?" she repeated, slowly, as she mimicked his words. She couldn't leave it alone.

He studied her expression for a moment, before realizing just how incongruous his statement had been. For dear, corpulent Cook, with her voluminous hips, could hardly be accused of having "little buns."

The sensuous little buns that Thad had referred to so passionately, were the "frightfully delicious" lighter-than-air jewels that Cook baked with pride each morning. The delicate aroma of these freshly baked croissants, plump with sticky rich raspberry centers, permeated the whole house in the wee morning hours. Early risers were embraced by the intoxicating aroma of a French bakery and the fruity gems had become the specialty of Sweetmeadow. Guests were willing to bribe Cook with pecuniary rewards for her under-lock-and-key recipe. Often she was begged to bake extras to accommodate those who hoped to extend the palate pampering experience by squirreling away a few morsels for the trip home.

Even Thad, who was a disciplined eater, found the buttery morsels irresistible and fell willing prey to the temptation.

They shared a good laugh.

"See you downstairs." He noticed she had a small calendar in her hand, milling over dates and knew she needed more time to sort out her schedule for the day.

"See you there." Pru headed to the desk in her bedroom.

The curved-leg desk had only one long drawer, more than ample for her needs. A beautiful French lace runner was pressed under a glass protector. On the top corner of the desk, Prunella had placed a slender crystal lamp crowned with a crisp white pleated shade. A small crystal bowl held a potpourri of last year's rose petals and a small frameless picture of Thad and her on their honeymoon in France completed the grouping. On the other corner, stood a dictionary disguised by a white linen cover, sandwiched between two glass bears with narrow silver bows around their chubby necks.

A needlepoint of her favorite saying by Henry Wadsworth Longfellow hung on the wall over her desk.

"In character, in manners, in style, in all things...supreme excellence is simplicity."

Mrs. Huntingwell sat at her desk and sorted through sundry letters from soon to arrive guests, matching dates to an already crowded calendar. The whirlwind had begun.

Who was arriving when, which rooms would suit which guests, who could not eat what, which couples were most compatible...on and on it went. She kept meticulous records in her journal of her visitor's likes and dislikes, making their stay at Sweetmeadow as stress free as possible.

After compiling a formidable array of data, she gathered up her notes and calendar and started down the main stairway in hopes of finding her husband in one of his rare talkative moods. She needed a little time to mull over ideas and hear his input.

The first week of the summer season was always the most hectic, until a basic format of guest lists could be solidified and indexed. She honestly sought his help in the initial planning stage.

As she rounded the corner to the breakfast alcove, she was greeted by the familiar strains of a Glenn Miller recording. Thad's favorite.

Ah, she mused, maybe the upbeat melodies indicate a mellow humor.

Through the years, Pru had learned not to intrude on her husband's early morning quiet hour. He had politely deemed it his private time and she fully honored his request. But there were days, like today, when she was faced with a staggering load of household business and felt a need to share the burden of responsibility with him.

The summers, although their vacation time away from the frantic bustle of New York, were fraught with endless entertaining. A constant flow of bodies coming and going at all hours of the day and night.

The mechanics of the social wheel were left entirely to her. She did a top rate job and Thaddeus assumed that she had all the help needed to carry out– what he thought– was an enjoyable undertaking.

But Prunella Huntingwell, as adept as she was at running a smooth ship, longed for his viewpoint. At times, she just needed to satiate her longing for his company to chat and visit a bit.

Did he have any preference for special meals that she could relay to Cook? What about this season's list of charity functions? Was he interested in attending Summer Stock again this season or the special opera performance of Madam Butterfly? The same questions every year.

Prunella liked to make arrangements in advance. Reserve seats, buy tickets, plan menus and table settings well before an event.

But during the few summer months, Thaddeus thrived on spontaneous socializing, often the source of great consternation, when interacting with his organized wife.

The Huntingwells had a strange union. It was known that they were faithful to their vows, so many of their circle were not, but there was no fire. It wasn't necessary. They had been married almost ten years and their ways were habit. He had his space...she, hers. Seldom did they share a common interest, but they were comfortable with the status of their love. She gave him all the freedom he needed without nagging, he showered her with extravagant gifts and afforded her the pinnacle of a pampered lifestyle.

Their friends often marveled at how they managed to stay together.

Pru also wished that Thad would take more interest in the nagging little problems with the servants; the upstairs maid, the downstairs maid, the butler, the chauffeur, the gardener and the volatile kitchen artists. It took constant policing to maintain a harmonious household. The egos of each employee who felt that his or her own position in the ranks, to be of the greatest importance in the overall running of the estate.

Mrs. Huntingwell loathed any form of conflict and did her level best to avoid discord. She was aware, from experience, that any strained relations among the hired help, unwittingly spilled on to work skills, leading to an undercurrent of tension and unpleasantness.

The first few mornings, after they had arrived from New York, Prunella courageously invaded the inner sanctum of Thad's morning retreat. She immediately regretted it. He had acknowledged her queries with toneless retorts in his gracious, yet condescending voice, without averting his eyes from whatever he was reading. He was truly an unselfish man, but amazingly oblivious to Prunella's hunger for emotional nourishment.

When he left New York on Friday afternoons for Narragansett, he chose to spend the weekends with his wife and friends, free from aggravation. He left his "working hat" in the city. Before stepping off the train at the Kingston Depot, he had completely divorced himself from the business "rat race" and adopted an aura of relaxation. The last things he wanted to involve himself in, were the picayune details of babysitting the staff. To waste the few precious hours at his ocean front retreat on silly nuisances, usually not worth the time it took to tell, was ludicrous. He honestly did not give a fig if the napkins were folded with the monogram to the left or the right, or if the sheets were cuffed down six or eight inches, or if the coffee cup was full or almost full. *Foolishness*, he would think to himself, if Pru ever confronted him with such matters.

Mrs. Huntingwell's job, although tedious at times, was hardly in the realm of earth shattering dimension, in Thad's eyes. Although, he secretly recognized that without her to oil the axle of his world, it would not run quite as smoothly.

Prunella Huntingwell had no complaints. He was a kind man, a faithful husband, a gentleman. They liked each other. They were comfortable friends. It worked.

"Hello, Tillie, have you seen Mr. Huntingwell?"

"He's out on the veranda, Ma'am."

"Thank you, Tillie."

Pru started toward the open area, but today, upon viewing Thad so peacefully enjoying his solitude, she reassessed her plan to annoy him with guest lists.

She turned, instead, and slipped through the swinging doors into the kitchen.

"Good morning, everyone."

"Oh, good mornin' Mrs. Huntingwell." The kitchen staff was always happy to see her. Some curtsied, others waved, a few just smiled. Poochy raced around the room in excitement upon seeing his mistress.

Pru thoroughly enjoyed the rumble of activity in the large cookroom as it geared up for the day's rendering of grandly prepared cuisine. An impressive display of breads and rolls hot from the ovens sat on racks off to the side of a long, marble top table. The wonderful morning aromas titillated her senses; rich imported coffees, bubbly hot fruit preserves, smokey smells of sizzling bacon, the yeasty fragrance of hot raspberry buns.

On a massive antique pine side board, Cook had in its usual place, a small crystal tray lined with a lace-edge linen napkin, a tiny tin of Chamomile tea, a white bone china cup and saucer with hand painted violets, one lump of sugar already in the cup and a sterling silver teaspoon. Upon seeing Mrs. Huntingwell, Cook readied the matching teapot with boiling water.

Prunella enjoyed personally greeting the help at the start of each new week. They were in awe of her genuine concern for their well-being. Everyone loved her. She listened with empathy to their grievances. She never flaunted her golden position or took advantage of their lesser station. Nor did she completely meld with them as equals. At times, Pru actually envied their license to be themselves, uncomplicated, free from the demands of social protocol.

At the long distressed pine work table, that centered the room, the servants quickly took their clue to join the lady of the house, as she took her seat. Cook brought a platter of her sticky biscuits and placed a large enamel pot of steaming coffee on a brass trivet in the middle of the old table. Every Monday morning, the same ritual was carried out, before the verbal encounter got underway.

"Is there anything that transpired during the week that needs my attention?" Mrs. Huntingwell asked, eyeing each with personal interest.

It was then that the symphony of voices, all talking at once, reached crescendo pitch. Each complaining, with polite discretion, of another's performance. Mrs. Huntingwell listened to valid criticism, discarding any useless gossip and made note of suggestions worth looking into.

It had been during last Monday's "kitchen talk" that Molly confronted Mrs. Huntingwell with Patrick, reliving the episode in the rose garden.

"A bold thing, he was, but seemin' a nice youn' lad, willin' t' work at 'bout anythin' to help out."

"Oh yes, Molly?" she asked. "And where does he come from?"

"Can't tell ya that, Missy, 'e neva said, jes' ga' me 'is phone numba."

"All right, Molly," Prunella had checked her calendar. "Have him come around on Monday at ten o'clock and I'll have a talk with him. A young back and an extra pair of hands will be welcomed."

"Oh, yes, Missy." Molly, for some unexplainable reason, found herself quite pleased to have another opportunity to confront her rose thief.

Today was the day...ten o'clock.

Tillie, the upstairs maid, perked up at the thought of having another young person around. It would be a pleasant addition.

"Oh, 'n by the by," Molly leaned in close to Mrs. Huntingwell, whispering in her ear as her eyes darted around the room. "Ah, 'erd 'er agin, ah did." Molly was tense. "Tha' ghost ...up in th' attic." She stole another look about the immediate facility, insuring the absence of any spies. "She's com' agin, 'nd jest s' bold as ever. I 'erd 'er up thar shufflin' about."

Prunella Huntingwell smiled, calming the dear lady with a pat on the shoulder.

"I'll have Nigel check the storage rooms again today so you can be at ease, Molly. I'm sure your attic ghost is only a part of your dreams."

The little Irish lady was a bundle of nerves. Over the years, Prunella coddled her whims, taking the fears and superstitions with a grain of salt.

A ghost in the attic? How quaint.

Hoping he had, in some miraculous way, escaped the smells and grime of his transportation, Patrick arrived at the highly decorative iron gates of the Sweetmeadow Estate around 9:30 AM, half an hour earlier than Molly had scheduled with Mrs. Huntingwell.

He was confronted by a polite, middle aged gentleman wearing green Bermuda shorts, a tan short sleeve shirt and sporting a visor with the blue, green and gold Sweetmeadow crest emblazoned on the bill. Beside him stood two rather formidable looking Dobermans, who did not appear quite as hospitable as their master. With ears starched straight up and turgid bodies, their trained silence spoke loudly.

The gatekeeper had been alerted to Patrick's arrival and from Molly's thorough description, there was no mistaking his identity.

"You're early" he noted scanning the day's guest sheet and checking his watch with obvious exaggeration.

"Had to rely on catchin' a ride. Couldn't count on anything, so I allowed plenty of time to get here." As he spoke, he kept his eyes on the black dogs who held him prisoner with menacing body language. "Got lucky early on, so here I am." Patrick shrugged his shoulders, lightheartedly. The gate keeper kept his eyes on his papers. For some reason he took an immediate liking to the candid, easy manner of the young man with a dirt smudge on his cheek.

The dogs remained erect. Legs straight and apart, poised, ready for their command. Their eyes were drilled on Patrick, unblinking, penetrating. His neck hairs prickled.

"Go ahead."

Patrick felt a sense of relief when allowed entrance through the grand gate. Tipping an imaginary hat to the gateman, he was careful not to make any sudden movement that might startle the dogs, as he passed. Once inside, Patrick turned around for a moment and walked backwards, giving a slight bow to the animals in gratitude for their restraint. The beasts had taken on the persona of docile house pets, flopping down on the cool pavement, even exuding a yawn for emphasis of their boredom.

As Patrick turned to follow the stately gravel driveway, the gateman smiled, in curiosity, at the grime on the back of the boy's trousers.

"Mighty impressive" Patrick thought as he walked through a tunnel of ancient old maples, splaying their graceful limbs overhead. A million hands reached out to him as he strode beneath their boughs, boasting the miracles of nature. He could only imagine the magnificence of this thickly foliated canopy in the fall, when nature's magic would fashion the leaves into a living kaleidoscope of autumn golds.

As he walked, his nostrils filled with a potpourri of earthy smells, freshly tilled loam, clipped hedges, newly mown grass. Since the mansion's occupants had arrived, the lawns were impeccably manicured, not one blade taller than another nor a fallen leaf seen anywhere; each flowering stem strategically placed at it's showiest advantage.

Later, Patrick would be more in awe of the landscape, when learning that only one man was responsible for it's near perfection. He began to think that he may not find a job here, after all. Everything seemed to be well under control.

As he came closer to the now fully visible mansion, he noticed an aging gentleman bent over, waxing the wooden sides of a dark red beach wagon. He was shining it with the care one might give to a precious jewel. The man was so intent on his work, that he did not see, nor hear, Patrick approach.

"Hello there," Patrick called.

No response.

"Hello there," Patrick shouted, upon noting a hearing aid tucked in the man's ear. He put him at about seventy.

"Who's there?" The laborer stood up, startled by the irreverence afforded his quiet space.

"Hello." Patrick smiled, trying to maneuver his face to make eye contact. The portly black man was attired in the same mode as the gatekeeper, except, he was sporting a wide pair of green suspenders clipped to beltless trousers. Patrick thought he was overdressed for the kind of work he was doing, but assumed it was a status symbol, to remain in uniform at all times, even when buffing the cars.

"Some piece of machinery you have there," Patrick made small talk.

"Yas suh, she's a beauty." The happy faced man laughingly acknowledged, clearly proud of the gleaming machine before him.

"Been working here long?" Patrick queried.

"O' yas suh. Long fo' you was born, ah 'spect." He chuckled again. A pleasant sort and Patrick found his friendliness inviting.

"Ah been drivin' fo' d' family since d' 30's. Yas suh, sho has." Another chuckle.

Patrick stretched out his hand.

"Patrick O'Shay, here."

"Marcus Washington, 'Max' is good 'nuff, yas suh." He flashed a large smile, accompanied by his signature chuckle.

It was a firm hand shake. Patrick was struck by the older man's strength.

"O.K. Max, good deal." Patrick smiled.

"Yas sur." Max was curious as to the identity and background of the young lad but knew it was not his place to question or interfere in the private lives of any guests of the Huntingwells. He said nothing.

"I'm here for a job interview with Mrs. Huntingwell, handyman or something, just for the summer." Patrick was feeling Max out, maybe he would get some insight as to the nature of his boss lady.

"Nice lady, tha' Miz Huntingwell. Gets on easy w' folks. Yas suh, sho do." The chuckle. Max continued polishing as he spoke, "Sho do."

"Well I'll let you know how it goes." Patrick turned to leave and gave a short wave to the amiable chauffeur, for whom he had instantly felt a warm attachment.

"Yas suh." Max stopped long enough to offer directions. "Nigel 'ill let yo' in, jus' rap the brass, he'll come," Max called after him, the chamois rag waving loosely in his hand.

An enormous hand carved replica of the estate's logo centered the wide wooden door.

Patrick thumped the heavy knocker twice. He did not have long to wait.

The door opened to reveal a tall, painfully thin man in his early sixties, an exaggerated handlebar mustache strategically distanced between the tip of a bony nose and a thin upper lip; his slick-back, thinning gray hair mirrored that of a 1920's matinee idol. Even though his crisp shirt had short sleeves and an open neck, the gentleman wore a royal blue silk ascot, reeking of old world refinement. He stood, unbent, heels together, head erect.

"Good day, Sir, how may I help you?" The low, resonant voice slid slowly over his lips in perfect Queen's English.

"I have an appointment with Mrs. Huntingwell at ten o'clock. I'm early." Patrick's smile was a bit uneasy.

Nigel remained expressionless. The butler scrutinized the young man's face, for just a moment, before stepping aside to allow him entrance.

"Yes, Sir, this way," he bowed, bending slightly from the waist. Nigel's head remained properly set. His steps were deliberate and unrushed. Robot-like, he led Patrick over a thick carpet to a set of French doors, off the grand entrance hall. With great precision he opened both doors at once, one would have been sufficient, and bid Patrick entrance. The room was dark, wood paneled, very masculine in feel.

Patrick stood awkwardly, watching the seasoned servant silently flick a switch that illuminated one whole wall of glassed-in shelves, showcasing artifacts from around the world. The apparent results of extensive travel. Nigel remained unsmiling as he methodically went to one lamp, then another until the musty smelling room was aglow with artificial light. The drapes remained closed.

Patrick noticed that as Nigel departed, he stepped backwards, never turning his back to his guest. In oiled movements, he closed the doors as he had opened them, without a sound.

Nigel had been Mr. Huntingwell's personal valet for ten years. He was English born and bred and had worked all his adult life as a man-servant. When he had met Thaddeus Huntingwell "on holiday" in England, by pure accident, the two had taken an immediate liking to each other.

Mr. Huntingwell offered him room, board and salary to come to America and hire on as butler and valet. Nigel had never married, he was alone. He had no one to answer to and gladly agreed to the offer.

Nigel accepted his "place" and had no fanciful notions of bettering his position. He was well taken care of and would never want for anything. He felt an unconditional allegiance to "The Mister." Although his boss was many years his junior, Nigel could not address him by his first name.

The loyal butler never retold a story or gossiped about internal house affairs. He would rather have been "sent to the tower" than betray what went on under the roof in Sweetmeadow. This home was sacred ground to him and he prided himself on his unshakable commitment to the family.

Patrick felt very small in the large, high ceiling room. The flavor was casual elegance, typifying in Patrick's mind a very prestigious men's club of the 1940's. Although he had come from an upper middle class family, this kind of exorbitant wealth was far beyond the realm of his world.

One end of the room was dedicated to an imposing stone fireplace, punctuated with a thick oak mantle; bookcases flanked the sides, crammed with a diverse collection of volumes on just about any subject one would wish to pursue. Oversized plump, well worn leather furniture invitingly begged a body to—come, sit by the fire. There were well stocked humidors within comfortable reach of sofas; ashtrays held monogrammed match boxes. Complimentary tables, tucked everywhere, were casually strewn with figurines, snapshots, smoking pipes, and framed pictures of happy travelers.

An enormous, carved rolltop desk rested like a contented giant in front of glassed-in shelves. Unlike the relaxed ambience of its surroundings, the desk was nicely organized. Neat, perfect bundles of files and correspondence, a general array of writing paraphernalia all stashed in unique containers, eye glasses posed on the current read. Patrick noticed the waste basket was almost full of crumpled papers and thought it odd, in a house boasting a fleet of servants, that this small detail should be overlooked.

A Persian rug slumbered beneath a mahogany pool table, its rich blues and reds giving the only color to an otherwise somber décor. An ornate oak bar, gun racks, an old world globe, the heavy smell of tobacco, all reeked of permanence.

Patrick was particularly interested in the paintings that occupied the remaining wall spaces. There were no great masters displayed, only an ill-matched collection of works by amateur artists, some personally signed to the Huntingwells and dated. Possible guest "thank yous."

"Mrs. Huntingwell will see you now, Mr. O'Shay. Please follow me."

Patrick was startled. He had not heard Nigel re-enter the room and wondered how long he had been observed. By the time Patrick walked the length of the private sanctum, Nigel had vanished. Patrick caught up with him in the grand hall and was directed to the next set of French doors. Again, opened in the same manner as before.

"Do step in, Sir. Lady Huntingwell is on her way." He stepped aside allowing Patrick to enter.

They entered a sitting room, four times the size of the last.

"Now, this has to be the party room," Patrick ventured a guess, upon eyeing the white grand piano and bare, highly waxed portion of floor at the west end of the room.

Nigel, cringing at the lovely Grand Parlor being referred to as a "party room" chose to remain silent. With almost ceremonial reverence, he drew open the ivory drapes on the east wall that immediately flooded the glorious space with sunlight and a most spectacular, panoramic view of the Atlantic Ocean. Patrick moved to the window for closer perusal.

Nigel left the room, once again unnoticed, without a word.

Patrick turned to take inventory of his surroundings. The greatest impact was the magnificent show of crystal vases and bowls spilling over with flowers. Fresh-cut flowers! Roses, tuberoses, lilacs. Enormous arrangements everywhere; fragrances mingling to offer the senses a surreal sensation.

The furniture was dressed in the palest shades of peach complimented by white and ivory...overstuffed couches in gentle floral pastels, puffy chairs in pastel stripes, honey colored wood floors framed white scattered rugs, fat cushioned ottomans nested in vacant cavities.

White walls were free of clutter. An occasional mirror was

strategically placed to reflect a sumptuous bouquet, magnifying it's beauty. The effect was stunning!

Eight, nine, ten. The hall clock struck the exact hour.

"Good morning, Mr. O'Shay."

Prunella Huntingwell approached him, dressed in a cool, white linen day dress. She held a small schedule book in the crook of her left arm. As she came toward him, she stretched out her right hand to his.

"I'm Prunella Huntingwell." She gave no indication of friendliness.

"Patrick O'Shay, here."

He gave her a smile.

She remained composed, unsmiling.

He assumed he was to follow her to the fragile-looking spindle-leg desk, that she strode toward on the opposite side of the room.

"Please be seated, Mr. O'Shay." Her lips never moved. Maybe her jaw was wired.

She motioned to the small gold filigree chair, in front of the writing table, for him to occupy. Why did she feel the necessity to point out where he was to sit? It was the only chair there. Did she think him not capable of figuring it out for himself?

He caught himself.

Why was he reacting to this literal stranger with hostility, it was not his nature. After all, wasn't it a standard courtesy on her part, a politeness, to invite him to be seated? Surely she did not mean to demean his intelligence or insult his manhood. What was it about this iron maiden that triggered his aggression?

Mrs. Huntingwell looked straight at him as she spoke.

"Molly tells me that you have some interest in helping out here, at Sweetmeadow, for the summer. Is that right, Mr. O'Shay?" Her tone was pleasant, gracious. Her manner, disciplined, mechanical.

Obviously, assessing a reply to be superfluous, she proceeded to give him a concise presentation of the jobs that might be in need of assistance. He listened and took in her aura. There was no interaction with him, what-so-ever, as a fellow human being. Patrick concluded that she must have been iced down somewhere, before she entered the room.

Mrs. Huntingwell paused to review her notes. Patrick noticed her ivory calling cards in a small footed crystal dish, shaded under a fragrant bunch of peach roses. Formal black scroll announced Prunella Catherine Huntingwell. Patrick deemed it farcical, that someone actually named this, seemingly flawless creature, Prunella. While amused by the thought, he wondered if the freckled face pubescences in fourth grade, ever called her "Prune face." It seemed inevitable.

Mrs. Huntingwell offered Patrick the opportunity to outline his ideas. What was it that he wanted from the job? Salary? Hours? His particular skills.

He would be willing to work wherever he was needed. She acknowledged his proposal with polite coolness and although she seemed porous to his ideas, it was without enthusiasm.

How does she do it? Not a hair out of place. Her dark mane was pulled back into a tight roll at the base of her neck. Every fingernail was the same length, perfectly manicured. She wore a minimum of makeup, none of that "pancake" stuff that Patrick hated on girls. Her dark eyes were clear and thickly lashed. He had to admit that she was a stunning woman, not beautiful, but definitely a head-turner. But cold. Damn, she was cold!

Patrick amused himself, privately. Did she ever long to run naked on a moonlit beach or dip herself in a vat of warm chocolate? Would she ever expose her alabaster skin to the punishing rays of the sun? or invite the wind to tangle her hair? Was the woman capable of screaming, belching, or any of the other natural things humans do? Would mosquitoes dare to bite her? He was enjoying the madness of his little mind game, when Prunella Huntingwell stood up. She felt the business at hand was well executed and again extended a hand to her guest. Her hand was thin, long, her flesh cool and dry.

"I'm sure we will be able to keep you busy, Mr. O'Shay. Some of our employees are getting up in years and will welcome a lightening of the load." No smile, her lips hardly moved.

The glacial lady took a few stately steps toward the French doors. She was about to exit, when she stopped and turned toward Patrick, who had stood up, but not left his place. Her eyes swept for a split second down Patrick's suntans. In the same expressionless controlled tone, she commented.

"You may wish to take your trousers to Molly. She will be glad to clean and mend them for you." She was gone before he could explain what had happened, leaving him with his mouth open. He spun around on his heels and pounded his fist into an open palm, in frustration and disbelief. God, she was irritating!

Patrick was left alone. His nerves, tense from the encounter, were ready to snap. As he started across the room, he caught sight of himself in a mirror, discovering the smudge on his cheek. The final blow to his ego.

To his surprise, the glass also reflected the image of a young uniformed girl. He had been unaware that he was being spied on. Tillie, the upstairs maid, had heard of the arrival of some "frisky rogue" from Molly at breakfast and was anxious to give him a "look-over."

Tillie had positioned herself behind one of the giant, fern-filled urns that guarded the French doors, where she would go unnoticed. She was stretching her neck, in hopes of stealing a closer peek, when Patrick had spotted her.

This was his kind of prank and the whole scene played right into the moment's pent up emotions. He became an actor. He turned nonchalantly toward her hide out, pretending no knowledge of her whereabouts and proceeded to slowly close the gap between them. Patrick knew she must be in a state of panic and continued to approach her.

As he came almost within touching distance, she dropped to her knees, in an effort to meld with the greenery. She closed her eyes, trying to quell her heart and remained very still, crouching as low as she could to the floor until he, hopefully, would depart.

She heard his footsteps pass her on the polished marble, feeling relieved that her camouflage had not betrayed her. With caution, she slowly rose.

"HA!" Patrick leapt out in front of her, knees bent, hands arched over his head, poised to attack. Scared the poor child witless! She fled up the stairs, uttering little moans of fear and embarrassment, at having been caught in such a compromising situation.

Patrick felt better after he had a good laugh. He only hoped the frightened maid would find it worthy of humor, after she settled herself down.

Still smiling at the success of his little prank, Patrick made his way through the grand hall to the front entrance. Nigel was waiting by the door to see him out.

"Good day, Sir." More of the same formality, that was beginning to make Patrick question what he was doing here among these stiffs. He had the urge to throw a grenade under the rug and wake the place up.

"Good day, Nigel," he returned, hopping down the steps onto the gravel driveway. He welcomed the sight of the sun burning off the morning fog. It would be a clear day after all.

The meeting had gone well enough. Short, to the point. Frustrating! There was no great warmth exchanged between the interviewer and the interviewee, but he was satisfied. It may well be a perfect solution to his need. No familiarity, no personal questions.

Prunella Catherine Huntingwell, the metallic woman void of emotion, who was she? He equated her with the lifeless stone statues of Roman goddesses, that reigned in silence on the glossy pages of his art history books. And yet, she had impregnated his senses with an overwhelming curiosity to investigate her world. An almost impulsive drive to "ruffle her feathers."

At that moment, Patrick Sean O'Shay, for some unexplainable, immature reason, decided to take on Prunella Catherine Huntingwell. He set out to crack her porcelain shell and release the imprisoned life within. Surely, there was a flickering pulse somewhere.

The tiny driveway stones made a grinding sound under his feet as Patrick turned to take one departing look at the lovely old mansion. He was now a member of the Sweetmeadow staff.

From an upstairs window a curtain fluttered as if having just been released by an inquisitive hand.

Prunella Catherine Huntingwell stepped softly back into the shadows of the room, and watched until the young man with the mischievous blue eyes, disappeared from view.

The first fresh weeks of summer at Sweetmeadow raced by amidst a constant flurry of goings-on, unleashing days at an accelerated pace. Patrick was inundated with new faces, new surroundings, and new dilemmas. His easy personality endeared him, not only to the Huntingwells, but to staff and guests alike. His heart did not distinguish between the wealthy and the less fortunate...king or commoner. He saw no distinction, that was his charm.

During his sprinkling of free hours, the ocean was Patrick's addiction. He gloried in the salt air, the palate of blues, greens and purples of the sea and the expanse of open sky, an ideal backdrop for the aerial antics of gray gulls. He often captured their acrobatics on film to later incorporate in a painting.

He positioned a hand-fashioned easel in a premium spot, a safe distance from unpredictable tidal sprays and lost himself in his art. Other times, a simple sketch pad and pencil his only need. Even on early mornings, like this one, when headaches invaded his sleep, he sought the peaceful solitude of the sea. Cool, pure air refreshed his consciousness and words flowed freely, enabling him to record his sensitive poetry.

It was Friday afternoon. Thad was due in soon from New York for his leisurely weekend at Sweetmeadow. It was going to be a busy one. Prunella hoped the weather would be cooperative for her guests.

She stood by the open window of her bedroom. Through a pair of opera glasses, she scanned the horizon, enjoying the ever-present parade of ships and sailing vessels, a delightful part of the summer scene. Huge shore rocks, normally under water, were now at low tide and fully exposed.

The pleasant day had suddenly turned dark. Angry clouds obscured the sun...the sky menacing. Ocean depths reflected a murky shade of gray-green, white caps tipped rising ripples. All typical forebodings of an oncoming warm-weather thunder storm.

Movements on the rocks caught her eye and Pru adjusted the lenses to focus in on the scene.

She caught Patrick, barefooted, toe dancing over the hot, dry rocks as if on burning coals to avoid blistering his soles. She watched him with simple pleasure, enthralled with his cat-like movements. He lept from rock to rock, grasping a rather bulky galvanized bucket brimming with a jumble of tools used to retrieve hard-to-get-at flotsam and jetsam wedged in rock crevices, tantalizingly out of reach of the seeker. Patrick was unaware of being closely scrutinized as he picked through the endless treasures that Neptune had hurled at his feet. An arrogant wave rammed the giant stone fortress, inundating him with a cold salt shower, causing him to lose his balance. With flailing arms, he fought to remain upright. As Pru stared, Patrick stepped on a patch of slimy seaweed freshly deposited by a delinquent wave, causing him to go down on the craggy surface. His leg slipped into an opening between boulders, scraping his shin on razor-sharp barnacles. Patrick rubbed his scratched flesh in obvious pain and continued on his way, trying to dodge another inevitable dousing.

Where did he come from?

A maverick gust of air lifted the sheer curtain and swiped at Pru's face. She smiled, eyes on the rocks. Her mind wandered. Why was the young man so drawn to that far end of the lawn? She had seen him in the same vicinity on numerous occasions. She noticed when off duty, he never wore shoes, reminding her of Whitier's line, "barefoot boy with cheeks of tan ..." Patrick seemed to celebrate the textures and temperatures of the earth he walked on.

Prunella scrutinized the expanse before her. Ominous clouds, blackening by the minute. She was not prying into his solitary world nor insensitive to his choice of aloneness. Being meddlesome was not her style, yet she could not tame her need to learn more about this Patrick O'Shay. She was hopelessly drawn into his carefree existence.

Clothed in a pair of pink silk slacks and matching shirt, white belt and sandals, she turned away from the now closed window, twisted her hair in a loose bun and stuffed it up under a floppy brim hat.

She unconsciously grabbed the flashlight by her bedside, kept close at hand in case of electrical storm blackouts, an occasional problem during summer months.

With a spring in her step, Prunella walked out across the veranda, down the wide steps, picking up speed as she traversed the plush lawn to the ocean rocks. The wind was coming up...rumbling echoed in the distance...the storm might break at any time.

The putrid stench of rotting seaweed was offensive. Prunella used her free hand to cover her nose in an attempt to mask the fetid air. She never had the desire to venture out this close to the ocean before.

Carefully she climbed onto the large stones, unfriendly to her slick leather soles and slowly made her way, using her arms for balance, to the end of the formation. There was an abrupt drop-off onto a small sandy beach abundant with shells. The open area, non-existent during high tide, exposed an entrance to what seemed to be a tunnel into the rocks.

She stopped short.

Imprinted on the velvet sand leading into the dark passage, was a strange pattern of jumbled footprints, freshly imprinted.

Dare she go further?

Before she could make a wise decision, she entered into a natural cave, bending her 5'7" frame to avoid the low ceiling. It was pitch black as she stepped inside, her eyes not yet adjusting to the darkness. The sound of pounding surf was unsettling. Her heart pulsated in her throat. Never had she had such an electrifying experience on her own. Prunella flicked on her flashlight to see the depths of the cavern and was stunned!

"Hey! Who's there!" a masculine voice assaulted.

The light quivered in her trembling hand and she was unable to speak. She could not even manage to push the button to douse the ray. She stood still.

Patrick approached the stranger who was blinding him with the light.

Snatching the flashlight out of Pru's hand, he turned it on her face. Pru squinted in the brightness.

"Hey!" Patrick's shock was apparent.

As she stared ahead at the yellow haired girl sitting on a low wooden box surrounded by mounds of colorful shells, Prunella's eyes adjusted to the inside light. Patrick had turned the penetrating beam off. It was then that she noticed the slim girl was wearing a bright yellow halter almost as skimpy as her white shorts. She, too, was barefoot. Angie was dumbfounded at the sight of the visitor from the sea. Who was this fine lady in pink silk?

Patrick was staring, not knowing exactly what to say, when Mrs. Huntingwell turned abruptly and fled out of the cave into the looming storm.

Once out in the threatening weather, she ascended the rocks, attacking the challenge like a madwoman. She stumbled, stubbing her toe and leaving a trail of blood droplets as she went. Not acknowledging the pain, she plodded on. Once again, her shoe caught on a jut-out and down she went. Flat out! Scraping her hands and knees, tearing her silk pants and marking her cheekbone with a rather long, superficial scratch.

As she went, wild gusts of air scooped off her hat, commanding the emancipated mane to whip across her face.

Prunella scrambled onward, bending and clawing at any protuberance that could assist her back to the grassy lawn.

She never looked back.

Mrs. Huntingwell hardly realized she was crying, half in disgust at her own foolishness and half in annoyance at seeing Patrick with the pretty young girl.

Why should it matter? Who cares? Was that his girlfriend? Why hadn't he mentioned her? Why should he? Who cares? Wild thoughts raced through her head. The lady was coming unglued.

As she neared the big house, she saw Thad still in his business attire, collar loosened, jacket casually flung over his shoulder, tie in hand. The wind played havoc with his usually perfect appearance. He leaned over, resting on the rail. His eyes were fixed on her.

How long had he been there? Had he seen her fall? What must he be thinking? Her behavior was so out of character. How dare the perfect

Mrs. Thaddeus Tilton Huntingwell the third, step out of character!

She picked up momentum, now, as she marched forward toward her husband, thrusting her arms out in pronounced rhythm with her pounding feet, looking like an embattled soldier on the charge. She was a sight ...almost comical.

As she neared Thad and the wide steps leading to the veranda, she was on fire! For once in her life she had been brave enough to venture out from her safe haven and it had backfired.

As her feet pounded the earth, she could hear her mother's soft spoken words resounding in her head. "A lady must always be a lady. You must carry the stamp of good breeding with you wherever you go, always groomed, always well spoken and mannerly, always perfumed. The lower classes of women allow themselves to be coarse like men. We must remain apart from that."

Her mother arranged the satin ribbons in her hair. "You may be excused, dear."

"Yes, Mommy," she would dutifully reply, as she was escorted to the nanny, who in turn, escorted her to her tutor for French lessons, who in turn, escorted her to her piano lesson.

"Yes, Mommy. Yes, Mommy."

NO, MOMMY! NO! NO! NO!

If only she had the nerve to buck the system, but there was no chance of that. She was the daughter of fortune and was to act accordingly. There was never any choice, she knew that in her heart. She belonged to no other community. She was beautifully clothed, fed the finest cuisine, schooled in the most prestigious schools and exposed to the most cultured people. It was a wonderful place to be, a world of pampering and wealth and she admittedly loved being a part of it. It was where she belonged.

So why, today, did she have those wild feelings to break free? Prunella, tight lipped, was still steaming as she stomped her way to the top step to greet Thad.

"Well, well, look at you." Thad came forward as she reached the veranda. He dropped his jacket on a nearby lounge, and held his tie in both hands. With a smile on his lips, he lassoed her neck and drew her close to him. After a wordless moment he stepped back and held her at arm's length.

"Nasty bruise," he teased, eyeing her swollen cheek. "Must have been quite a struggle." He laughed. She did not.

Prunella studied her partner. She squeezed his hand to acknowledge his presence while sending a message that she was not about to discuss her adventure. It was a closed matter.

She entered the house, walked pensively up the winding stairway, across the wide hall into her room. She hung the embroidered "Do not disturb" sign over the knob, shut the door and went directly to the window. Nasty weather. Rain drops tapped at the panes. The storm was fast approaching off the ocean. She could hear the distant rumble closing in. Lightening bolts flashed over the water.

Leaning against the window sash, Pru gazed out over the rock formations, reliving the ridiculous events of the past hour. Almost as if planned, in her line of vision Patrick emerged with his blond headed friend. Pru absent mindedly touched her own dark hair.

The pair made their way over the rocks, the young man's tanned limbs in stark contrast to the white-skinned form next to him. Patrick held Angie's hand, guiding her chivalrously whenever the need. They were laughing in carefree abandon as the winds threatened their footing. The enjoyment was real. They had found their place of rightness...their place of freedom.

Without warning, Patrick cast a glance to the upstairs window. Pru jerked back out of sight. There was no way he could have seen her from this distance. The absurdity of that reasoning, overlooked.

How many times had she scrutinized the rugged rock climber from her window, but never before had there been a woman. Prunella was loath to admit she was bothered by her presence.

Pru headed for her bath, stopping before a full length mirror. She laughed. It was her only recourse. Slowly the damaged togs were removed. Once down to her delicate undies, she stood before her reflection, twisting and turning, evaluating her thirty-six year old figure. She pulled in her already flat tummy and with an exaggerated straight back, puffed up her chest.

"Not bad, Mrs. Huntingwell, not bad at all."

Pru slipped off the lacy undergarments, reached for her satin penoire and headed for the bath. She drew her own tub, measured out violet bath beads, and slipped, gingerly into the warmer-than-usual fragrant water.

She would have time to gather herself before joining her husband for the ritual before-dinner cocktail.

Pru usually read while her body soaked in the benefits of the sweet vapors, but not today. She adjusted the terrycloth mask over her eyes and leaned her head back on the bath pillow.

For now, she chose to clear her head, to wipe her mind clean of even the tiniest of thoughts.

Preparation of the Feast

Patrick found Molly sitting on the window seat in the wide mid-stair landing. She often paused here for "a wee bit o' a nod" after a formidable morning routine. She gazed through the large window, taking in the full glory of the mansion's landscape, Poochy on her lap.

Molly was deep in thought. Patrick assumed she was reliving poignant memories just like Grams did. They were so much alike, these two vintage ladies.

"Oh! Wha tis it?" The skittish woman jumped with fright.

Patrick came up behind her planting an impish kiss on her cheek and delighting her with a freshly cut rose from the garden.

"Oh," she softened, "wha ta lov'ly tin ta be doin'."

Poochy opened his eyes, twitched his nose and upon seeing who it was went right back to sleep.

Molly reached up her hand to touch Patrick's arm in appreciation of his thoughtfulness, but with a wink and a smile, he was gone as quickly as he had come.

As Molly looked after him, soothed by the bloom's gentle fragrance, she thought of how often this young man had endeared himself to her heart. "He's a'ways up ta som'tin, thet one." She shared her whispered sentiment with the dozing pup.

Molly had no inkling how prophetic her words would be.

It was the 4th of July! The high celebration of the summer season.

Platters clattered ...pots shook...lids quivered...sauces simmered ...mixers roared. The enormous old kitchen at Sweetmeadow was ablaze with activity and titillating aromas, suggesting that the Huntingwells of New York were entertaining highly prized quests. An experience the honored attendees would not soon forget.

The wild cacophony of whirl-wind preparation could be heard all the way to the "back acre" where the prize rose gardens were expertly cared for by Angelo. He knew he must be very selective with his cuttings for the evening's soirée. The Missus insisted on perfection for the Wall Street guests, affording them glowing reports upon their return to the city of their stay at the Huntingwell's summer cottage at Narragansett Bay.

Back in the kitchen, Cook could be heard above the din spitting out orders in staccato outbursts without ever taking her eyes off the glorious plump goose she was lovingly preparing. As she fussed over the stuffing of the bird, she declared it to be the "most gorgeous goosey" she had ever encountered.

Cook ran her domain like clockwork and reveled in the production of such an extravaganza. She found great joy in working with well trained professionals and took comfort in the expertise of her staff. Each artisan knew precisely what his or her responsibility was and executed each duty with skillful precision. None deigned to infringe on another's station, less they risk firm reprimand and swift admonishment from the reigning kitchen queen.

From the dining room the low drone of activity could be heard. A plethora of "extra hands" swiftly polished silver ...buffed glasses ...folded linens with corner-to-corner exactness. It took two servants to sort out and place, with military precision, the impressive battery of flatware that guarded each precious silver-edge place setting like royal sentinels.

Dazzling in ornate splendor, an imposing silver tea service painstakingly polished, was flaunted shamelessly atop the marble server.

Great care was taken to position the heirloom pieces in front of the massive antique mirror at the most advantageous angle, reflecting its grandness out into the room.

Caressed to astonishing smoothness, yards of snow white damask clothed the long banquet table.

Imposing crystal candelabra, dripping with glistening teardrops and fitted with tall white tapers, towered over the guests so as not to obstruct across-the-table conversation; nor hinder the view of properly attired ladies evaluating each other's costume and secretively computing the value of displayed jewels in comparison to their own.

White place cards, scrolled in the blackest of ink from the calligrapher's pen, affirmed the legitimacy of each honored guest.

The final compliment, prized roses fresh from the garden. Angelo appeared cradling an enormous bundle of blossoms in his arms, exuding the same tenderness one might render a sleeping infant. A tantalizing fragrance lightly flavored the air.

Tonight Mrs. Huntingwell's décor called for all white roses. She had directed Angelo to choose only the most flawless blooms. Now he watched with quiet pride as the four dozen stems were artfully arranged in an immense footed crystal bowl and set down on center stage, completing the magnificent presentation.

The ambience of wealth permeated the lovely dining room. Refinement roared in silence.

In a few hours, fastidiously bedecked guests would encompass this splendid table and with willing hearts become a part of this memorable production.

All was as planned ...white ...serene ...elegant.

Indeed perfection.

Goosey Gets Loose

Tillie's heart beat wildly! For the past few days, her stomach was full of "collywobbles," as Molly would say, ever since she agreed to be a co-conspirator in, yet another, of Patrick's reckless schemes.

An upstairs maid and the youngest of the Sweetmeadow staff, she was now "training" to help out "in times of need" in the kitchen. She worked under the expert tutelage of the French pastry chef who spoke little English and had less interest in learning more. Tillie thought the job, at times, boring and dull.

As the summer unfolded, she found herself spending more time day-dreaming of how she could steal a few moments away from the kitchen far from the arduous task of mastering the art of folding layers of butter into puff pastry. She always looked forward to hearing about Patrick's latest plot to "liven the place up."

This evening was to be the most daring of all his pranks and the young maid was a bit qualmish. She was concerned about her daring friend. Could he really pull it off without a hitch? Tillie giggled in anticipation. She wouldn't miss it for the world. Patrick's fertile mind was incessantly concocting some sort of outrageous scheme, but to "crash" a formal dinner party might be a bit over the rim of sanity.

During the first weeks of summer season, Patrick had developed a congenial friendship with Mr. Huntingwell, who welcomed the young man's lighthearted humor and easy wit. The young prankster was always cognizant of crossing the boundary of employer and employee...never rude or overbearing. He was convinced that Thad would be amused by this evening's planned farce. Now, the lady of the house, that was a different matter.

As the guests slowly filtered into the main dining room, breathtaking by candlelight, they were escorted to their seats by college students hired expressly for this duty.

Tonight's gathering was an assemblage of powerful business associates and their spouses. The sort of affair that Thaddeus Huntingwell reveled in. He immensely enjoyed reigning at the head of the long table, regaling in the bounty of his harvest. How proud he was to present his exquisite home to this group of highly successful men and their wives...his peers.

Everything Thaddeus did was for a respectful appearance. He was of the belief that a man's worth was as substantial as his holdings. A philosophy passed on through several generations of Huntingwell men.

He was by no description a malicious man, but imbued by heritage to be the keeper of a fortune.

Thaddeus lived as a gentleman, always nicely groomed, well mannered and expectant of those hired to cater to his needs, to do exactly that. He was admittedly rather spoiled and inept at performing the most mundane tasks. Mr. Huntingwell was very good to his help. He paid them well. He believed in fairness and allowed his staff excessive fringe benefits for their intricate part in refining the household machinery. They, in turn, saw that "the master's" every request was performed with pride to his satisfaction.

Tonight, Thaddeus was in his glory. Every detail executed to perfection. His wife, draped simply in a white silk sheath was without question the "jewel in his crown."

In the kitchen, Cook was bent over a huge butcher block table fastidiously bestowing the final touches on "gorgeous goosey."

When the first courses were removed from the table, it was time to present the stuffed goose to the honored audience with great theatrical flair. Two white-gloved young men, ready to transport Goosey from the kitchen into the dining room, stood near Cook awaiting their cargo.

In the dining room, the stage was set by the appearance of a somber faced Nigel. With great aplomb and a swift flick of his wrist, he extinguished all but two candles. Thus, allowing the flaming bird to become the focal point of the sumptuous repast and heighten the drama of the presentation.

Nigel proceeded, Zombie-like, to the French doors of the kitchen and with exaggerated ceremony thrust them open.

Out came two stiff-walking lads carrying "gorgeous goosey" in all its regal splendor on an enormous silver tray. They strode in deliberate cadence around the table for all to gaze incredulously upon the masterful presentation. Gasps of admiration and "praises to the chef" echoed throughout. Mr. Huntingwell called for Cook to come from the kitchen and take a well-deserved bow.

Cook responded to the applause by portraying the humble undeserving servant, but had anticipated her moment in the spotlight and donned her most elaborate lace apron and cap. She stood proudly erect next to Nigel, directly behind "the master," to view the ceremonial "lighting of the goose."

The stage was set.

Tillie was beside herself with suspense. Every nerve in her body pulled taut. She was giddy with fear. From her vantage point, behind the pantry door, which was wedged open a sliver, she had full scope of the table allowing her to determine precisely when "goosey" was to be sacrificed by fire.

As the heavy platter was set down in front of Thaddeus, he arose from his chair to avoid collision with the festive bird. He raised a crystal decanter and with a slight tinge of drama, doused "goosey" with a lusty swash of 50 year old brandy.

This was Tillie's cue to alert Patrick that the goose was about to go up in a blaze of glory.

The moment was perfect.

Tillie pulled the shutter back from the side window alerting Patrick that the golden goose, was indeed, under siege.

To the horror of those in the kitchen, Patrick came charging through the back door crushing an ungainly squawking gander to his chest. The feathered fowl, visibly exasperated, audibly displayed outrage at being so dishonorably treated.

Patrick's plan was to meander calmly into the dining room for a few seconds with the bird under his arm. He would announce in his most pathetic voice to the unsuspecting guests that the poor grieving gander had come to pay his final respects to his dear, departed "gorgeous goosey." It was to produce a good laugh and be all over.

Unfortunately, grieving gander was in no mood to play the game. Patrick was unable to quell the powerful struggling creature. Just as he made his entrance into the sophisticated gathering, the gander exerted his full strength, freeing himself from Patrick's arms and lunged for the dark security under the table.

Patrick froze.

Tillie, upon seeing the disaster, began jumping up and down trying to cover her mouth in an attempt to quiet the gurgling sounds escaping from her lips. She was close to hysteria.

The kitchen help was aghast!

Feathers flew everywhere and the elegant flavor of the evening was instantly invaded with deafening screeches. Guests were thrown into a panic. Not knowing what was poking at their ankles or making such ear shattering protests, they were terrorized.

Chairs were recklessly shoved aside in an attempt to flee the menacing threat. Women screamed. Men stood in amazement. But, "The Missus," in semi-shock, never moved from her place at the end of the table. She remained in perfect defiance.

Servants tried in vain to retrieve the ornery bird who, by now was frightened out of his feathers.

Thaddeus stood like a marble statue and all he could muster was, "What in bloody hell is going on?."

No one knew. Tillie thought him so droll and wondered if he could see even a modicum of humor in the whole incident. She doubted it.

Through the whole farcical scene, Tillie's eyes were riveted on Patrick who was rummaging under the table on all fours randomly taking swips at gander and missing by a mile.

Prunella Huntingwell remained alone at the table, straight backed, poised. She was mesmerized by the goings on around her. Trying desperately to hide her expression, she coyly maneuvered her napkin over her mouth camouflaging her amusement.

As Tillie was studying her, in awe of the lady's self-control, she noticed Mrs. Huntingwell give a slight jump, but remain seated. Tillie assumed the gander had nipped at her ankle. What she could not see was Patrick taking full advantage of the temptation before his eyes. In an unthinking move, he playfully tapped his fingers, emulating pecking, over the silken ankles of the lady in the beautiful white dress.

She was shocked at such crass behavior and would certainly voice her displeasure. Or would she punish him with silence?

After a few hairy moments, Patrick was able to corner the shivering gander. He grasped it firmly in both arms, trying to soothe the traumatized creature whose heart was beating out of control.

Patrick stood before the stunned group, some of whom had slowly begun to reappear and seek out their places; several guests going all around the room to avoid any more contact with the unruly pair. Patrick apologized for the antics of the disruptive bird and conjuring up a pitiful expression explained that gander had just "come to pay his last respects to his departed friend, gorgeous goosey." His head slowly shaking, eyes lowered.

After his sterling performance, Patrick bowed ceremoniously to the lady in white, coyly sending her that lazy rakish grin. She returned a mannequin-like nod, her breeding not allowing her to flinch a nerve.

Patrick was amused to see her bravely fighting to maintain her composure. She remained outwardly provoked at his childish antics, but the glint in her eyes betrayed her.

Thaddeus, still peeved and too annoyed to see any humor in the whole absurd episode, impatiently waved Patrick off with the back of his hand. He was too above it all to even notice the innocent flirtatious exchange between his wife and the young handyman.

As Patrick took one quick glance back into the room, he noticed that all eyes were riveted on the silver tray and the glistening goose. His few seconds plan had turned into a thirty minute disaster. Not at all as he had envisioned and he felt badly. Patrick knew he would hear from Thaddeus on this one.

Molly hurried down the stairs upon hearing the commotion, knowing intuitively that Patrick was at it again, "stirrin' tins up." She was waiting for him in the kitchen.

"Wha tem ah goin' t' do wit ya?" she scolded.

The agitated lady did not know whether to laugh or cry at "th' likes o' 'im" doing battle with a squawking bird.

"A'ways jollyin'...stirrin' up one shenanigan o' t'other." Molly looked up into those impish blue eyes and knew there would be no changing him.

On his way out to free the gander, Patrick winked at her with sweet affection.

"Can't help it, me darlin' Molly," he whispered. "'Tis the Irish in me soul."

Her heart constricted.

Needless to say, the gaiety was at a low ebb for the remainder of the meal and not much of the delicious entré was consumed by the more tender hearted.

But the events of the evening were just beginning. Red, white and blue ice cream parfaits would be served out on the lawn where guests would be treated to an impressive show of fireworks. Later in the Great Room, live music and dancing would top off the annual 4th of July celebration at Sweetmeadow.

Change of Plans

The mid-day sun was grueling. Heat emanating from the old house's blistering siding made Patrick's job more trying. Changing the shutters on these sizable windows was no simple task and he was relieved to be nearing the end of the project. Only two more windows. He would finish up sometime when the guests were at play away from the premises.

As Patrick dismounted the ladder, he noticed Thad coming toward him in haste across the lawn.

"Patrick," he hailed, "been looking for you." He approached with an extended hand. "Wonder if I could impose on you."

"Sure," he wiped his brow. "What's up?"

"As you know, our tenth wedding anniversary is coming up next Sunday and I promised Mrs. Huntingwell that I'd take her to the opera on Friday. Had the tickets for several weeks." He paused. "Just received word that a good business friend had a fatal heart attack in New York." Thad shook his head in disbelief and went on. "Younger than I am ...hard worker ...four kids. Shame, damn shame!"

Thad glanced at the sky as if to seek an explanation. There was a brief silence. Patrick started to speak, but his boss continued.

"Need to catch the next train back out." It was Saturday and Thad had just arrived from the city last evening. He had planned to enjoy the whole week at the estate before the devastating phone call. "Might be of some help to the family, funeral arrangements, whatever they need." He shrugged his shoulders. "Damn, shame, damn shame," trying to make some sense of the loss. "If you would escort Mrs. Huntingwell to the performance, I'd be grateful. Hate her to miss it. Puccini, one of her favorites. I'll have a tux sent by. Nigel will get it to the tailor, if need be. Max will be informed of the evening's event."

Patrick, astounded at what his ears were absorbing, stared with blank expression. Was Thaddeus unaware of his wife's innate appeal? Was he so sure of her devotion to him that he would send her off with a younger man? Or, did he think Patrick to be a mere boy. Was a middle age man just plain naïve about such things?

Patrick was unable to find words to refuse, for after all, he had been hired on as a "boy Friday" to fill in anywhere he was needed. He agreed to help out.

Although his love for classical music took him in many directions, he had never developed a particular fondness for opera. At times he found it non-inspiring to listen to actors performing lyrics in a language he could not readily comprehend. For his new friend, he would suffer through.

Above all, he loathed being mummified in a monkey suit, but having a stunning show piece on his arm should soften the mood. He was familiar with the story and arias of Madam Butterfly, which would add considerably in lightening the evening's tedium.

When confronted with the last minute change of partners, Prunella just laughed.

"Spend an evening with that clown?" She refused. But seeing how intent her husband was to assuage the sudden canceling of plans, she made the best of it and agreed to just "go and come."

Side Trip

Emulating a pair of novice detectives, the aging maid and Patrick huddled together obscured by generous folds of curtain that dressed the tall dining room windows. They peered with guarded excitement through the sparkling panes at the sleek limousine purring motionlessly in front of Sweetmeadow's front entrance.

Max, poised in his dark green uniform, legs apart, hands behind his back ...rocking slightly back and forth ...awaited the arrival of his second morning passenger. The congenial chauffeur had already returned from his first regularly scheduled Monday morning jaunt ...a short trip to the Kingston Depot with Thaddeus.

It was Max's job to make certain every Monday morning of the summer that his boss boarded the express train to New York City on time for another spirited week on Wall Street.

It always pleased Max to see Mr. Huntingwell refreshed after a relaxing weekend with his wife and friends at the glorious estate. He was amazed at how short a time it took Mr. Huntingwell to slip back into the work mode. Five minutes into the fifteen minute trip, Mr. Huntingwell's expression became intense. He was already geared to take on any bustling challenges the market would offer.

Max unselfishly envied his boss. Thaddeus had been dealt a trump hand from life's deck of cards. The ultimate privilege of living two separate lives ...each as satisfying as the other; one stimulating the mind, the other soothing the senses, and Mr. Huntingwell possessed the unique ability to divorce one from the other ...work from play. Max admired that.

The amiable driver had always accepted his blackness, feeling the strong self-respect his mother had instilled in him as a young barefoot boy. Yet, he couldn't keep his mind from fantasizing what it must be like to be white; to have such riches ...to know the great luxury of choice. He was imprisoned in a world behind invisible bars ...a world of duty where choices were meager, but Max was a contented man and took great pride in performing his services well.

Doing any honest job with dignity as long as "it don't hurt nobody" was worthy of the Lord's praises, the old folks would preach.

Max was employed by the Huntingwells only through the three summer months they were in residence at Sweetmeadow. It was the perfect arrangement. Max held a job at the local high school during the school year doing janitorial work and at night took on a night watchman's duties for a car dealership in Wakefield. With a wife and children to support, the work load was a necessity.

Max had lived his entire life in what was carelessly referred to by the white community as "Niggatown." The term nigger was an offensive appellation carried over from slave days. Over the decades, it had evolved as the name of an area, with no intentional slander or derogatory connection attached to it, but still odious to those who struggled within it's boundaries.

The hard working dark skinned souls who crammed into tiny run down shacks fought daily for a part in the white drama. They had a difficult time being accepted for their merit and not judged for the color of their skin. It was uncomfortable to push their way onto the pompous stage of light skinned players.

Max had known severe times as a young father...money was scarce and living conditions less than desirable. He had agonized through a horrendous home fire ...the result of an overturned gasoline heater ...which culminated in the loss of his two sons and leaving him with ugly, deformed scars on both hands...a constant reminder of the tragedy.

Although Max was only forty-two, his woolly hair had grayed and the years of toil already lined his pleasant face.

The saddest element of his life, and hardest to cope with, was that his wife, "a whisper of a woman," had to work so hard. It tore at his heart to see the piles of mending and laundry she faithfully did every evening to supplement his income. The morning hours she cleaned house for a gracious couple in Kingston who had two daughters a few years older than their own girls. Her employers generously passed down any usable clothing that would help ease the gloomy pressures of survival for the young black family.

Max looked forward to "The Season" at Narragansett. He was treated with respect and generosity. "The Missus" always had a stack of last seasons fashions for his wife ..."fine fabrics" that she could restyle to suit her own simple needs.

"The Mistah," time after time padded his paycheck without explanation and on occasion Max would find an extra twenty dollar bill stuffed in his cap. Dear "Cook" never let him leave the premises without a bulging sack of fragrant delicacies "for the little ones."

His days at Sweetmeadow were his happiest ...literally rubbing elbows with the world's elite. A steady stream of fascinating characters graced the manor each season; actors, politicians, dancers, musicians, novelists, corporate executives. The ultra-rich, many paralyzed by the soft ease of their lifestyle, perpetually seeking to add new texture to the threads of their luxurious hours by forever searching for a more stimulating kind of entertainment, a more daring feat.

Max experienced, firsthand, the visual splendor of humanity in all of its multitudinous forms; life at its most spectacular, life at its most desolate.

His wife found profound joy in the fairy-tale accounts that he brought home to her. He purposely embellished each episode and watched her dark eyes dance with excitement. Tales of a kingdom she would never know.

"Thar she is! Thar she is!" the old servantess whispered almost outloud.

"Who, Molly, your ghost?"

Patrick took a swift shot in the ribs from Molly's elbow.

"B'hav yerself! It's Missus Huntin'well" Molly gave him a look of reproach. "Oh-h-h look at 'er." Another blow to the ribs. Patrick grimaced without averting his eyes from the window.

Mrs. Huntingwell appeared in a summery pale yellow frock with matching sandals exuding an aura of controlled joy. She almost ran down the wide cement steps, with Poochy leading the way, giving Max a "this is our secret" kind of smile.

"Hello, Max, beautiful morning," a lilting tone.

"Mornin' Missus." He touched the rim of his cap, returning her greeting. "Sure do look like it gonna be a purty one" he paused, assisting her with his white gloved hands into the spacious middle backseat of the limousine. Poochy had already chosen his spot by the window. "Yas 'um, it sure do."

Inside the house Molly was in a dither.

"Wha tin th'world d'yeh suspect th'two o'thim t'be up t'on these

Mond'y mornin's, eh?" Molly was now unconsciously prodding Patrick's arm with little staccato-like jabs from her index finger as she spoke.

"Easy, easy." Patrick tried to dodge the latest attack. Molly ceased her poking and went right on with her thought.

"Seems mighty suspect t'me, thet it's th' same thin' ev'ry Mond'y, ev'ry Mond'y." She quizzed him with her eyes. "Wha d'ya make o'fit, eh, Paddy?"

Molly was secretly hurt that "her lady" had not confided in her as to the nature of these weekly excursions. After all, hadn't Mrs. Huntingwell always trusted the older woman like a mother with the most personal aspects of her life? It was odd and although Molly respected her boss's right to privacy, her own curiosity was insatiable.

"Wher' does sh' romp off to so secret, eh?" Molly couldn't let it go.

"Beats me." Patrick offered vigorously rubbing his arm to ease the pain from the latest pummeling. No sooner had the words left his lips when he turned and bolted from the room.

"Whar 'n hell's fire do ya' think yar goin'?" Molly engaged her short legs in a half run, trying in desperation to catch him. He had vanished. She scurried back to her lookout post at the wide window just as Patrick jumped into the wood-sided station wagon in hot pursuit of the curious couple.

Monday was Angelo's day off, and the keys were purposely left in the ignition of the "Town and Country" handy to any member of the staff who might need to run personal errands.

"Foolish, Lad!" Molly wished she were quicker on her feet. She would have sneaked off with him.

Patrick stayed on the gravel drive far enough behind the luxury car until it turned north onto the narrow Ocean Drive. He stayed within spying distance for about thirty minutes to the outskirts of Providence and a pitifully deteriorated tenement district. The area reeked of poverty and suffering.

Patrick, at first, accepted the rundown streets as part of a detour assuming Max wanted to avoid the more trafficked roads of the city. But as they continued on he deduced that the chauffeur had simply lost his way. Still trying to interpret the meaning of the current circumstances, Patrick was shocked out of his thoughts as the sleek limo deliberately turned down a narrow street and pulled up in front of a run-down, three story apartment building and stopped.

Patrick remained at a safe distance, not chancing a discovery and continued to take inventory of the puzzling events unfolding before him.

The big car's engine quieted. A gaggle of little children...some black, some white, bombarded from the scuffed-up doorway. They spilled down the chipped brick steps, waving and jumping up and down at the sight of their visitors. Patrick watched, unable to draw any immediate conclusion. As the drama played out, he noted with intrigue that the tots were all amazingly clean and well-clothed, in sharp contrast to the despicable conditions that surrounded them.

At their heels appeared a large, jovial looking black lady holding a tiny infant clad in what seemed from a distance to be a white cloth diaper.

Prunella Huntingwell bounded from her seat, not waiting for Max to open her door, and ran to the children, stooping to gather up as many of the squealing tots as her arms could embrace. Poochy was right in the middle of the mix, wagging his tail in happy reunion. They greeted each other as the dearest of dear old friends.

"Well, I'll be damned," Patrick breathed in a whispered voice, subconsciously protecting himself from being overheard. He remained open-mouthed in utter confusion at this impeccably dressed woman who was now on her knees allowing, even welcoming, the army of "playful pups" to assault her immaculate clothing. He remained mesmerized with wonder.

The rotund mamma, a calico apron swaying over her big belly, hurried forth. She extended her free arm to hug Mrs. Huntingwell who was fighting to be free of the clinging children and avail herself to return the jovial woman's warm gesture.

Patrick was overwhelmed at the poignant scene that had transpired in the most unlikely of places. What was it all about? Who were these children"? This kind looking woman who cradled the helpless infant so lovingly in her arms? How did they meet? As questions flooded his mind, another strange twist took place.

Prunella stood on her tiptoes. With a raised hand she motioned to Max, who had not left his post by the curb, to open the rear trunk. She hurriedly left the milling little group and joined Max at the back of the limo. The top sprung open, exposing an eclectic array of grocery bags, toys, books, boxes...miniature clothes still on hangers.

Max handed Mrs. Huntingwell several lighter, odd-shaped parcels, all she could manage with ease. She went ahead into the house followed by the nursemaid and the noisy troop of little ones comically resembling Mexican jumping beans.

Max, himself laden with a hefty load of cartons, also disappeared into the deteriorating dwelling. He came back and forth several more times until every cavity of the vehicle had been emptied.

Max again took his dutiful place behind the steering wheel to await his boss lady.

Ah...Mrs. Huntingwell...you are a study, thought Patrick.

As Patrick sat, anxious to add the next link to this chain of discoveries, it suddenly became clear to him. Of course! This was her own personal charity...an intimate warming of the heart. It was her private way of giving a portion of her wealth without fanfare. To boast of it's merit in public would violate the very nobility of the deed.

She reminded him of the exquisite white shelled creatures he often discovered hiding in the deepest crevices of the rocks. Their thick exteriors hard and cold to the touch, belying their interiors lined with the richest, most exquisite depth of colors and designs the sea could offer. Their outer surface impenetrable, yet cradled beneath the crusty casing was a soft fragile heart nesting within its walls, tentative to expose its vulnerability for fear of being devoured.

A good thirty minutes later, Mrs. Huntingwell, with Poochy in her arms, appeared at the front entrance, still surrounded by the flock of waving children who now had colorful lollipops in their mouths. She kissed the cheek of the aproned lady and hurried down the steps waving back and smiling as she approached her waiting chariot.

Max saw her coming and instinctively jumped out onto the cracked sidewalk to open the door.

Max had the engine idling and it was only a few seconds before they were on their way again, with Patrick on his trail. Down another street bordered on both sides by crumbling doorless old buildings. Yards strewn with broken toys, sagging upholstered couches crammed onto small cement stoops, street gutters were resting spots for overfull barrels of decaying garbage. Every yard had a full sagging clothesline. Most areas were peppered with tiny shoeless children playing with carefree abandon among rusted out remains of old stripped-down car chassis.

How many would make it to adulthood? He was saddened by the reality that these innocents were thrust, without choice, into such harsh conditions. Patrick saw the children laughing and running about, making do with what was available. They knew no other lifestyle. They could not long for things they were unaware existed. It was their prison of poverty and they were likely to die here within the neighborhood confines. Their happy little faces were mercifully oblivious to the opulence that bejeweled the earth, but a tear drop away.

Golden opportunity would be offered to only a few of their color, although times were slowly beginning to change. Where was the justice in such a contrast in human conditions? Patrick agonized.

The rich lady ...the poor lady...how did they meet? Patrick was burning with curiosity. He knew he might never garner the details of such an unlikely friendship and he vowed never to inquire. He would not expose her cover.

To have discovered the human portion of Prunella Catherine Huntingwell's heart was reward enough.

The Dress

Patrick sped up. He strategically designed his maneuvers to assure the limo was framed well within viewing range. He empowered Max to lead him like a leashed spaniel through a maze of tangled streets.

The big car finally oiled it's way to the corner of a bustling avenue lined with an odd mix of struggling businesses; haberdasheries, shrouded with amazingly awful displays of unpressed garments...tiny "hole-in-the-wall" ethnic restaurants...shoe makers...pawn brokers..."mom 'n pop" donut shops...and a mishmash of trendy, if not sleazy, dress boutiques. A few shop owners were sweeping the sidewalks in front of their establishments out of boredom, others stood in open doorways eyeballing foot traffic in hopes of luring in would-be buyers.

Only seconds after Max brought the limo to an idle, a back door opened and the slender lady stepped out. This time, without her fluffy companion. In haste, she flung the door closed behind her and fidgeting with an oversized purse, fled down a cluttered alleyway.

Max stealthily moved a few blocks away to an undeveloped overgrown area on the outer fringe of the merchandising district, a polite distance from the carnival atmosphere, to await his passenger. Here out-of-sight, the car, a showy display of wealth, would not be a conspicuous target for vandals.

Patrick, once again was at a loss to make sense of what he considered to be rather odd behavior. If the couple had chosen to travel incognito, why did they opt for the limo in the first place? But nothing would surprise him...not after the morning's revelation.

Patrick followed suit and parked just out of Max's range. The shade of an obliging oak offered him camouflage and a hope that he would not be discovered.

He set out on foot, determined not to lose the swift fleeting lady in the crowd. She was on a definite mission, but for what? This was hardly the home of Lord and Taylor.

Patrick's initial stirring of guilt was quickly quelled by the energy of the chase. He deemed it prudent to insure against recognition and chose to travel a parallel route. He would catch up with her at the far end.

He raced down the crowded sidewalk unaware of bumping passersby, none of whom took kindly to the unsuspected jostling. Consumed with the task of keeping her in sight, he unconsciously ran through the spray of a faulty fire hydrant.

Patrick rounded the corner. There she stood in front of a garishly appointed store front. It's door and window frames screamed a vivid hot pink and gaudy purple flowers had been emblazoned by some fledging artist on "Pepto-Bismol pink" shutters.

He tried in vain to make some logic of the picture in front of him.

In the window, a pair of mannequins stared expressionless, flaunting dazzling flame-red fashions. Patrick opined that this outlandish clashing of colors could only be repulsive to someone as refined as Mrs. Thaddeus Huntingwell and found it baffling to observe her scrutinizing the window display with such intensity.

As he continued his vigil from across the street, hidden by a healthy cluster of hedges, he saw Mrs. Huntingwell position herself deliberately in front of the dress on the left, a blaring siren-flavored teaser. The strapless dress slunk in shamelessly sleek lines, featuring a wide jeweled band designed to accentuate the slimmest of waistlines and a bold side slit that slithered halfway to the hip. The figure was wittingly posed in a most seductive posture to titillate the senses. Spot lights, strategically stationed, exaggerated the fire of the faux jewels evincing a stage effect even in the middle of the day.

Patrick had no trouble pouring Prunella's slim fluid body into the flashy costume and envisioned the result sensational.

He could barely see her profile. Did he imagine it, or was there a slight smile on her lips. He hoped she was fantasizing a wild night on the town, then laughed to himself at his lunacy. For although she might enjoy wearing the spicy garment, she wouldn't dare to adorn herself in such risqué wrappings for fear of appearing too brazen, vain...bourgeois. Poor Prunella Catherine, he empathized with her. She was a prisoner jailed in a much more elegant world than this brazen show-piece would tolerate.

After viewing the window display for a few minutes, she stole quick secretive glances up and down the sidewalk, scanning the area as if for a familiar face that may witness her surrender to this irresistible invitation to serendipity. Satisfied that all was clear, she slipped through the garish entrance.

Patrick found it amusing that Mrs. Huntingwell actually surveyed her surroundings. Surely, none of her high-class friends would be found shopping in this tawdry part of town.

Still damp from his recent dousing, he made his way with caution across the street and guardedly positioned himself with his back pressed flat against the outside wall of the shop. He edged as close to the window opening as he could to peruse the interior.

Patrick caught a glimpse of Queen Catherine following a sales lady who was holding a duplicate of the scanty "window dress" into the dressing room.

Would she dare?

Patrick found himself inwardly cheering for Prunella.

"Yes! Yes!" he made a half-hidden pumping gesture with his fist. "Go for it!"

Dodging traffic, Patrick retreated to his spying post behind the clump of greenery and waited. In short order, the lovely lady made her exit without a parcel and instantly melted into the stream of shoppers.

"No dress?" Maybe she didn't like the fit. "Yea, right! Sure she didn't."

He contemplated his next move for all of thirty seconds before deciding to check out the dress shop.

Sheepishly slipping into the "house of fashion," he was all but blinded by the vulgar pink carpet and mirrored walls. Forcing himself not to gag from the sickly-sweet fumes of cheap perfume, he inquired of the overly made-up clerk about her last customer and the celebrated garment.

She affirmed that the lady had certainly approved the fit of the dress and would be giving it some thought.

BUNK! She didn't have the nerve to face her "blue blood" friends or blatantly embarrass her high brow husband. She had no right to regale herself in a smashing get-up that would undeniably loosen a few shocked heads, possibly even get herself written up in the social columns as "the hottest dish of the season."

"God forbid she should feel alive!" Patrick found his innards agitated. It jarred his sense of fairness that Prunella was trapped into living her life by someone else's rules, programmed into a world so vividly colored by those who, duty bound, designed her lifestyle. Her boundaries were set. It irked him.

He was annoyed with himself for wasting precious time trying to decode the combination to Mrs. Huntingwell's inner vault. Why was he so driven? What was she to him, anyway? His employer. That was all.

Patrick decided to forget it...the insane spying. It was time to head back to the estate. His emotions had been stimulated enough for one day. He had discovered that the steel mistress of Sweetmeadow was wearing several disguises.

He was certain, in spite of all his pompous good intentions, that the need to learn more about her charade would not end today. He had wrestled with these promises before and lost.

Molly's Ghost

"T'was 'er agin!" T'was 'er agin!

Molly, usually happy and mild mannered, bounded into the grand parlor wildly waving her feather duster in an uncharacteristic outburst. She stopped, wide eyed and frenzied, inches from the graceful little Queen Anne's desk, almost knocking over a tiny crystal sleigh that Mrs. Huntingwell's grandmother had lavished her with on her sixteenth Christmas. She was face to face with "the missus" before she realized her faux-pas. To overstep her bounds as a maid and invade her lady's private space without knocking was unthinkable.

Mrs. Huntingwell, hardly expecting a boisterous intrusion, glanced up from her letter writing in bewildered curiosity. She rose from her slender gold leaf chair to pay immediate mind to the overwrought woman displaying odd signs of excessive strain.

"There, there now, Molly, what is it?" the younger woman pacified as she rounded her desk to calm the obviously shaken servantess.

"T'was 'er, ah'm sw'arin it on me mether's grave, ah em." Molly, nervously made a tiny sign of the cross over her heart and raved on. "T'is th' ghost, all'righ, ah 'erd 'er, up thar over me 'ed." She pointed the duster ominously to the ceiling above them. "Las' nite...ah did."

"Now, now Molly dear" Mrs. Huntingwell soothed in a tranquil tone, placing an arm lovingly around the shoulders of her long time friend. "There are no ghosts in this house, honestly there aren't. You mustn't be disturbed. I'm sure it was the wind."

"No, no 'Missy'" (an appellation Molly lovingly called her mistress when she felt the need of extra closeness.) "She w'sup thar. Ah 'erd 'er footsteps, ah did." She looked straight up at her employer who stood several inches taller than she.

Molly was not going to be talked out of her ghost.

"T'was thet young Clara Doolaine, it t'was" Molly vented with authority. "Yes, Ma'am, thet's who it t'was!"

Years ago, the first inhabitants of Sweetmeadow Estate were a young couple by the name of Mr. and Mrs. Samuel Paul Doolaine. He was twenty three, his child-bride Clara only sixteen.

Although heart broken over his daughter's decision to marry the chauffeur's son, an inferior choice of mate, Clara's adoring father indulged his rather homely pampered little girl with the enviable mansion for a wedding gift. He had made his millions importing the finest silks and brocades from around the world, featuring them "as a lure" for his chain of classy department stores.

After only a meager interlude in the beautiful home, the shy child-bride, little Clara Doolaine was mysteriously found dead in the summer attic, her clothes neatly folded by her side. Her unclad body was partially veiled by a lustrous swarth of scarlet silk, presumed to have been chosen from a nearby trunk.

No evidence of foul play was ever unearthed; no pills, no weapon, no note, simply the serene presence of a young maiden peacefully slumbering in the arms of death.

It was common knowledge that the handsome looking bridegroom had trapped the innocent lass solely for her fortune and although she became adoring of him, the love was never returned.

A plethora of puzzling suspicions sizzled among Naragansett's high society and sundry carelessly concocted motives were speculated. With quiet retinence, it was concluded that the frail child who suffered the "wasting effects of asthma" had plausibly succumbed to the overpowering fumes of mothballs coupled with the oppressive heat in the unventilated attic. The conditions placing too much demand on her delicate constitution.

Nothing was ever confirmed. Generations of Sweetmeadow visitors were introduced to an insipid ferrotype of the mystery child hanging in the entry hall and left to their own conclusions as to the fate of the celebrated Clara Doolaine.

Prunella Huntingwell, seeing that the headstrong woman was not about to recant her ghost claim, decided it best to humor her.

"I am quite sure, if she is there, that she is a kind friendly ghost, Molly, and certainly not up to any harm."

"I'd like t'be thinkin' so" mumbled Molly almost inaudibly as she turned to leave.

Patrick was out in the main entrance hall polishing the filigree finials that reigned on the grand mahogany staircase when he was startled by Molly's rather boisterous outburst.

"Hey, what's this I hear about a ghost?" He entered cautiously through the French doors, rescrewing the lid on a tin of metal cleaner.

Molly repeated her story with just as much conviction and enthusiasm as originally expressed.

Patrick smiled skeptically. He shot a quick inquisitive glance at Mrs. Huntingwell who was trying her level best to dissuade him from erupting with any sinister comments that might set the dear little woman off on a tangent again. But before he could utter a sound, Molly was at him.

"Don' yar be mockin' me now, ya hear?" she warned, shaking the feather duster vigorously at his face as she turned to leave the room. He realized that she was serious and decided, wisely, not to provoke her further.

Patrick and Prunella exchanged sympathetic looks, chalking it up to just one more of Molly's Irish superstitions. For after all, wasn't it the same sweet lady who believed that finding a green snake on the grass was an omen that another soul had departed from the soil of Ireland?

It was several weeks later, the universe glowing from a full moon, that Patrick was having a fitful bout with sleep. His head throbbed and he had migrated to the open window for a refreshing interlude of night air. Moon glow cast intriguing shadows over the still grounds of the mansion, giving fuel to his fertile imagination. As he raised his head to drink in the full grandeur of the celestial spotlight, his eye caught a glimpse of a wavering form dart past a window on the fourth floor of the main house, an attic room.

"What the—" He didn't move. His eyes incredulously glued to the narrow window. There was nothing! But as if teasing him, the shadow reappeared for a fleeting moment and again retreated from view.

Patrick was flabbergasted, ablaze with curiosity. He gave himself a hearty slap on the face to assure he was not in some dream mode. He felt the sting of pain verifying his awake state.

"Molly's ghost? Could it be?"

Without giving a scintilla of thought to the consequences of his actions, he grabbed his flashlight and flew down the outside stairs, across the damp spongy lawn to the north side of the big house. He quickly scaled the fire escape that led to the wide hall on the second floor and let himself in through the open window. Counting heavily on everyone's being asleep at this ungainly hour, he tiptoed over the thick rugs directly to a narrow stairway at the end of the dimly lit hall. It led to the third and fourth floors.

Patrick raced up the two flights of stairs staying in the middle of the rubber treads. He tried to make himself weightless in an effort to avoid any telltale creaks that would announce his presence.

He entered the enormous expanse with a feeling of anxiety. The air was hot, stuffy, oppressive. He stayed close to the splintered rafters. Protruding nails were garnished with a variety of roosting old hats and vintage clothing which sporadic slivers of moonlight transformed into grotesque characters lurking in the night. Patrick was painfully tense.

Pieces of wicker furniture occupying the area a few weeks ago, had been moved to the outside veranda, granting him full view of the endless space. He prowled on all fours in the eerie darkness, slithering with the silken prowess of a jungle cat, to a more sheltered vantage point under the eaves.

"Holy saints!"

He stopped short in his tracks.

There was a woman at the most distant end of the room ...or was it?

Patrick froze. The only part of his being that was still working was his heart, and he thought it too, might cease to function at any moment. His body tightened.

Who was she? WHAT was she?

An icy shiver of disbelief washed over him in the simmering heat.

Who was this phantom being? A witch? A demon? And where did she come from?

The moon's rays filtered in through slender dormer windows, casting just enough light on the svelte figure to make her visible, although he was unable to identify her features.

Patrick stared, unable to avert his eyes.

The alluring seductress was flagrantly enthralled in some sort of choreographic rhapsody, almost ethereal. She moved like an angel. Was she?

Patrick was astounded by her obvious sense of freedom. His eyes unblinking, fixed on her performance. He found himself spellbound as he watched her twirl around the room at dizzying speed, pirouetting rhythmically to a silent symphony that only she was privileged to hear. In and out of the shadows she swirled, enraptured by the consuming enchantment of her whimsy. On and on and on she danced with unrelenting energy, skillfully exuding an illusion of weightlessness. Patrick was convinced that her feet were not touching the floor.

With every nerve in his body strained to the breaking point, he inched his way closer to the alluring prima donna, staying well within the protective shadows of the night. His heart was now pounding with such fury he was sure she would hear it.

As he snuggled into an airless nook, as close as he dared to venture, he noticed for the first time that the lithe silhouette was unclothed. His immediate reaction was to avert his eyes from the scene, but he was too stunned to stir.

This was not a lurid, bawdy display of lustful immodesty, but a portrait of innocence...guiltless and pure.

As time passed, the child-like simplicity of her dance became more and more erratic. She waltzed over to an open trunk and without stopping, scooped up several veils of sheer fabric which she gracefully balanced on her finger's tips and commenced to manipulate with sultry skill.

Patrick's senses churned as her dynamics slowly accelerated. Little by little the fever of her emotions began to surface and the tempo of her mood soared. The once gentle flowing movements became more pronounced; her body undulating in waves of exhilaration, swaying from side to side, as if possessed by some sensual demon. She caressed and hugged her body with supple arms as if some imaginary lover were within their bounds, captive under her spell.

Her long mane turned into a wild mass of tangled coils as she reeled across the sweltering room in reckless surrender. Runaway tresses clung tenuously to the moist flesh of her neck and arms.

Patrick, energized by a new intensity, looked on with raw pleasure. Drinking in the headiness of this free spirit, he envisioned her performing exclusively for him. His body quivered, his own stifled hungers allowing him to be her willing captive. She had unknowingly inveigled him into her world of desire.

Hot blood pulsed through his temple veins. He felt himself weaken with a sudden rush of fervor. His throat tightened, warning him to flee, but he was helpless to move. He remained motionless trying desperately to find the slightest clue to her identity. She was still too far away.

All at once, her exhaustive performance ended with a dramatic series of leaps and spins. With one abrupt theatrical gyration she dropped to the floor where she remained in a lifeless heap for what Patrick thought was a frighteningly long period. Was she breathing?

A macabre stillness roared throughout the stifling attic. Deathlike, foreboding.

He waited...waited...perspiration blinding him.

Slowly the graceful "ghost" rose to a sitting position. Her whole mood mellowed, the demon slain. Picking up a small piece of cloth that was nearby, the wearied dancer lightly patted her face.

Then, without warning, she sprang to her feet discarding the flimsy veils and tossing them haphazardly back into the open trunk. She lowered the lid without sound.

In the streaked darkness he could see her start toward him. "Oh God, spare me," he begged. She stopped as if remembering something and turned back to the spot where she had been resting. She bent down to retrieve what looked to Patrick like a small book. She maneuvered the object in her hands, studying it for a few moments with great intensity. Lifting the lid of the old cedar box with painstaking care, she gently stowed her curious treasure deep within it's secretive walls. She turned, scurrying on the balls of her feet, again in his direction.

He was trapped!

Soaked in sweat, Patrick folded his arms over his head, balled himself up as tightly as he could and prayed, as he never had before, that she would not discover his refuge. He fought to remain stone-like, hoping she would see no movement and continue on.

It was too late! She stopped within inches of him. She was traumatized with fright at the sight of an unidentifiable mass under the dark eave, possibly planning to pounce on her. She jolted back and stared, panic struck, into the threatening ominousness of the recess.

Patrick's worst fears had been realized. But he mustn't lose her before he discovered who she was. He struggled to set his body in motion, forcing himself to uncoil his twisted limbs in measured movements as not to scare her away. He cautiously straightened himself out, standing to meet her head on. Eye to eye.

He was shaken beyond description.

"YOU?" He gasped in utter disblief. "My God ...Mrs. Huntingwell?" He stared into her eyes, long and hard, assuring he had made no mistake.

She remained mute, suffering the unbearable shock of discovery. His presence unnerved her and she came to life, fumbling awkwardly with the small towel she carried in a vain effort to cover strategic bits of her naked body.

He had never been this close to her. Stray shafts of light caught beads of dew trickle down her neck. Her arms glistened in the heat of the suffocating closeness. He had never seen her sweat. Patrick was amazed to discover that this elegant thoroughbred was actually capable of such common earthiness. He found it oddly appealing.

They stood painfully awkward in their nearness, breathing in unplanned cadence.

Prunella Huntingwell's look turned scalding. To have encountered him at such close range, compounded her embarrassment.

How dare he invite himself into her private retreat, trespassing on her chosen solitude.

Had he been spying on her? And what exactly was he doing up here? How dare he? Her eyes watered in anger. She was blinded by prideful contempt. Her sacred space had been violated and she was enraged.

The cave. Had she not invaded his secluded retreat?

Their eyes held. She in cold resentment, he in blatant disbelief. Neither in sufficient control of their own emotions to break the agonizing silence.

Mrs. Huntingwell, forced to deal with a circumstance she could not change, fought fiercely to reweave any remaining threads of her frayed dignity.

She unglued her eyes from his and lowered her lids, giving herself a moment to rally. Gradually the lines in her face softened, her aura relaxed. Her face lifted to his again.

She implored him to honor her secret, begging him without words, to be her confidant. She, looking uncharacteristically vulnerable and much like a little girl, had innocently wound herself around his heart.

Before he could pledge his allegiance, she had fled down a secret stairway right behind him that led to her private chambers. She was gone and with her the reality of the evening's events.

Patrick Sean O'Shay and Prunella Catherine Huntingwell had stood a heartbeat apart, two hungry souls, entombed in a tiny cubicle of the universe. They had silently shared a moment of touchless intimacy that would throw them, inescapably, into a maze of dead ends, of silent longings.

Each belonged to another; she to a caring husband, he to an insidious disease. Each dealing with their private prison of fate.

Patrick remained in the attic for awhile, trying to extract a modicum of sense from the events of the past hour; a drama in which he had, unwittingly, become involved.

He walked with cautious steps to the far end of the open space where moments before, such energy had been exuded. He bent to touch the still wet drops of perspiration that speckled the hot dry floor boards.

For the first time in the past hour, Patrick realized he still clung to his flashlight. Kneeling on one knee, he illuminated the old trunk that had played such a key role in the evening's puzzling spectacle. He tried to lessen the glaring beam of light by partially shielding the powerful bulb with an open hand.

Patrick scrutinized the elaborately embossed metal strips that embellished the wooden trunk's exterior and recognized it as a masterful example of old world craftsmanship.

The vintage piece taunted him. He harbored an insatiable urge to explore the secrets of its stowage and yet he wrestled with the ethical censorship of his conscience.

Did he have the authority to trespass into another's private world without invitation? And yet, had she not, by her own blatant sensuality, bid him entrance into her fantasy? He had become entangled in a tightening net of intrigue. He could not free himself now.

Patrick was convinced that the majestic trunk was dutifully chaperoning a vital passage of time, guarding with patient loyalty the missing bits of Sweetmeadow history.

Overpowered by the intensity of his own intuition, his hand reached for the trunk's tarnished brass latch. He glanced around the room, ensuring that he was indeed alone, then lifted the heavy hinged lid. He was momentarily stunned by the assaulting fumes of mothballs that emanated from within.

Patrick's heart quickened.

He had exposed yards and yards of brilliantly dyed silks stored loosely in random heaps. Under his tiny spotlight the colors were breathtaking! Scarlets, royals, emeralds, purples, a baffling range of shades; some intricately embroidered with golden threads that came alive under the waves of light. Finery, the likes of which Patrick had never seen in such abundance.

He caressed the delicate fibers in appreciative reverence of the weaver's skill and wondered from whence they had come. Who would have abandoned these exquisite materials in such an ignoble, out-of-the-way corner of the attic.

Patrick's curiosity raged on.

With controlled excitement he probed further under the airy layers, in hopes of finding whatever it was that Mrs. Huntingwell retraced her steps to deliberately seek.

At almost the very bottom of the grand trunk, his fingers grazed over an ungiving surface. It was obvious to his touch that he had come upon a thin little book.

The hairs on his arms prickled.

The attic was so still...so expectant.

He turned off his flashlight, a cautionary measure. Then tenuously lifted the treasure from its nesting place. Tiptoeing toward a stream of light, he carried his find as though any moment it would turn to powder in his hand. At the window, he positioned the book's cover in the moon glow for better viewing.

Elaborately scrolled across the faded old façade were the words. "The Voice of Clara Doolaine."

Patrick felt like a thousand fluttering moths had alighted on his skin. He shivered.

Clara Doolaine! The frail, unhappy looking young bride in the hall tintype?

Had he inadvertently stumbled on more than he had bargained for? The fragile journal seemed to open automatically in willing response to his touch. A pale lavender ribbon dozed between two dogeared pages of transparent paper, stained with amber hues of time. Although the years had grayed the black ink, the beautiful Victorian scripted sentiment was still boldly legible.

The mellifluous words read like a prayer;

> *Sweet darkness ...deliver*
> *me from the cruel truth of light.*
> *Disguise me in thy regal robes.*

Grant me beauty worthy of
being your queen.
O honest blackness, allow
me the splendor of love's passion.
Night's shadow, I implore thee,
Set me free.

Patrick read the poignant passage a second time aloud. Slowly, softly. Such unmasked pleas of love and despair. He looked away as he closed the diary, convinced that the hand painted borders profuse with hearts and flowers, could only be the endearing expression of a very young, lovesick girl. No other pages had been written on.

Patrick took a few moments to digest the gripping message, one so full of despair. With a finger still marking his place, he sat down on the bare floor and rested his head back against the rough hewn timbers. He closed his eyes, feeling great compassion for the disparaging heart who had innocently penned her secret agonies so many years ago.

He opened his eyes and sat straight up. A bolt of discovery shot through his heart! It was all too clear.

Two young women, decades apart, yet bound together by a common yearning to be free. Both trapped in the same web of fragility; both bound so subtly by their own prisons of fate. Clara by deficient beauty, a loveless marriage, ...Prunella by the rigidity of her station, her class.

Patrick thought of his own frustrations and hungers. He longed for all the same things; love's passion, freedom from illness, and time. Time to do his beloved writing, time to paint. But was that not the universal cry of all humanity? Each to discover his own place of rightness, of true peace, unbridled freedom?

He got up, carefully placing the diary back in the protective care of the loyal old trunk and retraced his steps back to the carriage house. He was feeling old, heavy with longing. He was emotionally drained.

From the window of his loft room, Patrick stared woodenly out into the stillness of the night. There was a certain sadness about the evening that he could not shake.

The night had been a brutal one. His head had throbbed with terrifying images of death. If only he could ingest some elixir capable of obliterating the portion of his psyche that came alive in the darkness.

Patrick struggled so with his inner conflicts. His dispassionate family...aging Grams...the attic ghost...Frankie...his art, writing, music...his cursed disease...and time.

He found his greatest peace when adopting his grandmother's iron will.

"Face your demons head on! Slay them!"

It was working for him...so far.

Patrick knew he would find the kitchen crew up at this early hour. Food preparation was always in progress before the light of day.

He needed an emotional outlet from the tenseness of the night...the ache in his head had slowly retreated.

He picked up his guitar and headed for the main house. As he surmised, they were all there just beginning their daily routine.

Patrick was greeted with hearty welcomes and soon crafted a medley of lively tunes. Cook immediately led the almost-on-key carolers in hearty song.

Molly came down the back stairs in response to the music and joined the party.

Patrick, upon seeing her, left his guitar and approached her.

"Wal, wal, if i' tisn't me darlin' Molly" he teased.

"O go on w'ya, sil'y lad" pretending to wave him away.

Patrick took her in his arms and smiled mischievously at the unsuspecting maid who was a bit befuddled by this familiar behavior. He serenaded Molly with an animated version of Sweet Molly Malone, complete in a rather fine Irish brogue.

In Dublin's Fair City
Where the girls are so pretty
I first set my eyes on sweet Molly
Malone.

A spin around the big work table was initiated before releasing her with a formal bow.

"O, th' likes o' 'im" Molly panted, a bit out of breath. She spoke for the benefit of her audience, all of whom had picked up the levity of the moment and joined in a rousing chorus.

Alive, alive o! Alive, alive o!
Crying cockles and mussels alive, alive o!

"Enough! Enough!" Cook raised a long wooden rolling pin over her head. "Let's get busy."

Molly's heart was renewed by the unabashed antics of this spirited young man.

If only she could know how he suffered behind his perfected masquerade.

"Good morning, Cook" a chipper Mrs. Huntingwell pushed through the swinging kitchen doors, looking fresh and cool in a navy blue sleeveless blouse and white cotton slacks. No matter how informally dressed she was, Patrick thought she always looked like those girls on the cover of a fashion magazine. Picture perfect and untouchable.

He had just finished tying his laces, with one leg still up on an unopened wooden crate of French wine. He straightened out from his bent position to take notice of this magnificent actress, wondering if she would give any admittance to their attic encounter.

She waved lightheartedly, covering everyone in the room, not to risk the awkward interaction of eye contact with Patrick. Poor Queen Catherine. He studied her face with open honesty as she continued to ignore him. The events of the previous night had never taken place.

"Hey, Paddy-O. Sorry I'm late." Tillie came barreling down the back stairs into the kitchen, grabbing a sweet roll off the baking stone, fresh from the oven.

"Yeow! Hot!" She juggled the pastry from one hand to the other, attempting to cool it. She turned to Patrick.

"I'm ready when you are" her blue eyes flashed. She gave him a teasing shove.

"I'm ready, I'm ready" he responded with equal alacrity as she sent him sprawling off balance.

They laughed.

Tillie was Patrick's match. She never walked. She ran everywhere, always game for an adventure. Their relationship was platonic. She had a boyfriend in Providence and although she saw him only once a month during the summer season, she wrote to him every day. Patrick felt the few hours spent with Tillie to be a leveling antidote. She was great fun.

Today they were scheduled to take a couple of horses for a run on the equestrian trail through winding back woods, maybe explore a barn or two. Patrick was continually in search of a new plot of turf to set his easel.

Mrs. Huntingwell pretended not to notice the playful interaction between the two. She went about her chosen routine of pouring her own hot water from the samovar into her special violet tea cup and choosing just the right fixings for the brew. Today, instead of sitting at the work table with cook, Prunella left without ceremony through the swinging door.

Patrick had watched her little charade with interest. So that's the game she's chosen to play. He would grant her wish and stick to the rules.

He would honor the secret of the attic ghost.

Peeping Tom

Patrick hoisted the last shutter up the ladder to the second floor ocean front window. Mrs. Huntingwell's room. The day was overcast, making working conditions palatable. These jobs were usually taken care of before the Huntingwells were "in house" for the summer, but the new replacements had arrived late from the manufacturer.

It had been a hearty task and Patrick was relieved to be nearing it's end. He had taken the cumbersome pieces down the ladder, unscrewing old hinges, replacing with new and then hauled them back up again. While balancing the hefty pieces in place, he administered the long screws.

The grand old home was quiet. He guessed everyone was out relaxing at the club. The usual afternoon fare.

As he struggled to tighten the bottom hinge, forcibly turning the stubborn screw, a dangerous thought floated across his mind. He had never seen the interior of the lady's quarters. What better time than right now. He paused to wipe his brow with the work rag trailing from his short's pocket. His eyes went to the large window. He was so close.

Inside, unknown to Patrick, was Prunella Huntingwell, choosing her dress for tomorrow evening's opera. She had selected three outfits, holding each up to her as she faced the white framed cheval mirror; the decision, as always, made the day before all upcoming social events. It was the way she ran every aspect of her life. Always astutely prepared, avoiding any last minute stress.

The peach silk, Thad's favorite or the unadorned black with a diamond broach? Perhaps the ivory crepe.

One by one, the lady rehung the garments in an enormous armoire expressly designated for evening attire.

She returned to the bed and with a pleased look on her face, reached under the bed skirt and removed a carefully hidden hot pink box. In a daring moment, Prunella, after giving it some thought, had reassessed her decision, asking the kind sales girl at the brazen boutique in Providence to send her that dress,

Patrick stepped to the edge of the rung. With one foot remaining on the ladder, he stretched his body as far as safely permitted and sneaked a peek inside the enormous white room. His eyes scanned the portion of space available to his range of vision.

He was shocked to find it occupied! With sudden reflexes, he jerked back, never cementing an image in his mind of exactly what it was he had seen, except to be certain that someone was present in the room.

Patrick turned away from the window, still balancing himself at a rather precarious angle. His eyes dotted swiftly in every direction reassessing the security of his perch. He would be humiliated if caught like an adolescent schoolboy gawking through a peep hole.

He was overpowered by sheer adrenalin to risk one more quick look. He leaned toward the window and could view the lower half of the bed. Fully exposed, glared a hot pink box, a slim hand slowly lifting the lid. The vivid container blasted an immediate memory through his brain. The secretive trip to Providence.

Mrs. Huntingwell was by no means naked, but scantily decent in ivory satin and lace undergarments, her beloved violets hand embroidered on the silky camisole, one of her indulgences from a little shop on the Champs-Elysées.

She had moved to the center of the room, the red dress held up to her svelte body, gracing Patrick with a side view of her silhouette. The full length glass reflected an approving smile. Was she envisioning herself in the deliciously scandalous frock, entering the theater as all eyes bulged out of their sockets in shocked admiration? For one moment, she seemed lost in a make-believe place of unedited freedom.

As she cradled the red creation close to the front of her, the forbidden garment seemed to come alive, spinning her around the room in a dizzying journey to a magical land where no rules existed. A place where the titillation of bawdy fantasies was accepted.

Prunella Huntingwell was boldly snapped out of her daydream by a sound on her window. She froze! Innately pulling the red dress tightly up under her chin in a futile stab at covering herself. Her initial thought was that the knocking had come from the bedroom door and instinctly turned in that direction, affording the window watcher an unsuspecting view of the lady's barely shrouded back.

Prunella suddenly realizing where the noise originated, swung around in horror to see Patrick's embarrassed face slide out of view.

"I don't believe it!" She was livid, flushed with anger, at the defiant intrusion. The nerve of him. Now he was taking on the role of a peeping tom! Despicable! She turned from the window with indignation. She would show him that she was not flustered by his juvenile antics.

Without ever looking back to see if Patrick had returned to the window, she flung the red dress across a white lounge chair. Slowly, Mrs. Huntingwell straightened her body, holding her head erect and strutted in calculated steps into her dressing room. What the miffed actress failed to know, was that her captive audience of one had left the scene and entirely missed her stellar performance.

Opera

The evening of the opera arrived with disarming alacrity.

Patrick found himself pacing Sweetmeadow's spacious front entrance hall, annoyed at his own inability to control his physical tenseness. He was feeling strangely like a pimpled face pubescent on prom night, awkwardly anticipating the appearance of his frilled-up date.

He tried to sort out in his mind exactly what had tangled up his thought process long enough to accept Thad's ludicrous proposal.

And now, here he was, diabolically strangled by an over starched collar cutting off his air supply and tweaked by shoes slowly remolding the structure of his feet.

"Nice job, O'Shay, you really did it this time." He reprimanded himself for his childish lack of good judgment.

Patrick rechecked his watch. She would appear any moment. Punctuality was one of her valued disciplines.

As he waited, Patrick noted that the reflective images thrown back at him from a lavish display of mirrors, validated his assessment that he cut a fairly acceptable figure in his fine fitting black suit.

He positioned his arms out to his sides in modeling fashion and turned a complete circle.

"Well, wha-d-ya think?" he queried of the gloomy gray ghosts imprisoned in garish frames on the opposite wall. They gazed back without expression from another century.

"That great, huh?" Patrick smiled to himself at the absurdity of the moment.

Once again he reminded himself that the sole purpose for his presence at the mansion this evening was to be an escort to Mrs. Huntingwell; to remain at all times as a prop...collected, conversational if necessary and a gentleman of blasé composure, nothing more.

Absentmindedly scanning the room, he spotted a small nosegay of tea roses carefully placed on the mahogany pedestal by the front entrance.

Nice touch, Patrick thought, *so like Thaddeus Huntingwell to remember "his lady" with flowers in his absence.* On the same stand, propped against a tall cut-crystal vase dripping with feathery fern, was a long white envelope, the Sweetmeadow crest embossed in gold on the upper left corner. In Thad's hurried hand was scrolled—*theater tickets.* Patrick removed the envelope, checked the contents and slid the packet into the inside pocket of his jacket.

Before Thad left for New York he had seen to every detail, ensuring the evening's venture to run without incident, free of stressful decisions.

When Nigel delivered the perfectly tailored tuxedo to his carriage house room earlier in the day, it was accessorized with a crisp, one hundred dollar bill protruding from the handkerchief pocket. Patrick was not at all sure exactly what was expected of him to do with the cash. It was to be a cut and dry, "go and come" evening. He would see that the money was returned.

Patrick was executing a last minute minor adjustment to his collar in a small oval mirror, when he caught the reflection of Prunella Huntingwell gliding almost without movement down the wide staircase behind him.

She was stunningly wrapped in a high neck, floor length evening coat of summer-weight white taffeta. Light from the newel post candelabra sparked the solitaire diamonds that pierced her ears. The utter simplicity of her costume broken only by a dazzling set of three diamond studded initials worn as a monogram on the cuff of her three quarter length sleeve.

As he turned from the mirror to greet her, she politely floated past him, this white angel, coolly acknowledging his presence. She strode directly to the pedestal, removed the nosegay and without breaking her stride, continued through the front door held open by a non-judgmental Nigel.

As she passed, Patrick noticed the splendid diamond comb that accented the severity of her dark swept back hair, coiled as usual, into a flawless bun at the base of her neck.

He bristled at her hoity-toity attitude.

"So, what am I, the invisible man?" he asked of Nigel not expecting an answer. The gall! Wasn't it he, who was giving up his Friday evening for her precious opera?

He followed her through the open door held rigid by the stoic butler, who deliberately avoided any eye contact. Patrick slowly paced his stride, taking his sweet time in descending the stone steps to the familiar limousine. Another open door, this time manned by the ever-pleasant, Max.

"Good evening, Max." Patrick exaggerated his speech in his most affected high-brow.

"Evenin', Mr. Pat." Max was a bit confused at the sudden formality of his friend.

"A fine evening at that," Patrick continued, sounding much like an eccentric English professor.

"O'Yas, Sah," the chauffeur returned a respectful nod and the two exchanged winks.

Patrick slid onto the cool leather noticing that the duchess had claimed her territory at the farthest end of the seat. He took her clue and remained near the opposite door, leaving enough space for a B-17 to land between them.

Neither did much verbalizing during the ride to Providence, except for a cordial exchange of small talk. Prunella positioned her head to look away from him, out the window. She had traveled this route a hundred times and surely was not intent on discovering new surroundings. She was, obviously, using her standoffish manner as a way of letting him know from the start that she was not thrilled with this arrangement any more than he was.

Fine!

He went along with the frosty mood she dictated. Every so often he caught a glimpse of her gloved hands fidgeting with the thin clutch nested in her lap.

What was she really thinking? This lady of disguises.

When they arrived at the opera house, Patrick noticed that she deliberately ignored the peach colored roses. They remained on the seat. He assessed the gesture odd as he followed the fast moving lady into the theater.

Patrick was duly impressed with the artistic presentation of the Puccini masterpiece, especially the exquisite wedding scene. The stage was magical. Oriental costumes, gloriously fashioned of white silk brocades, seemed to come alive under the skillful hands of lighting technicians. Hundreds of delicate cherry trees, magnificently laden with a profusion of sheer silk blossoms and tiny lights gave the all-white presentation an almost ethereal mood. It brought rave applause from the appreciative patrons.

Patrick had disciplined himself to sit attentively through most of the performance, but when the curtain finally came down and the lights went up for intermission, he found a sense of relief. He welcomed the chance to readjust his legs.

He turned casually toward Mrs. Huntingwell to exchange a few pleasantries and was struck dumb! He did a double-take to assure his eyes were not playing tricks on him. The white coat was stiffly propped against the back of the gold velvet chair, coyly framing her bare white shoulders and boldly displaying, who would have dared to believe it, the forbidden red dress!

His immediate reaction was to jump onto his seat and shout "at a go girl!", but assessed such behavior grossly inappropriate under the rigid code of opera house protocol.

It was clear now, why the sweet peach roses were left in the limousine. They certainly would not compliment the evening's brazen attire.

Prunella could feel her skin prickle as she sensed Patrick's eyes ogling her and refused to look his way. She would not watch him gloat. She envisioned that cocky half-smile on his lips and she must, under all conditions, hold herself in check and protect herself from any tell-tale sign that might indicate her pleasure in having "shocked the stuffing out of him."

"Enjoying it?" he ventured, his tone flat. He stared directly into her eyes as she turned in response to his question.

"Oh yes," a matter-of-fact reply. "Magnificent cast, very polished." She knew all too well that he was inquiring of the dress, not the opera, and she was not about to give him one inch.

"I agree" he almost whispered his words, "magnificent."

Prunella immediately opened her program, pretending to lose herself in its pages.

Near the end of the final act, Patrick was unnerved by a bout of claustrophobia. In the darkened theater, he unfastened his tie and buried it in his jacket pocket and loosened his shrinking collar, experiencing immediate relief. Earlier, he managed to slip off one of his patent leather opera slippers, that had been biting his toes for two hours and promptly lost track of it under the seat in front of him. He'd get it later.

Prunella, totally enthralled with the performance was oblivious to Patrick's restless discomfort.

After what seemed an eternity, the curtain came down on the final act. The audience flew to it's feet, applauding vigorously, calling the players back over and over again, encore after encore.

"BRAVO!"

"BRAVO!"

"Enough is enough, let's get out of here." Patrick mumbled under his breath and Prunella, thinking he had said something complimentary nodded her agreement as she enthusiastically continued to pound together her gloved hands.

To Patrick's dismay, when the gentleman in front of him stood to applaud, he inadvertently kicked Patrick's stray shoe another few feet under the next row of seats. Patrick was forced to tap the unsuspecting gent on the shoulder and ask him if he would be kind enough to retrieve the runaway slipper.

The man obliged, reacting in a rather confused disbelieving manner, setting the stage for Patrick's creative mind to develop. He decided not to make an issue of his shoeless foot by trying to squeeze the swollen appendage back into the shiny vice. Instead, he reasoned, being in black socks who would ever notice if he had both shoes on or not.

The well-mannered audience filed out of the hall in an orderly procession. Patrick and Mrs. Huntingwell, in turn, joined the ranks of quietly animated guests. He had wedged his loose shoe up into his arm pit, hoping to conceal it's presence well away from his escort's view. Together they walked, side by side, in tandem with the slow moving crowd.

Patrick could hardly contain his amusement when Mrs. Huntingwell first caught notice of his shed tie. Her expression of utter disdain and annoyance at his plebeian behavior was priceless. Almost in the same glance she was appalled to find his gait tottering and on still closer inspection, realized he actually had on only one shoe.

"Honestly!"

Her horrified reaction only invited him to play it for all it was worth. He deliberately exaggerated his movements, hobbling up and down more conspicuously, heaving his shoulders in rhythm with the feigned limp.

She shot him a repugnant look.

Patrick was undaunted. He was on a roll. Whipping the missing shoe out from its coverture, he proceeded to nonchalantly adorn his hand with it, waving solicitously to those in the immediate area with the shod appendage.

Faces turned ashen in horror.

Mrs. Huntingwell paled. There was a limit to one's tolerance. Her acceptance of his juvenile behavior must come to a halt. Mrs. Huntingwell, the modest coat once again concealing the tasty frock, tried in vain to wedge herself discreetly through the solid crowd. She met with resistance every inch of the way. She had no choice but to stay with this ridiculous clowning clod by her side making a consummate fool of himself. She was on the verge of losing her control but refused to give him the satisfaction of seeing her flustered by his outrageous stunts.

How dare he humiliate her! If only she had the nerve to whack some sense into him with her purse! Good God, now she was thinking on his level.

As the crowd oozed into the loggia, Patrick intensified his antics, catching icy stares from several appalled guests. They, too, were intolerant of such uncouth behavior rendered in this time honored hall. Patrick was enjoying the spontaneous gig, the purity of the moment and continued to playfully acknowledge the unbelieving stares of dazed sophisticates.

She could feel them closing in, smothering her, all vying for closer inspection of the crazed half-wit.

Once outside, Mrs. Huntingwell raced down the mountain of marble steps, highly resentful of her involuntary entrapment in a preposterous sideshow.

Max, standing guard beside the door of the limo, was a bit mystified at seeing Mrs. Huntingwell, who always carried herself with great aplomb, race toward him at break-neck speed with skirt hiked above her knees, she bolted through the open door into the vehicle's protective cover.

It was only when he saw Patrick limping about, wearing his shoe as a glove, that he understood her behavior. Patrick arrived at the limo. He paused a moment to remove the shoe from his hand with a flurry of exaggerated motions. Still playing to the crowd, he tossed it theatrically into the limo. Then the jacket was shed and with the grace of a magician, folded it into a tidy bundle over his arm. He bowed to the onlookers and nonchalantly passed in front of Max, flashing him a "what-the-hell" smile before settling himself on the slick upholstery.

The chauffeur was all too familiar with the lad's penchant for frivolity, having shared many an hour in the boy's company. As he carefully closed the heavy door, all he could do was shake his head in resigned acceptance, remaining as always, expeditiously on the outer rim of involvement.

Once inside the cruising car, Patrick avoided any direct contact with Mrs. Huntingwell. He did manage to observe her, unnoticed.

Her chest was heaving with labored breaths, her lips pursed, brows knit, eyes narrowed and focused straight ahead. She was obviously, more than a little peeved with his feckless behavior.

"Aw lighten-up, cement face." The words never left his lips.

Neither spoke as they rolled out onto the highway. Patrick used his program as a shoehorn to maneuver his foot back into it's cage.

A short time into the drive he felt her eyes boring holes into the side of his head. He turned to look at her and met with an icy glare. She was silently excoriating him with a clear expression of disgust. A look that could have only one interpretation.

They rode on into the warm summer evening for an undetermined span of time without a word. How could she be so bent out of shape. He was just having a little fun.

Patrick decided to be Mr. Nice guy, opting to adjudicate the cold war that had developed between them. He would make the first move toward civility.

"Nice dress."

She said nothing.

"Lovely evening."

Silence.

He opened the window, allowing the crescendo of the cricket's choir that invaded the balmy summer night to fill the stifling cavity they occupied.

"Looks like snow."

She raised her program to hide her face, continuing to look away from him in hopes he would not see her desperately trying to stifle even the slightest reaction to his nonsense.

He is a madman, she thought to herself, still visibly unflinching.

He was batting zero, but had no intentions of retreating. Instead, he took it upon himself to open the tiny refrigerator that housed two long stem glasses and a chilled bottle of Asti Spumonte. Nigel had stocked the mini-bar as was usual for formal evenings.

Patrick lowered the tray table from the back of the seat in front of them while keeping a sneaky eye on her highness.

"Champagne?"

Receiving no acknowledgement to his offer, he quickly answered himself.

"Ah, don't mind if I do, old boy." He did not look her way. "Certainly a most pleasurable experience and indeed one to be shared." Purposefully exaggerating his speech, he continued to uncork the bubbly.

POW!

The cork prematurely shot to the ceiling, causing Max to almost swerve off the road. Mrs. Huntingwell jumped and instinctively raised her arm in front of her face for protection.

"Whoa. A live one!" Patrick reacted quickly, pouring the effervescent liquid into frosty stems before it spilled over. He held one of the sparkling glasses out to her. She did not move.

Patrick urgently wrapped on the glass partition to signal Max.

"Head for the morgue."

Then, contorting his face in Frankenstein manner and using a low Peter Lori rendition, he slowly turned toward her, cutting his words in deliberate syllables.

"Take… this… med…i…cine… for… your… con…di…tion."

She finally turned to look at him, somberly, still fighting to hold on to her last thread of dignity, and again, managed to look away, proving to him that she was not at all taken by his ridiculous drama.

He continued to bait her with the Champagne glass, holding it near her cheek. He tried again, still in character, this time undulating his eyebrows and fashioning his eyes into narrow slits as he spoke.

"Doctor's orders" he whispered, sliding toward her just a trifle, closing the gap between them by a few millimeters.

She stiffened.

Prunella Huntingwell turned to meet her jester head on. She held his eyes in hers. His laughing, warm…hers controlled, cold. This time she could feel herself losing ground. Her chin quivered. Then, as though a dam had suddenly burst within her heart, a reservoir of pent-up emotions flooded over into gales of uncontrolled laughter.

"Praise God! The woman lives."

The mood was immediately contagious and Patrick burst into a round of knee-slapping and hooting until they were both near hysteria. Every time the laughter would subside and they were able to regain an inkling of composure, a mere glance would throw them into a deeper abyss of convulsive folly, leaving them gasping for breath.

Max watched his passengers from the rearview window and assessed that they were both acting rather oddly. The mood had changed dramatically.

They were half-way home when Patrick slid open the glass panel he had closed only moments before and directed Max to take them back to the city.

Max tried to get an approving gesture from his boss lady before turning the grand car around, but she pretended not to notice. Max assumed her silence was a sign of agreement.

Mrs. Huntingwell had made a feeble attempt to protest at first, then softly succumbed to Patrick's well chosen words, agreeing that it might be interesting to discover a corner of his world.

It was only ten o'clock. They had no deadline to meet, no one was waiting for them at home. There was no reason to cut the evening short. No reason, at all.

The Trattoria

As the limousine purred, retracing it's way over route 138 back to Providence, Patrick relived the first visit to Frankie's neighborhood, "The Hill," as it was affectionately labeled. How he had been stunned by the ethnic richness emanating from the narrow bustling streets. Crowded sidewalks were stuffed with bins of perfectly sculptured fruits and vegetables. Pyramids of golden onions, boxes of plump mushrooms, succulent clusters of purple grapes. Tomatoes and peppers in a myriad of colors. Crates of greens...dandelion, chicory, spinach...all picked from gardens that very morning.

Long strands of braided garlic hung near doorways. Inside these little one room groceries were shelves lined with olive oils and vinegars. Row upon row of pasta, all shapes and sizes; racks of tin boxes containing tuna fish, anchovies, sardines. Overhead hung globes of cheese, salami, strips of baccala and sausages.

Long loaves of crusty breads filled paper-lined baskets. In show cases, trays of olives glistened in brine or herbed-olive oil. The floor, stacked with wooden cases of wine, had an offering for every palate. The cakes, the candies, the creams! These meager, family-run operations had presented Patrick a canvas of unrivaled dimension.

He found the fervor of activity an entertainment in itself. There was a certain playfulness in the bright pink gelato wagon, or the over-laden flower cart, or even Luigi's hand-concocted roaster full of hot chestnuts.

Patrick's heart sang!

The Italians lived lives of celebration. He liked that.

A short way beyond the Italian district the aura changed dramatically. The air was filled with equally delightful, but decidedly different aromas of corned beef and cabbage.

Patrick was jolted back to the moment as Max slowed down in a familiar area of the city.

"This is fine, Max. Thanks."

The young man and the lady made the rounds of the city's night spots, stepping in each just long enough to sample the flavor of its ambience. Some seedy, some presentable, but all holding unique new experiences for Prunella. She became a willing captive, fascinated to explore this segment of his world, one she had little knowledge of.

They were overdressed. No one cared. Drinks were ordered, but hardly touched, a sip now and then. They observed, talked, exchanged experiences. How different they were, how alike.

Throughout the evening they remained as acquaintances, nothing more. Nothing was ever mentioned of the cave nor the "Peeping Tom" incident. The attic meeting was definitely off limits. She did not confess to listening to him sing as he worked or divulge how she had spied on him from her window as he explored the rocks. Best not to glorify these episodes with an air of importance.

Now, sharing these few unplanned hours with this playful spirit, she was astonished at the pure honesty of him. His total freedom of expression. His child-like acceptance of all forms and colors of humanity, the ability to slip in and out of any set of circumstances without hesitation, enjoying each new encounter as it was presented. Prunella delighted in the very essence of him.

Before heading back to Sweetmeadow, there was one more stop that Patrick saved for last. A special little spot where his heart was always soothed, welcomed with open arms, and where he was truly family. It was the second sweatest place on earth, after Gram's place.

The red neon sign blared out "Zaffini's Trattoria." It was a small eatery and grocery store crammed into the heart of "the Hill." To Patrick, it was a time of refueling. Wonderful food, genuine interaction and unconditional acceptance. Love was freely given. No strings. A warm shelter where comfort from the uncluttered goodnesses of life were commonplace.

The "Tori" was run by Mamma and Pappa Zaffini, first generation Italian immigrants. Still speaking in murderous English, struggling to master the harsher sounds of a new language so foreign to the fluidity of their own.

Mamma Zaffini suffered with enormous swollen legs. Varicose veins, the doctor called it. But she continued to stand over hot pots of tomato sauce "sugo" and prepare her superb dishes for her family and clientele.

She was a short pudgy woman with a constant spark in her eyes. Always in a black dress, her heavily veined legs were bound in thick, black stockings. A weighty silver cross hung around her neck.

Patrick loved the Zaffinis. They were so joyous in their work. Pappa was a naturally shy man and even more subdued since his stroke. But Mamma remained cheerful, singing and interacting with all who visited...so different from his own family, where wealth was ferociously sought and openly flaunted. Happiness did not figure into the O'Shay equation.

For Mamma Zaffini it was different. For her it was the Lord's work. The Zaffini's labored for God and "la famiglia," holding great love and pride for each member. That was their dedication, their fulfillment. A simple way. No child could ever feel worthless or unloved in this unselfish atmosphere.

Patrick felt such a burst of emotion when he visited these generous people, and harbored a strange need to share this unmatched hospitality with Mrs. Huntingwell. He hoped she would be receptive to their overflowing hearts.

"Hey Max, wanna come in? Meet my friends?" Patrick knew he would be welcomed with open arms.

"Oh, no, no, Sah. Ah stay righ' heah." Max had decided at the evening's birth that he would not be a party to this risky plan.

"Mama Mia! Patricio! Ah-h-h...mio figlio."

Mamma Zaff left the stove and came hobbling toward Patrick, her weighty arms outstretched, her eyes brimming with gladness.

"So good-a see you."

They hugged in a tight embrace as he swung her around.

"Eh! Mio figlio, where-a you been-a?"

"It has been too long," Patrick acknowledged.

"Frankie a gonn-a be sad-da he miss-a you."

Her son was away on a holy retreat with the church for the weekend and would not be home until tomorrow night.

"Ah, che bella." Mamma turned her attention to the lovely stranger that had come in with Patrick. Her womanly intuition told her not to question him about her.

"Come-a in, come-a in, make-a you'self-a happy," Mamma invited Prunella, after proper introductions. The older woman took the beautiful white coat and gingerly hung the elegant garment on a wooden peg, arranging the folds with finiky care.

Upon seeing the red dress with naked shoulders, Mamma reached for a black lace shawl and offered it to Prunella.

"Here-a wear-a this, you not be chilly." The temperature of the lady's arms was hardly the determining factor for the cover-up.

"Pappa, Pappa, vieni qui. Subito! Patricio has-a come-a home-a."

Pappa's graying hair lent him an air of distinction. Slightly bent now, he maneuvered with valiant effort, using two rough canes that Frankie had adapted from small tree limbs.

He greeted Patrick with the same emotions as did Mamma. Tears and hugs of old friends. With a more serious look, he scrutinized Patrick's lady friend over his wire frame glasses. He offered her a congenial "come sta?" before dropping his frail frame into a padded rocker.

Pappa Zaffini pulled the gold chain from his vest pocket, slowly checked the large time piece attached, snapped its case closed and returned it back to its refuge of darkness. This ritual had taken place every fifteen minutes for the past ten years.

The old rocker was positioned in full viewing range of the cash register and front door. From this angle, Pappa could unobtrusively keep an eagle eye on the whole business operation.

Four tables, covered in oil cloth and circled by an eclectic assortment of chairs donated from garages and attics of relatives, occupied the main room. A glass display case featured a tempting assemblage of home cooked specialties.

Pappa Zaffini noted, with interest, the blaring absence of touching between his two guests, a seemingly calculated behavior, to stay distant, thus portraying the appearance of plutonic friends. He was too old and wise in the ways of the heart to buy that charade. Pappa Zaff felt the uneasiness of something not quite right. She was older. It troubled him.

Tonight Mamma invited them into the private back room, she motioned both to sit down. Pru was taken with the rows of fresh pasta draped over wooden racks to dry and marveled at the painstaking process. A true labor of love.

Although the hour was late, Mamma Zaffini filled the intimate table with a squash flower and onion frittata, made earlier in the day, sliced tomatoes with fresh basil and olive oil, a pottery bowl of cured black olives, chunks of pungent cheese and thick slices of homemade bread. In the middle of the humble table, a few stems of yellow dandelions wilted in a blue glass vase.

She brought out a bottle of fine sparkling white wine and instructed Patrick to get down the long stem glasses from the top shelf in the cupboard. The "company" glasses, gold-edged and hand cut, were kept for special occasions.

Prunella Huntingwell absorbed the scene before her; one of such contradictions. She was so moved by the genuine interaction with these newly made friends, who made her feel an instant part of their inner circle.

"Here, Mamma." Patrick, taking the bottle from her, "Here, let me do that." He reached for the cork screw and proceeded to uncork the wine. With glasses filled, he raised his own in a toast.

He looked at the aging Zaffinis with great admiration.

"To my dear friends...a life of continued love."

They all drank to that.

He paused. His eyes fixed on Mrs. Huntingwell, who was astonished at the poise and sudden seriousness of this young man.

As he looked at her, not a telltale emotion revealed, his glass was raised again. Prunella could sense he was fighting to conjure up something to say. Words did not come. He barely touched her glass. The chime of the crystal spoke for him. She lowered her eyes.

The conversation, once again, became animated. While they chatted, Mamma made her luscious "Zabaglione." The evening called for it.

Holding an oversized copper bowl over boiling water, she vigorously whisked the sugar and egg yolks until they were a thick, pale yellow fluff, before adding the Marsala wine. Her heavy arms jiggling in tandem with each stroke, pausing every few minutes to accommodate the need to use her hands in emphasis of a word. The ambrosial cream was doled out in small amber, ruffled edge glass bowls. These were kept aside expressly for this special dessert.

A platter of assorted biscotti, a dish of plump figs and a pot of aromatic coffee completed the presentation. Patrick always savored the delicate wine pudding but tonight it seemed particularly flavorful.

It was 2:30 in the morning before they realized that time had kidnapped them. They exchanged hurried "goodbyes" vowing to return soon. As Patrick passed the rocker, now stilled, he patted Pappa's arm lightly in silent parting not to disturb the sleeping man, who had nodded off only moments before.

They had all but forgotten poor Max and found him asleep with the door locked, windows up.

Patrick rapped on the window to awaken him. Max abruptly stumbled out of the driver's seat, trying to regain some measure of aplomb, fumbling to open the door for the lady who seemed to be moving rather loosely. There seemed to be an unabashed free air about her, a posture Max had never seen her adopt before. He pretended not to notice. It was surely none of his business. He assumed she knew what she was doing.

Patrick handed the driver a small parcel of Mama's biscotti.

"Home, Max." Patrick whispered, as Mrs. Huntingwell arranged herself comfortably on the plush backseat.

"The scenic route by the ocean."

Max did not question why one would choose the "scenic route" in the middle of the night when one could not see the scenery.

"Yas, Sah," stealing a quick glance in the rear mirror at the unlikely couple in his care.

Patrick slowly pulled close the separating glass panel.

Max pretended not to notice.

The Gift

The well-recognized crunching sound of wheels over gravel announced their arrival back at Sweetmeadow. Time, once again, had melted away unnoticed. The limo came to a slow stop.

"I'll get the door, Max. No need to get out."

"Oh... ah ... ah, yas, Sah. Good nuf... yas, Sah." Max was bewildered. "Eve'nin, Sah, 'n' Missus." tipping his cap. The old gent did not much like what he was a party to.

"Good night, Max. Thanks." Patrick moved quickly to offer a hand to Mrs. Huntingwell, helping her from the limousine.

"Good evening, Max" politely whispered the lady who was gathering her shoes. Somewhere along the way they had slipped off her feet.

The pair watched until the limo made its way around the circle and out of sight.

The house was dark. Guests tucked in for the night.

As Mrs. Huntingwell fumbled for her keys, knowing Nigel would not be up at this hour, Patrick gently guided her away from the entrance.

"I want to show you something I did for you a few weeks ago," he urged.

Prunella was momentarily caught off guard and allowed herself to be languidly, strong-armed onto the lawn.

"Wait just one moment." she pulled back, dallying. "Exactly what are you doing? It is dreadfully late. Someone may see us." She hesitated, hardly in a stable condition in stocking feet on the thick spongy grass.

Patrick wondered if she even realized she was sans shoes and looking so irresistibly vulnerable.

"It'll just take a minute." he continued to guide her along the way as he spoke. "And besides, who would be up at 3:30 in the morning, anyway?"

She allowed herself, with some qualm, to be piloted toward the carriage house. Prunella felt she was not in complete control at the moment, a rare condition that both baffled and frightened her. She found herself tiptoeing cat-like up the outside stairs to the loft room, leaning on Patrick and oddly trusting him for guidance in the bazaar venture.

The door was open. Patrick never locked up. He figured if anyone wanted to steal his meager belongings, they probably needed them more than he did.

He opened the door cautiously, mindful of Angelo who occupied the far end of the building and put his finger over his smiling lips, signaling Pru to be very quiet.

She looked at him, beginning to enjoy the intrigue of the "break in" and played along with his theatrics by mimicking his motion to be silent with great exaggeration.

Immediately inside the door, he made his way to a small lamp beside his bed. It proffered a skimpy supply of light. He shed his tuxedo jacket on the bed.

Mrs. Huntingwell was shocked by the flavor of the room. Not at all what she envisioned a bachelor's place to look like.

There was a profusion of flowers bursting forth from baked bean cans and sundry odd containers in every available space. Some fresh, some dried.

In front of the open window, facing the ocean stood a tall easel spattered with paints and exhibiting a half-finished watercolor of a bouquet of zinnias in a dented copper pot.

In one corner, near the bed, a wooden crate stood alone with a well-worn cushion on top, obviously being used as a stool. A guitar leaned on it's side. A splash of music sheets and pencils strewn over an excess of oddly shaped carpet scraps in a variety of colors. Pillows were propped against the wall.

A wooden bookcase sporting many years of usage, dominated the other side of the bed. It was crammed with a surprising selection. The classics, books on horticulture, works of old prophets, musicians, French painters. A formidable collection of poetry. She had no clue, from his attitude toward tonight's opera, that he was enamored with the arts.

On the bookcase ledge, posed lazily, were rough sculptures of little children, birds and horses. Over a black iron bed hung a large ceramic crucifix from Italy. An acquisition from Mama Zaffino.

The yellow walls were covered with spring-like paintings of gardens, seascapes...woodlands. All his own works. Haphazardly nailed to walls were interesting swatches of fabrics, rusted horse shoes, brass bells hanging from leather strips.

A wooden tennis racket and press, a crude set of homemade barbells, and a cluttered desk. Everything to indulge the creative mind.

Patrick's bed was covered with a khaki army blanket accented with two blue and white ticking pillows. Prunella Huntingwell could not fathom resting her head on a naked pillow or her limbs resting under such a scratchy covering.

This room blared the tastes and interests of a sensitive talented soul. She found herself helplessly drawn to this young man and for the first time in her life, allowed a raw river of passion to flood her heart. These sensations went against everything she stood for, everything she was programmed to feel, all that was forbidden in her world. Her impulses told her to retreat, leave the scene of temptation. But as she watched him, so at home in this den of simplicity, she ignored inner warnings to flee, veiling the truth with taking an honest interest in a plutonic friend.

He passed by her, warming her with a wink and that sideway smile. Her heart contracted. She had not moved a centimeter from the door, mesmerized by his quick movements from one area of the room to another.

After removing the borrowed cufflinks and rolling up the starched shirt sleeves, he retrieved his guitar and a penciled sheet of music from the floor. He sat on the side of the bed.

Patrick patted the bed with his free hand silently inviting her to sit beside him. She moved toward him, hypnotized by the depth of pleading his eyes begged, and sat softly on the prickly covering ...U.S. Army stamped in black. Hardly the white satin monogrammed bed dressing she was accustomed to.

Prunella was astounded at how comfortable she felt, here in surroundings so foreign to her own. Patrick filled the room with electricity. This magical creature, so tender, so masculine, so in command, without in any way contributing to a thought of forced captivity.

"This is my gift to you." His fingers plucked out a few random cords. Without warning he began to softly render the ballad he had composed expressly for her.

"*When did it happen?*" the words asked. "*This love of ours? When did it happen?*"

She scrutinized him as he sang and noticed in his eyes a dimension of intensity that overwhelmed as much as frightened her. She found herself reacting to him. He was so secure in who he was. He reveled in what made him happy, and did not harbor a need to put on a front or be someone he was not for appearance sake. He lived his life in total honesty and openness, giving freely of himself and his talents to all who had the unequaled privilege of crossing his path.

She was spellbound by this unique being who sat so tantalizingly close to her. A rugged, grown man...an impish little boy...the ferocious lion laced with the tranquil lamb...all fashioned so superbly into one wonderous man-child.

She watched his muscled arms hold the stringed instrument so tenderly, plucking the melancholy ballad with unprogrammed ease. Somewhere between the edge of the lawn and the entry into Patrick's room, she had unconsciously crossed the boundaries of good reason and drifted into his domain without any notice of transition.

Mrs. Huntingwell was baffled with the role she found herself playing. Submissive...free of care. She, the staunch sophisticate, so self controlled and disciplined. She who had traveled the world over...Rome, Paris, Monte Carlo. She had skied the Alps, climbed the stairs of the Eiffel Tower, gloried in the Sistine Chapel. And yet, tonight, here in this square of unpretentious space, passions stirred within untouched zones of her soul she had not known held life. For once she had nurtured a forbidden moment, giving vent to foolish, self-gratifying weakness and she had succumbed to the splendor of its energy.

She was suddenly aware of the deafening thunder of silence. The room was tomb-like. The music had ceased.

Patrick's eyes were soft, his face turned to hers, waiting for her response to his offering. She sat mute. Still. She felt awkward, not able to gel one sensible set of words together. She summoned the courage to meet his eyes. Neither daring to move, fearing an accidental touch might unleash the dreaded demon of want. They had made the ultimate misjudgment. Leaving the door of temptation open, inviting in the insidious seductress to test their wills.

Patrick bent to replace his guitar against the wall. Mrs. Huntingwell tried to move, but her body did not respond. Patrick stood in front of her, offering her his hands. He sensed her urgency to flee from this smoldering circumstance.

Pru ignored his outstretched arms and turned to collect her shoes that she, obviously had placed on the bed. She could not remember. Avoiding any contact with his skin, she moved past him and was out of the door, and down the steps, before he could make a judgment call.

His initial response was to go after her. He did not have the right.

Patrick stepped out onto the tiny deck at the top of the stairs and watched her fade away from him.

She ran on, as if possessed, toward the main house. Tears streaked her cheeks. Her heart pounded.

Smells of the sea flavored the soft summer air, heavy with dew, adding a tantalizing perfume to the evening's surreal interlude.

Patrick stood motionless.

The huge mansion door closed...ever so slowly...and with it the cold reality that their golden interlude had come to an end.

Tonight Prunella had luxuriated in an amazing experience of joy.

To be a part of a loving family, privy to old stories of the past, the nostalgia of generations of loyalty, the beautiful food and wine. A simple sharing of life. How she rejoiced in its pureness.

And Patrick...he was, in himself, a celebration.

Prunella felt the strings of her soul being tenderly plucked, as if by the sensitive fingertips of an expert harpist. Each note played to perfection, each emotion tweaked, one at a time, deliberately chosen in perfect harmony with the other.

Patrick and the lady had shared an extraordinary journey of discovery. Each nourished forever by its essence. They had managed to scale the confining walls of their personal prisons, stealing a few moments of pure freedom.

Together they indulged, with curious delight, in the sweet mysteries of their own self-designed kingdom, losing themselves for an infinitesimal beat of time in the whirling clock of eternity.

Tonight, two hearts were joined by desire...by passion.

Without a word.

Without a touch.

Tenth Anniversary

It was Sunday, the Huntingwell's tenth anniversary... Thaddeus had returned home late last evening after an emotional week with the family of his late friend.

This evening she was eager to be with him, her husband, to reinforce their tethered state and to quell her gnawing twinges of silent betrayal. This was where she belonged. He was her vow. It was a good union, a comfortable partnership. She knew all that. She berated herself for allowing her hungry heart to mimic a selfish, undisciplined child.

As he walked, expectantly, to his wife's bed-chamber, Thaddeus smiled to himself. For convenience, they had planned separate sleeping quarters to accommodate their incompatible sleep schedules. At times, Prunella wished his visits were more frequent, that their love making was nurtured by spontaneity and lust rather than presumed appropriate ritual.

She was, after all, the product of a "school of thought" that dictated the female of the species wait demurely, and non-aggressively, to be wooed. She could never adopt the role of seducer, although there was a smoldering corner of her being kept under lock and key that could easily become wildly provocative, given the slightest hint of encouragement.

Earlier in the day, Mrs. Huntingwell had confided in her trusted servant. "It's funny, Molly, we humans are all sculptured from the same clay and yet, our lives are governed by the people we encounter on our journey, especially those intimate souls who are in a position to safeguard our vulnerabilities."

Molly knew, at times like this, she was expected to be still and listen...the role of sounding board.

Prunella continued pacing the floor, as though giving a speech to the ladies' club. Her evening with Patrick still warm in her heart.

"If we are touched by gentleness, our softer nature will respond. If we are governed through harshness, our heart will answer with bitterness."

She paused. Her words came slowly, softly...as though from some far away place that she alone was privy to. "If we choose to couple ourselves with indifference, we become cold. But, if the spirit is nurtured by kindness and respect, the worth of our own existence is profoundly validated, inviting us to rejoice unencumbered in our own innate sensuality."

"Heavenly Fathah!" Molly groaned to herself...those were a lot of words and wondered why the Missus was in such a preachin' mood today. Although Prunella could talk to Molly about almost anything, she would never divulge her unbelievable escape with Patrick. Nor could she ever feel totally free from its innocent guilt. It would be her private, sweet agony.

She was able to clear her thoughts and visualize Thaddeus weaving his way through the cozy library sitting room that separated their facing doorways. This room did not open to the hall, only to the bedrooms. It was truly their private sanctum. A place where they could steal a brief, intimate parcel of time away from the petty trials of the day. A rendezvous...pleasant for both.

He would be carrying a bottle of vintage bubbly under his left arm, leaving his hand free to grasp two stemmed glasses. With his right hand, he would balance a small silver tray presenting a nosegay of fresh violets, (echoing those she carried on her wedding day and he special ordered every year since) ...and a tiny white moiré taffeta box, held captive by a narrow white cord. It would contain a sumptuous scoop of precious jewels from a jewelry shop he frequented on 5th Avenue. The same lovely scenario every year.

Thaddeus would be fresh from the shower, barefooted, cocooned in the ever-so-faint muskiness of cologne and wrapped only in his black silk lounging robe, sashed loosely around his hips...a gift from her several Christmases ago.

Tonight she would celebrate with honesty. He was deserving.

As most nights, Prunella's door was loosely closed, never locked. There were evenings when she deliberately left the wide carved door ajar, in hopes he would accept her wordless invitation to enter. The blatant clue was often overlooked.

She was timid in this regard, lacking the ability to comfortably express her intimate needs to him. Things continued without change, year after year. Prunella always enjoyed his nearness and although their romantic interludes were rather mechanical and uncreative, his gentleness was soothing.

Tonight, Thad was feeling a bit culpable after being forced to renege on the long planned opera weekend. He wanted her to know how much he loved her after ten years of marriage. He did love her, in his own way, and couldn't conceive of his life without her in it.

He knocked his usual three knocks.

"Come in, Thad."

She had just slipped off a white lace peignoir and with deliberate care, placed it over the back of a chair, as he entered. She could not help but notice how his black monogrammed robe was in powerful contrast to her all white roomscape. Prunella's slim, fluid limbs did justice to the white silk negligee that flowed like liquid over her body.

Flirty panels of French lace adorned the bodice while narrow shoulder ribbons offered access to acres of white skin, beckoning to be caressed.

"Oh my, what have we here?" A slight sway of the hips. A coy eye on the tray.

He came toward her without a word, kissed her shoulders, lingering a moment to luxuriate in the delicate scent of her. She laughed with guarded emotion, toying a bit with his psyche.

After finding a home for the wine bottle and glasses, with an exaggerated bow, he extended the little tray. She slowly reached for the nosegay. With closed eyes, she brought it to her face, smothering her nostrils to fully appreciate the faint woodland fragrance it held. That was the dearest thing he did each year, to remember her violets.

She caressed the little box.

"What have you done, Thad?" knowing it would be his usual extravagant offering. The cord slid easily from the shiny fabric. She gently wedged the lid up with her thumb to an explosion of sparkling lights, a spectacular multi-faceted amethyst framed by ten perfect diamonds. The ring was a masterpiece!! She knew it must have been designed for her by Thad's old jeweler friend in New York, expressly to commemorate their tenth anniversary. It was so like him. Classy, elegant and so in keeping with his extraordinary compunction to favor her with expensive gifts. He pleasured in the sight of her obvious approval.

Prunella wrapped her arms around his neck. No words were needed. He could feel her slimness through the silken layer of fabric.

Fate had blanketed him with enormous good fortune, but she was, by far, his most coveted trophy.

The morning hours shed light on the circumstance, that Mr. Huntingwell's bed had not been touched. The upstairs maids, all a twitter behind the linen room doors, took giddy delight in charting the master's moods.

"Go on wi'ya, now" Molly protested, raising an arm to shoo them away. "Be off! Thars work t'be done" she directed. But as the young girls, in their freshly starched aprons, scampered off down the long hall, Molly couldn't resist a slight smile of her own.

Wedding

Clip-clop ... Clip-clop ... Clip-clop ...

Newly shod hooves trod rhythmically over Nantucket Island's narrow cobblestone streets, tapping out poignant memories of an era past. A passage of time, so long ago, in which a slower pace of living was embraced. When folks took pride in helping a neighbor, a bucket of maple syrup exchanged for a mended fence post, when manners were taught and kindness expected.

Today, the steady clatter of heavy wooden wheels echoed throughout the sleepy, picturesque township. A shiny black wedding carriage meandered along at a lethargic pace, laggardly maneuvered by an unsmiling stiff-backed driver. By plan, he was formally attired in black suit, black gloves, black top hat, to meld unobtrusively into the blackness of the elegant surrey. Across his knees, a long, slender, wisp-like whip lay almost unnoticed. His hands relaxed, slackening tension on narrow leather reins, inviting the seasoned steed to seek out his own lackadaisical stride over familiar ground.

The glistening shay methodically wove its way through a maze of quiet lanes. They passed several grand old saltboxes with their stiff frontages and slopping back roofs, that had for generations gallantly braced against the poundings of inhospitable New England winters.

The carriage rolled on along the familiar way. Every so often, a small doll-like cottage, frosted with weather-bleached shakes, coyly bared its face from behind a white picket fence. It revealed brightly painted window boxes pregnant with cascading blue lobelia or a potpourri of colorful petunias in pink, lavender, yellow.

The moors were blanketed with heather. Summer's lilacs lightly sweetened the air with their ambrosial scent, occasionally mingling with the earthy essence of freshly tilled soil to titillate the nostrils with their bewitching incense.

The bride, bedecked in ivory lace, sat proudly erect against a background of black tufted leather...a flawless diamond exquisitely displayed on a jeweler's velvet tray. Prunella Catherine serene and beautiful bathed in a glow of unspoken contentment. Her eyes softly focused ahead exuding an aura of inner peace, seemingly mesmerized by the breathtaking wonders of the world around her.

As she rode on, a whimsical thought serendipitously captured her imagination. She envisioned herself being chauffeured through the enchanting Giverny gardens of a Monet canvas. The slightest smile curled her lips.

Her gown was fashioned of vintage lace; the same dress that was hand-sewn and worn by her grandmother two generations before on this very land. Its delicate fibers stained and warmly tinted by time, added a touch of sentiment and permanence to the flavor of the moment. She wore her hair combed back into a cluster of soft curls, sweetly intertwined with satin ribbons and rose buds.

In her lap rested a grand assemblage of the palest pink and ivory roses furbished with fragile sprigs of babies breath. All gathered in a soft ruffle of French lace; lovingly hugged by yards of narrow ivory ribbons that floated aimlessly in the air, playfully tickled by a whisper-soft breeze. The heady fragrance, intoxicating.

For a moment, the bride's eyes were averted to her bouquet to catch a glimpse of an exquisite white butterfly alight on the sheer rippled edge of a rose petal. Seeming to feel its presence to be intrusive, fluttered off as quickly as it had come.

The carriage brushed beneath the sweeping boughs of ancient maples. Warblers and jays heralded the lady in lace with deafening twittering in appreciative applause of the gracious cargo.

Clip-clop ... Clip-clop ... Clip-clop ...

On the opposite side of the island an anxious groom paced expectantly at the road's end. His black boots crunched noisily over the pebbled shoulder. He stretched his five feet, eleven inches as tall as his might would allow in an effort to peer over the bobbing heads of a gathering crowd. He craned his neck, straining every muscle in hopes of catching the first glimpse of the voiture that would round the bend and deliver his love to his side.

Patrick Sean O'Shay fidgeted with the lapels of his cutaway, and sporadically checked his watch as though to magically dissolve the remaining moments. His eyes dotted to the ever growing swarm of guests. Clusters of small circles formed as new invitees arrived amidst warm cheers of instant recognition.

Patrick was fraught with nerve splitting anticipation. Although his timepiece reassured him she was not late, his heart relayed a different message.

What's taking her so long? Maybe the horse went lame. It could happen. Silent misgivings halted his heart. *Could she have changed her mind?* He laughed out loud. What an absurd thought.

"There she is!" someone shouted.

An invisible straight-jacket snapped around Patrick's body at first he felt the tightening, immobilizing, and finally transforming all his joints to steel. He was locked inside a tomb of desensitized flesh. He had waited so unbearably long for this glorious sight and as he had fantasized a million times, it was about to become a reality.

"Look! It's comin' 'round now!" another called out.

"Here she comes, ol'boy. Not too late to bolt," a deep voice heckled.

Patrick did not turn to identify the joker who had so vigorously whacked him on the back. He was too involved in his own web of simmering thoughts to care. He could feel the power of passion pulsate through his loins and knew he had to pull himself together.

The carriage was approaching at a painfully slow rate.

"Let's start, Patrick." The voice was low, deliberate, assuring. The kindly old minister gently nudged Patrick's elbow. He motioned him to take his place behind the three animated fiddlers who had been hired to lead the procession to a rock peak that dramatically jutted up from the ocean floor. The summit was the highest point on the island, the same romantic spot he had chosen to ask her to be his bride.

"Wait! Wait!" Patrick insisted without turning his head. His voice hushed. His hand automatically clutched the minister's arm to stay himself.

The man of the cloth was gently insistent. Patrick, with eyes still riveted in the direction of the oncoming buggy, allowed himself to be guided by the determined hand of the mild-mannered preacher. They dutifully took their places several yards behind the frolicking musicians, who had already begun the long trek over a rough rutted path to the mount.

They began the symbolic walk; the groom...the minister...shoulder to shoulder...in silence. A mellow apple-cheeked aging gentleman, and the young tanned confident boy; one relaxed, one tense; one old, one so very young; each walking through a different passage of time; each secretly moved by his own intimate interpretation of love, colored by personal beliefs and experiences. But both hearts in full accord with the solemnity of the day.

As if rehearsed, the crowd of well-wishers filed into a single line behind the odd looking couple, mindful of remaining a respectful distance from the slow-gaited man, thus setting the cast appropriately back from the lead players. For all had become willing actors in the poignant drama unfolding before them.

Up ahead the jaunty fiddlers hopped about, spirited by the lively strains of their own bows. The elixir of joy reverberated through the large group bidding each soul to recapture the innocence of their own youth. Even the most dispassionate among them experienced renewed stirrings of warm heartedness as they were inescapably amalgamated into the dizzying atmosphere that had wafted through the fields. Love's fire had heated the earth on this fine day.

One of the fiddlers, noticing the strained lines furrowing Patrick's brow, left his place at the top of the procession and jigged his way back down to the serious looking young lad. He removed his dark green felt hat and with an exaggerated low sweeping motion, made a deep bow in front of Patrick continuing to hop to and fro, first on one foot then the other. He skipped around the stiffly moving bridegroom, lightheartedly taunting him as he sawed his fiddle with a flurry of comical movements in an effort to relax the rigid young man.

"Loosen up, my man, loosen up!" he gibed.

With a twinkle in his eye, "Little Red" as he was appropriately nicknamed in tribute to his diminutive stature and flaming mane, was able to eke out a slight smile from the boyishly handsome face. Mission accomplished, he wedged his fiddle further up under his lavish beard and danced his way back to the energetic musicians, who after a lengthy hike had reached the designated spot on the promontory. They veered off to the right, leaving an open space for the groom and preacher who had both chosen to travel the way in silent communion.

Continuing forward, the solemn pair stepped up onto an enormous flat rock that protruded out over the ocean like a giant stage. Surely it had been placed there expressly for this day. The two men turned to face the long silent procession as it continued to creep forward, reverently snaking over a narrow uneven ribbon of dirt, slithering noiselessly through the flower-studded field like a curious serpent.

One by one, guests reached the wedding rock that had elevated Patrick and the preacher above the heads of the crowd. As each left the line they dispersed, passing directly in front of the groom, some went left, others right as though choosing invisible pews in a phantom chapel. Some nodded, some politely smiled, others kept their head lowered considerate not to intrude into Patrick's private thoughts. All stepping from the rough path onto the uncut grasses, instinctively leaving a natural aisle for the bride.

Patrick was resplendent in his vintage black coat, tan knickers, knee-high black boots. A vibrant blue sash she had so lovingly hand woven for him, drew the color of sapphires from the sky matching his eyes so perfectly, as though nature had purposely tinted the heavens from the same palette.

Patrick unconsciously wedged an index finger into the neck of his shirt, running it around his strangled flesh in an attempt to pry loose the damp skin that had adhered to the wide starched collar. The tip of his finger touched the chain holding Gram's cherished Claddagh. A shiver ran through him. Someday the treasured talisman would belong to his beloved as the tradition dictates. To be passed on "from heart to heart."

Grams could not be here today in person, the terrain much too arduous for her aging bones, but Patrick could feel her beautiful soul blanketing him like the warmth of a country quilt.

At the distant edge of the field glistening in the noonday sun, the highly polished carriage could be seen veering off the macadam onto the road's edge. The crunching sound of heavy wooden wheels crackling over graveled ground, shot out over the sprawling grassland and pierced the quietude like machine gun fire. The horse came to an abrupt halt. Once again silence reigned.

On the mount, standing like hundreds of placed mannequins, the gatherers came to life at the sight of the bridal buggy. As if on cue, all heads turned in unison toward the shay's two costumed occupants who, from a distance resembled two tiny porcelain figurines.

A few random whispers rustled through the hypnotic stillness. Mindful of being minutely scrutinized, the gentleman driver was bent on executing a performance of which his audience would be duly impressed.

With ridiculous overtures, he unwound his lanky limbs, each motion executed to the fullest. He stepped stiffly from the narrow running board onto a slippery carpet of tiny round pebbles. He had played this role a hundred times and by now it was second nature. As a proclaimed actor worth his salt, he took enormous care never to allow his job to become mundane.

A tall, deceivingly awkward looking man, he gathered the slack leather reins in his nimble fingers. With head held high, back arrow straight, eyes fixed ahead, he walked to the hitching post, disciplining himself to use slow leaden paces. As he strode past the lowered head of the bored looking horse, the animal turned slightly to grace his master with a lazy bray exposing a corn row of large brown-stained teeth.

With a wild flourish, engaging in far more theatrics than necessary, he tethered the grateful animal to within drinking distance of the watering hole.

The man's expression remained frozen, yet always cognizant of distant eyes evaluating his every move. In long measured strides, he returned to the carriage and flamboyantly offered a gloved hand to the statuesque lace angel. With calculated grace she accepted his assistance.

As her brocaded satin slippers touched the dusty earth, acclamations of approval rippled through the throng on the summit. The sun's brilliance set aflame a profusion of opalescent sequins and pearls that had been precisely spattered on the bodice and sleeves of the antique dress, inviting it to come alive as she moved.

Cradling her oversized bouquet lightly in both hands, she began her long solitary stroll through the fairytale landscape up to the wedding rock. Lost in her own fantasies, she was truly unaware that every inch of her countenance was being devoured by the appreciative crowd.

"Isn't she glorious!" a whisper carefully uttered.

The women were on tiptoes swaying this way and that in hopes of viewing the heavenly creature from a more advantageous angle.

"Oh my, how beautiful!"

"Lovely."

"Her grandmother's dress, you know."

"And imagine, all sewn by hand." Gossamer wisps of salty air wafted over the sunlit meadow nudging the tall willowed grasses, gently turning their shafts into delicately swaying wands of gold. The gauzy fields were a sublime tribute to nature's masterful creation, a surreal paradise for lovers.

Unmindful of the passing of time, Prunella approached... unhurried...serene...gliding over the challenging ground with steps so fluid one could only surmise she was being transported on the wings of butterflies.

After what Patrick determined was forever, his radiant Queen Catherine stood before him. For one fleeting moment their eyes touched...misted...and in that divine drop of time, held the secrets of eternity. The golden cloak of love shielded them from the ogling eyes of the crowd.

Patrick was about to explode! Never had he known the power of want so urgently. This perfect creature had actually agreed to be his; to love, to hold, to cherish for a lifetime. His mind was a mish-mash of disbelief. How did this incredible blessing come to be bestowed upon him...an ordinary man. Surely the gods had some gargantuan mission in store for him equal in depth to his unprecedented good fortune. He would deal with that later.

Prunella lifted her dress a bit, exposing thin ankles sheathed in the sheerest ivory stockings. She gracefully raised her foot onto the rock platform. Patrick was totally helpless, unable to unlock his limbs and offer her assistance. She placed her hand in the outstretched hand of the knowing old minister. Patrick's entire body had literally shut down. He could feel her nearness, smell her perfume, each playing havoc with his senses, and yet he could not muster even the slightest twinge of movement. She remained astonishingly calm. In turn, his own fever was mildly tempered by her gentle composure.

The minister's aging joints creaked as he painfully hobbled off the stone stage. He turned his back to the guests and faced the perfect couple elevated a foot above the crowd.

"Would the bride and groom please join hands?"

Patrick remained frozen. He could hear the words in a tunnel of filtered sound, but was unable to react. He was mortified. The preacher, savvy to the ways of nervous grooms, once again struggled to step back onto the rock and with as little notice as possible, positioned Patrick's hand in that of his bride. Patrick felt foolish, helpless to maneuver his own body.

"We are all gathered here today to witness an exchanging of the sacred vows of marriage between ..."

The monotone voice hummed on in synchronized accompaniment to the ocean tide rhythmically lapping the cliff's foundation fifty feet below.

The little gray-haired man extended his bony arms to the heavens and with an all encompassing gesture toward the vast horizon proclaimed "This is your universe" indicating that the world was theirs. "Your life will be as the potter's clay. Mold it as you will."

As the words hung in space, Patrick, unthinking, stepped backward toward the ridge of the precipice. Panic gripped his throat! He could feel the solid foundation crumble beneath his weight. The shattered crackle of splitting rock slapped at the caressing wind.

"Oh God ...GOD!"

Fighting frantically to keep his balance as the earth gave way, he made a futile attempt to right himself by grabbing for the trembling hand of his terror stricken bride. Their finger tips barely touched. She was a breath out of reach.

He searched desperately for a familiar face in the crowd. All had vanished! The minister? Gone! His bride quickly fading out of sight.

He was alone...alone...alone.

Like a bag of wet cement he plummeted with lightening velocity toward the jagged unyielding rocks below.

A horrific, blood-chilling cry pierced the air!

Patrick, bathed in cold sweat, shot straight up in his bed, blinded by the dread black pitch of night. Grotesque demons clawed at his flesh...jerking his bones...leaving him quivering with insufferable pain. The choking cries that reverberated through the night were his own.

There was no sun...no carriage...no grassy meadow...no rings...no guests...and the most twisted of all agonies, no bride! No bride...no bride...no bride. It was the same cruel dream he had experienced time and time again. The worst of worst nightmares. But this moment...here...tonight...he hungered passionately...more than ever before...for it to be a reality.

A compendium of emotions hemorrhaged from his gut. He felt like vomiting, crying, laughing, yelling! In a raging surge of fury, he stood up on his bed wildly hurling his pillows, one after the other, at the wall beside him, dislodging his guitar which spat out an eerie discord as it hit the floor. He was out of control, sobbing, fighting bouts of hysteria. He jumped off the bed...on again...off again...rampaging around the small cluttered room. Pounding a wall. Kicking a chair. Venting his anger like a rabid animal.

Patrick flung himself onto his bed again. Anger poured from his mouth in the violent wrath of a madman. He thrust a clenched fist to the heavens. A surge of bile erupted in his throat.

"Why? Why?" he bawled. "Why are You tormenting me?" His breathing had become more labored, sweat oozed from his pores. "Why?" Patrick ranted for an exhaustible interim, breaking into abusive attacks on a God he was convinced took diabolical pleasure in persecuting him and watching him bleed.

Spent, he flopped onto the damp twisted sheets face down, hands soothing his throbbing head. He remained in that position with his eyes closed for a long calming interlude.

Patrick rolled over slowly. His sobbing almost inaudible and stared up at the ceiling, invisible in the darkness. His arms folded under his head, tears slid across his temples in silent resentment. His chest convulsed at irregular intervals. He felt nauseous.

Raising his torso to a sitting position, he sought refuge in the oppressive blackness. He hugged his knees, rocking back and forth attempting to sooth his crucified heart. Finally, his strength had totally evaporated and he flopped back onto the pillowless bed. In reconciled desperation, he slid into the open arms of Morpheus.

The naked blare of morning rescued him from the night's horrors. He dragged himself into the bathroom to shower and was greeted by a roughly scribbled note he had taped to the medicine cabinet several weeks before.

He read it.

"WE HALLORANS DO NOT BUCKLE UNDER."

He smiled. Dear Grams. Dear, dear Grams.

Going Home

The frequency and strength of his paralyzing headaches had lessened over the past few months until the presence of pain had virtually subsided. But of late, Patrick began to experience a familiar throbbing behind his eyes and instinctively feared for the worst. He abhorred what was happening to his body. The prospect of losing the battle altogether was the bitterest dimension of his fight and he vowed to keep punching until the sound of the last bell.

In his valorous efforts to ward off mental depression, Patrick often beseeched the solace of his grandmother's words. Her tough message pulsed through the convoluted tunnels of his mind, over and over, the same powerful litany which had in the past been so successful in reinforcing his will to forge on.

Patrick smiled. He pictured eighty year old Grams pounding the table with her bony fist to emphasize her heartfelt beliefs, beliefs that she, a well-seasoned warrior fiercely lived by.

"We Hallorans do NOT buckle under!" she would expound. "Life is a game of seemingly irrational little scrimmages." Her eyes would narrow. "Fiendishly wicked mazes with stumbling blocks placed in strategic spots along our path. All for a purpose ...a purpose!" Her fist hammered the table for emphasis. "To test our fortitude ...our courage ...bolster our confidence." A pause. "Testing ...always testing ...molding us into stout-hearted soldiers of virtue ...separating the weak from the hardy."

Her tone softened.

"We should be forever grateful for its challenge."

Grams would be forced to gasp for a much needed breath, her voice becoming thinner and higher pitched as she spoke.

She was not preaching ...she never preached. The old lady was merely passing on lessons she had painfully learned in hopes of lessening life's burdens for those who might take heed. She was eminently qualified to testify to human trial.

"We learn to stand up to adversity. Defy her! Meet her head on!" A tightly clenched blue veined fist shot into the air, "We Hallorans" repeating her proclamation with fervor, "do not buckle under."

Her performance would leave her shaking all over. Grams, always stalwart, suggested she might sit awhile and that a "small glass of claret would not be out of order" to reprogram her heartbeat.

It was mid summer and Patrick had not seen his grandmother in over a month. He missed her. Since taking on work at Narragansett, his days became increasingly long ...hardly designed for leisure time. Although her spirit was with him always, now and again he needed to be nourished by her presence. He promised himself he would honor his mother's invitation for the weekend. His summer job contract allowed two free weekends during the three whirlwind months of employment.

"Dah-ling, do try to pop up for din-ah on Saturday." His mother begged. "Puff is doing her mah-va-lous thing with venison," Heather O'Shay oozed into the phone.

Patrick was not enamored with the gamey taste of wild meat and wasn't convinced his family was either. He learned early on that one must always tout the spoils of the hunt as "glorious eating." Rule number two was never insult the bearer of such bounty, especially if the aforementioned was one of the prosperous clients who seasonally stocked the O'Shay freezer with a plenteous stash of neatly wrapped and labeled packages containing the flesh of sundry wild creatures. Patrick never understood the hypocritical interplay between the firm and its auspicious clientele.

"It's good for business, dah-ling," his mother once winked while delivering a maudlin pat on his cheek.

"Name of the game, son." John J. echoed. "One hand washes the other. You know."

Patrick didn't know, but guessed it was a small sacrifice on the O'Shay's part to develop a taste for venison to coddle a wealthy client. So be it.

Patrick believed these beautiful animals should be left to roam free. He detested the concept of slaughtering any of nature's masterpieces for the sheer pleasure of man's primitive need to conquer, to fan his ego, boast of his virile skills.

As a young lad, his stomach would churn as he listened to vivid accounts of a grisly kill; hunters, trying to justify their sport by convincing each other that they were humanitarians. "Weeding out" the herds that would over-populate, causing many poor animals to succumb to death from lack of food, disease and old age.

Patrick marveled that he had never seen any of those poor shaggy, old sick-looking bucks with broken racks and mottled fur mounted on mahogany paneled trophy room walls. Only the largest, strongest of the breed, the most perfect specimens with the largest racks and the most points were worthy of the bragging ritual.

He kept quiet. His feelings would never be understood.

Puff, who Heather O'Shay had alluded to, was the family's jovial Norwegian cook. She looked like a plump dumpling and when she wasn't laughing, she was singing or dancing. She sang folk tunes from the "old country" in her native tongue or newly learned songs in her broken English.

She was famed for her rich cream layered puff-pastries and when the boys were little they would beg. "More puff." Hence the endearing pet name. They all had great affection for her and she, in turn, cared for them as mine own. Puff even cheerfully took on the often overbearing priggishness of Mrs. O'Shay with a light spirit.

One of the few fond memories Patrick had of his childhood was of racing home from school in hopes of arriving before his brothers did to eat the left-over pastry that Puff would declare might just have to be "tosst oot" if it didn't "get e-tup qwik." He remembered how jealous he felt, if perchance, someone entered the kitchen before he was able to receive his final treat, a tall cold frothy glass of molasses milk.

Patrick never interacted with Puff about anything serious as he did with Grams. The happy cook was a warm soft spot in a house so full of cold hard personalities.

He should pay a visit.

It was time.

Making the Rounds

Late Friday evening the taxi pulled up in front of the imposing brick Victorian on Benefit Street. Patrick paid the driver, gathered his few belongings and stepped into the twilight. He paused a moment to survey the large home, his childhood residence. It stood deathly still. No sign of life.

In an unhurried manner, Patrick ascended the wide brick steps, automatically counting each rise as he did as a child. Five...six...seven. He approached the over-sized walnut door. O'SHAY tastefully engraved on the enormous brass knocker quietly screamed of success.

With as little sound as possible, he turned his key and entered the grand foyer, crossing gingerly over the black and white marble squares in hopes of avoiding a premature announcement of his arrival. He made his way directly to the hall elevator, a direct route to the cozy third floor rooms. Gram's place.

There was a sliver of light dozing at the bottom of Gram's door. This was no indication of her slumberous state, for since the death of her young son, she had chosen to keep the light burning. Darkness brought too many uninvited ghosts of the past into her heart.

Patrick rested an ear against the white painted door in an effort to discern any sign of stirring therein. All was quiet. He would postpone his visit until tomorrow.

Returning to the first floor, he took refuge in the elaborately decorated guest room off the main hall. Opting not to disturb the mountain of designer pillows, artfully positioned on the antique oak bed, Patrick curled up on the wide over-stuffed chintz lounge. It would do nicely.

Early rays of light seeped through the tall wood shutters, acting as a wake-up call. Familiar aromas of freshly baked pastry awakened his senses. He threw on his sun-tans and made his way to the kitchen.

"Patkee! Patkee!...is you! Com'ere."

"Hey, Puff."

Before he could say more, the corpulent cook, overcome with pure delight came toward him, arms reaching out to hug "her Patkee." They danced around the spacious room, both laughing out loud like two silly children. Wonderful Puff. Always the same.

They exchanged a few light-hearted thoughts while Patrick surveyed his surroundings. The butcher block work table was strewn with assorted paraphernalia in preparation for the evening's culinary presentation. He observed two coffee cups near the sink. One wearing the unmistakable bright red imprint of his mother's freshly applied lipstick. Signs of a hasty departure. Racing to the office even on Saturday.

"Folks gone already?" He knew the answer.

"O'sure. They go." Puff sensed his disappointment. "Ah, lookee ova heer. Nice afpal strudel, eh?"

Patrick felt a warm sense of connection in Puff's kitchen and never refused a hefty portion of her "best-in-world" apple delight.

The rest of the day he spent almost entirely by himself, except for the few relished hours enjoyed with his grandmother. He never tired of her delightful tales, many of which he jotted down upon leaving her rooms in hopes of weaving the priceless vignettes into book form. Someday, if time permitted.

Saturday evening, as promised, they supped on Puff's famous roast of venison. But instead of a quiet private family gathering, as his mother had intimated, the O'Shay table was crammed with an eclectic collection of invited guests, rendering intimate family dialogue virtually impossible.

Sunday rolled lazily around and it was time to bid his goodbyes. It annoyed the fire out of him that the two days he was home, he was hardly granted a private moment with any member of his family. And when Sunday rolled around, it was he who made the rounds of farewells. His presence was acknowledged just long enough to utter the same old pat remarks.

Patrick bolted up the winding stairway, two steps at a time, in hopes of catching John J. O'Shay in his library. He collided full force with his impeccably dressed mother who was headed down at that precise moment.

Heather O'Shay was shaken by the sudden encounter with her youngest son.

"Oh dah-ling, I didn't see you!"

She was balancing an armload of neatly stacked papers, a tin box of paper clips precariously perched atop the pile. The unsuspected collision forced the tiny container to escape her grasp. Mother and son watched helplessly as the lid popped open on impact, sending the freed contents to tumble downward, spattering a hundred shiny coils over the marble steps below.

"Oh my, De-ah," she dramatized, nervously taking a quick inventory of her precious business papers before assessing the run-away clips. "What an awful mess," she purred, pressing her hand over her rapidly pounding heart, as if to hold it in place while she caught her breath.

"Sorry, Mom, you alright?" He steadied her, bracing her arms until he was certain she had regained her balance.

"Oh yes, De-ah, perfectly fine." Heather put a loose folder to use as a fan.

As Patrick began to retrieve the clips and methodically re-box them,

Heather noticed her son's overnight satchel and several books positioned at the bottom of the stairs.

"Goodness dah-ling, where did the weekend go?" she cooed dolefully in her acquired "upper class" drawl. "It seems we barely get to see you when you are home for such a tiny stay" she added in awe of the time lost.

"Yeah, I know. Everyone around here is pretty tied-up."

"Well then, you will just have to plan on staying a stretch longer next time."

Heather had already started down the remaining stairs as she spoke, the white silk scarf that accented her tailored black suit floating after her as she went. Never turning around, she blew him a theatrical kiss over her shoulder and continued waving her hand mechanically in the air, as a queen might deliver from her royal carriage. Stepping quickly into the sun-filled foyer, she vanished around the corner, leaving him alone with the lingering scent of expensive perfume.

No hug. No goodbye. No inquiry of his academics. No encouraging word.

Patrick shook his head and smiled in resigned acceptance. That was all the expression of love that Heather Halloran O'Shay was capable of. Oddly, he understood and pitied her inability to feel any deeper emotional stirrings. It was her loss.

He continued back up to the second floor.

"Well, well now, off again?" John J. O'Shay responded in a jocular tone to his son's surprise appearance.

Patrick stood in the door frame of the lavish at-home office absorbing the mellow ambience of the cherry-paneled room. His father sat forward in a high-back, made-to-order leather chair. Patrick rightly presumed the stacks of files before him were portfolios belonging to extra-pampered clients. It was of no concern that today was Sunday, a day of rest. It was imperative to John J. that all accounts be kept current. That was of prime importance.

The business, thought Patrick. *The almighty business.*

John J. got up and rounded the huge desk offering to shake his son's hand. Patrick approached a few steps onto the deep red pile and returned the gesture.

"Leaving so soon? Next time you're in town, let's get caught up. Take you to the club, lunch, meet some of the new boys. Play any golf?"

Not allowing his son the time to respond, he released his grip and gave Patrick the all-too-familiar "end-of-conversation" pat on the shoulder and returned to his work, leaving his youngest son in awkward silence. Without looking up from the papers he was perusing, asked in a flat tone "How does that sound, hmm?" He pulled his weighty chair closer to the carved teak desk.

"Sounds great, Dad. Great. Look forward to it."

But John J. O'Shay had already switched mental gears back into a work mode and never heard his son's reply. Only the grandfather clock dared to penetrate the room's morgue-like silence. Tick-tock...tick-tock. Even the beauty of its melodious chimes was wasted on the oblivious ears of the room's occupant.

Dolorously, Patrick left, full of sadness for these rigid hearts. He caught sight of his "Hollywood handsome" brother at the end of the hall. Michael, the middle O'Shay son, had just returned from the weekly basketball game, a long standing tradition; same ol' gang, same ol' high school gym, same ol' bravado banter, same ol', same ol'. Every Sunday, rain or shine, no excuses accepted short of death. And like a dutiful son, Michael paid the folks that unspoken, yet expected, Sunday visit even though they worked together all week long.

Michael was enroute to the shower to freshen up before going home to Gwen and the twins.

"Hey Mike!" He approached with a rapid gate. Patrick was unable to ignore the grossly scarred legs of his older brother. The thin, misshapen limbs, were the result of a gruesome accident. "How's everything going, good buddy?" A trite figure of speech, they had never been buddies. "Haven't seen your ugly face all weekend."

"Pat, my man. Lookin' good. Lookin' good." Michael, normally reserved, jabbed Patrick in the stomach with more force than he intended. "Oh Ho! Tight!" A typical male interaction.

Before Patrick could recover enough from the unsuspecting blow to his mid-section and retaliate, Michael had evaporated in thin air. Once again, leaving him with a mouth full of unspoken words.

The empty space, that seconds before had been filled with his brother's presence, was now cluttered with a kaleidoscope of images; memories of a war...a disfigured soldier...a snow storm ...a tragic mishap...a funeral...a young girl...the miracle of love. All woven together in Patrick's head like an intricate tapestry.

Guinevere

Patrick piloted his body back toward the stairwell, pausing for a moment before he made his descent. He found it incomprehensible that the past months had rolled over with such astonishing swiftness.

His mind became a whirlpool of memories as he relived that extraordinary emotional block of time the O'Shays were forced to live through. It read more like fiction than fact.

He sat down on the top landing. His memory flashed back to the incredible chain of events that began, here in this very house. Time had passed so quickly. It seemed like yesterday.

R-r-r-ing ... R-r-r-ing ... R-r-r-ing.

The shrill cry of the doorbell impatiently sliced through the silence of the downstairs rooms.

From the parlor, where he was reassessing the last few lines of his latest poem, Patrick stole an inquiring glance at his mother. His mother had neglected to inform him of the evening's expected company. So typical not to feel the importance of making him a participant in family plans. He noticed Heather O'Shay nervously peering into a narrow portion of the tall gilt edged mirror, the last bit of glass left unobstructed by an overflowing arrangement of red roses and pine boughs, gracefully supported by a fancy 18th century Hepplewhite table.

It had been several years since Mrs. O'Shay had actually seen her old Vassar roommate, although, they had remained in close contact through lengthy letters, pictures and gossipy phone exchanges. Tonight she was driven to present a flawless "first" impression.

"Oh dah-ling...that must be the Moores now. Will you get it? Please, De-ah?" She spoke in hurried, little gaspy wisps and turned immediately back to recheck her coiffured reflection, fancying herself as "hardly changed."

"On my way."

"I'll be right there, dah-ling" Heather sing-songed.

The opened door introduced an assaulting gush of icy air into the warm room. Standing before him, as if professionally posed, were three smiling faces perfectly centered in the doorframe. An overhead lantern spot-lighted the trio, transposing them onto center stage. A background of gently falling snow-flakes gave an illusion of diamond dust blithely powdering the heads and shoulders of the performers. For a moment Patrick felt the scene to be directly from a Dicken's novel.

Father ... Mother ... Daughter.

Mr. Moore came to life, removed a fur-lined leather glove and offered his warm hand.

"Bart Moore here." Handshake firm, sure.

"Patrick O'Shay, come on in."

"And I'm Violet" handshake cold, weak, smile sincere. Her arms were laden with little fancy, wrapped packages. "Your mother and I were college roo ..."

"Vi! Oh, Vi! Dah-ling!" Heather, perfectly groomed in matching winter-white sweater and slacks, came quickly toward the small group, who had begun to exchange polite greetings. With arms outstretched, she literally pounced on her old friend in a burst of girlish enthusiasm, almost hurling her off balance. "My word! Look at you! You're gorgeous!" Heather secretly thoughther old friend was showing her age a bit.

The two remained locked in each other's arms crying, squealing, laughing, adopting for the moment the role of two young collegiates.

Patrick recalled how oddly he had evaluated the visiting threesome. Dad, richly dressed in a light tan, double-breasted camel's hair Chesterfield, black velvet collar, black felt homburg, rim softly rolled; mother regally wrapped in mink from head to ankles, make-up flawless, bright red lipstick, matching fingernails, jewelry extraordinary yet tasteful. Patrick thought, *One might adorn a more practical style of dress in a winter snow fall.*

And then there was daughter Guinevere. She was named, Patrick later learned, after King Arthur's beautiful Queen. Her mother, an English major "just fell in love" with the name, hence, Guinevere.

Unlike her beautiful namesake, Guinevere Moore was a plain looking young woman. Twenty, maybe twenty-one. Clear fresh skin, naturally rosy cheeks, lips unenhanced by paint, blue eyes, vibrant, large, heavily lashed without the assistance of mascara. Her clothes were comfortable, blue jeans, brown hiking boots, cuffed with thick red wool socks. A red turtle-neck sweater hugged her long neck beneath a navy blue corduroy jacket, left open in December. She was making a definite statement of individuality. Patrick liked her immediately, even before she spoke.

Guinevere was certainly no raving beauty, but her vitality and honesty later proved to far outweigh her ordinary appearance.

She carried one large, rather grubby canvas duffel-bag that hardly needed the label checked to determine it was not purchased from Bloomingdales. Patrick made a guess that the khaki sack was a find from some army surplus store. The one small case, with V.L.M. embossed in gold letters near the handle, was obviously borrowed from her mother.

Patrick remembered thinking it incredible that a young girl, who was planning to live away from home for one whole year, had so few belongings. He found it nicely refreshing.

Almost as an afterthought, Heather remembered the sole reason for the visit. She turned to acknowledge Violet's daughter, who had chosen to remain in the background while they got reacquainted.

"Oh my, and just look at you. You have grown to be quite a young lady." In reality, adornment conscious Heather found the girl to be pathetically plain and promised herself, over the next few months to doll the poor thing up.

Heather positioned her jeweled fingers around Guinevere's waist and held her at arms length as a buyer would scrutinize a horse. Patrick was fearful she might ask to see her teeth.

"My, my, aren't you the slim one." Heather struggled to find an outstanding feature to compliment her guest on and felt that thinness was always praise worthy.

Smiling, Guinevere sensed her hostess' disappointment in procuring such an unglamorous house guest.

Heather directed her eyes to her longtime friend. "We are going to get along wonderfully." Turning to Guinevere "aren't we, De-ah?"

Guinevere managed a nod. She evinced a good humored glance at Patrick who was standing on the outer circle digesting the interplay of personalities. He returned her silent message with a "might-as-well-accept-her-as-she-is" look. He was assured that was exactly what Guinevere Moore intended to do. Yes, things would most certainly be just fine.

In her senior year of college, an elective course on Egyptology had birthed Guinevere's insatiable interest in Egypt's ancient civilization, much to the dismay and puzzlement of her obtrusive parents. Years spent on the culture of a dead society seemed ludicrous.

"King Khafre? Queen Nofretari?" Bart Moore would query his daughter. "Who were they and who cares anyway? What possible difference do they make to the twentieth century? Waste of time, if you ask me." Mr. Moore hardly felt a kinship to these mummified souls who walked the earth some five thousand years ago.

"But Dad, the Egyptians have left us with wonderful legacies. They were fabulous artisans, builders, inventors, and politicians." She defended her choice bravely.

Bart Moore pooh-poohed his daughter's enthusiasm at first, trying his utmost to dissuade her from her course of study, deeming it "an egregious waste of time." Realizing that Guinevere remained unyielding in her decision, he ceased his campaign of words and bowed to her wishes.

"After all," he voiced privately to his wife, "putting undo pressure on the young girl to succeed in the corporate world was certainly not necessary" and far from fashionable for the times. She could be a teacher, find a nice school in the neighborhood. She would more than likely marry and raise a family, become a dutiful homemaker, a loving mother, a good wife and not tarry too far from home. For now, let her study whatever her heart desired.

If darling Guinevere had been a male child it would have been, naturally, a whole different kettle of fish.

Guinevere was serious about her studies. That is why she applied, on a suggestion from her teacher, to the Rhode Island School of Design in Providence. Her appetite had been whetted when she found that a formidable collection of Egyptian ornamentations and artifacts of archaeological interest were available. The school offered guest lectures, slides, a vast library of books and from time to time even unwrapped a real mummy for observation and study.

When Heather O'Shay had received the call from her old school chum, she was thrilled to be of assistance. She had not seen Violet Moore since she had moved from the area ten years ago with her husband to Washington D.C., where he was an active figure in the political scene.

"Of course, De-ah. Guinevere may stay with us. Of course we have extra room. Of course she would be no trouble. Of course having a daughter for a spell would be great fun. Of course. Of course. Of course, De-ah. Of course he won't mind." Heather was flattered that Violet chose to place her precious only daughter in her home. "Why, De-ah, it would be foolish for her to stay anywhere else when we are only a stone's throw from the school. Don't you agree, dah-ling?"

And so it was planned, by the two dear friends, indeed, the young girl would benefit by boarding in a safe environment while specializing in her field. It had been settled to the happy approval of Guinevere.

Michael

In the living room John O'Shay was already twirling two brandy snifters over separate flames to "take the chill out of one's innards." Bart Moore helped himself to a handful of cashews from a shallow cloisonné dish. They had left "the girls" to chat while they made themselves comfortable in the great room. Flames flickered lazily in the expansive stone fireplace offering an ambience of congeniality and welcome to the room's occupants.

In the foyer, the group still had not moved. With a slight wave of her hand Heather beckoned to Guinevere.

"Come, De-ah, let me show you your room." But instead of escorting Guinevere, Heather reached for Violet and together they ascended the flight of steps to the second floor, chatting a-mile-a-minute, still reminiscing of old times and common acquaintances. They mounted the stairway in tandem, arms linked. The girl in blue jeans momentarily forgotten.

"Oh well," Guinevere laughed with a shrug of her shoulders.

Patrick bent to lift her bags and she promptly stopped him.

"Thanks, they're light. I can manage."

She slid the shoulder strap of the clumsy duffel over one shoulder as if it were weightless, then stooped to draw up the smaller case before beginning the climb several steps behind the animated women.

That evening, the O'Shays and the Moores meshed smoothly, exchanging stories, retelling old jokes, sharing business experiences. They enjoyed an amiable fellowship, most comfortable in each other's company.

As the hour drew late, the front door opened in the hall. Heather turned to call out.

"Michael? Is that you, De-ah?" She craned her neck to identify her middle son, who was unwinding a snow-encrusted scarf from around his neck, gloves tucked up under his arm, just in from the new falling snow.

"Eh, Mom." He strode into the warm room filled with relaxing bodies. For a startled moment he was at a loss as to their identity, forgetting that today was the day the boarder was to arrive.

"Oh dah-ling, you are traipsing wet all over the floor," Heather protested politely. The highly polished oak floors were her pride and joy.

"Sorry." Michael was cordial and in tune to his mother's need for order. He granted her request and retreated.

Executing great care in removing his navy pea-coat, not to dislodge the fast melting flakes, he hung the long jacket on one of the ornamental hooks of the hall tree.

Rubbing his hands together, to revive circulation, Michael re-entered the room.

"This is my son, Michael" Heather presented her handsome son with due pride.

Everyone began to stir.

"Don't get up...please," Michael instructed, both hands in the air to stop them from rising. "You all look pretty settled in."

Soft snickers of agreement.

Bart Moore, disregarding the young man's suggestion, stood to introduce himself as Michael made the rounds.

"And Michael, De-ah, you do remember Violet, my college roommate."

"Oh yes, pleasure." He lied, offering his hand to Mrs. Moore. She straightened herself a trifle from her curled position on the white overstuffed couch, pleasantly noticing how the bright blue of his sweater accentuated the color in his eyes.

"Hello, Michael, how nice to see you again. I feel as though I know all of you so well through Heather's letters." She was a pleasant sort.

Violet motioned toward the girl sitting on the hearth in her stocking feet. She was snuggled against the stone fireplace, her arms cozily wrapped around her knees.

"Don't get up. Don't get up." Michael came around the couch. He bent over to shake Guinevere's hand and extended a felicitous welcome.

"Don't move" he lightly commanded again, still looking down at her.

"Don't worry, I couldn't get up if I had to," she teased. "I think my legs are dead."

Everyone laughed.

Patrick noticed a spontaneous exchange of pleasure radiating from both faces, an immediate look of approval between the two. Michael and Guinevere's eyes met and held a moment too long, the handshake a trifle more lingering than necessary. Definitely a delicious moment.

Michael made a move toward the empty place next to her on the long hearth, but as if the hand of some unseen spirit pulled him away from her, he rerouted his body to the bar and poured himself a Coke. His expression clouded, and the flush in his cheeks faded. He seemed to sense danger. To stir up a closer acquaintance with the sweet looking lady on the hearth, was the last thing he wanted.

Patrick noticed Guinevere silently questioning the abrupt mood swing of his brother. She looked confused by his behavior, keeping her eyes focused in his direction. Michael purposely avoided her. Very shortly he said his good-nights and retired for the evening.

Michael had been in Korea for only six weeks when the freak accident occurred. He was carrying a small drum of muriatic acid between his gloved hands when it slipped from his grip. Upon impact with the ground, the container burst open, exploding its deadly chemicals over the defenseless soldier's lower torso, instantly causing irreversible damage to his body. The potent liquid absorbed into the skin like a sponge. Although he was quickly disrobed and washed down with gallons of water, by the time he was rushed to the medics, his flesh was already beginning to be eaten away.

From his waist down, his body was a mass of scarlet blistered flesh. His feet had been mercifully less affected, protected by heavy army boots, of little consolation for the agonies he was to endure.

Although successful in reconstructing his maleness, he remained monstrously scarred and rendered impotent.

With the help of a team of psychiatrists, therapists, potent drugs and skilled doctors, Michael was able to accept the torturous salt baths, where dead skin was softened and scraped off to expose new raw flesh. He agonized through the trauma of skin grafts, hundreds of them, with rows of fresh skin taken from his buttocks, minute sections at a time and the eternal waiting to determine if the patch took. The ordeal was a ghoulish nightmare.

It had been almost two years ago, his body was still in the healing process. It would take years for the scars to harden and the red discoloration to fade. He wore elastic coverings on his legs to hold the skin in position. Still vivid in his mind was the excruciating pain of long therapy sessions, atrophied muscles stretched back to suppleness, joints twisted into movement again.

Michael had made up his mind, never to be seen by a woman. He had known enough degradation. He had nothing to offer, he could never father a child. He evaluated his body to be repulsive.

Guinevere melded politely into the O'Shay household and guarded against getting underfoot or being bothersome. She was most grateful for the opportunity afforded her. She could walk to her classes and come and go, as she pleased.

She settled into the spare bedroom down the hall that was John Jr.'s room when he was at home. John Jr. was the oldest O'Shay son and had married his high school sweetheart. They had produced a beautiful set of twin girls, much to the joy of their grandmother, who kept them clothed in the most expensive outfits money could buy.

Regardless of his stoic intentions during the months that Guinevere roomed in his home, Michael had yearned to approach her. He disciplined himself to structure the time with her in a formal, uncomplicated manner. They might enjoy an occasional foreign film together. She might invite him to an interesting lecture at the college and once in awhile she accompanied him on a museum tour, if there was a unique exhibit of interest to both.

Each recognized a quickening heart beat between them, yet each leery of misinterpretation as time together became increasingly needful. Guinevere found herself gearing her schedule more in concert with his routine. Intuitively, she realized that some sort of an emotional explosion was iminent. Her heart could no longer tolerate this cat and mouse game they were playing.

Silently she began to critique his behavior when they were together. She concluded her evaluation, determining that he was slowly exhibiting tell-tale signs of a captive heart. She also noticed, that if their togetherness took on the slightest flavor of entanglement, he masterfully shifted the mood to something less threatening.

Baffled she was!

Why was this basically shy, unassuming man, ostensibly unnerved by their quiet interludes of closeness. Why did he battle so to retain his blasted distance. It irked her.

Self-admittedly, she was no raving beauty, but she was confident that Michael did not deem outer appearances to be a salient consideration when choosing a partner. They enjoyed the same taste in music, literature, humor, political and religious philosophies and even food. What could be holding him captive? She found it impossible to read him.

Guinevere decided she must talk to someone in the family who could, honestly, give her insight into Michael's psyche. She thought he might be secretly married, or running from the law, harboring some awful disease or maybe he just didn't like women. Her imagination ran amuck. She must have answers.

Grams. She would consult Grams, who had quickly stolen her heart. Her own grandmother died when she was a tiny tot and she had adopted Grams as her own.

On weekends that Patrick was able to visit, she willingly shared the sweet lady, knowing how dearly the woman needed to be refueled by her grandson's vitality. He is the "core of my heart" she once told Guinevere of Patrick.

Through their mutual love for Haddie Kelly Halloran, Guinevere and Patrick developed an unanticipated closeness, one of bonded siblings. They were able to sincerely trust and confide in each other.

On one of those infrequent weekends, while Patrick and she were visiting Grams, Guinevere brought up the subject of Michael, her secret love for him, his seemingly caring for her, and her stoic determination to figure out why his mannerisms were so bewildering.

To her chagrin and sadness she was lovingly made aware of Michael's private world, his devastating ordeal, how far he had come in slaying his personal demons. Yes, she would honor his privacy, but her heart could not be trusted.

No advice was offered her, only facts. Although unspoken, Patrick craved to see Michael invite this rare young woman into his inner sanctum. Her intentions were honest, her needs simple.

The officer said that John, Jr. and his wife had died instantly. The young couple never having seen the semi that plowed into them head on in the most dire of blinding snow storms.

It had been only a few weeks before Christmas, when the tragic news ripped through the core of the O'Shays existence.

Why had they chosen such a night to go out in? Why? Why?

John, Jr. and his wife had come to leave off their babies with Heather and John O'Shay, who rarely offered to babysit for their four month old granddaughters. Heather declaring that the twins were "too much stress for a woman in her late forties." The truth of the matter was, that the O'Shay weekend calendar was overflowing with social obligations, allotting no time for diaper changes.

This night had been a "special treat" for the young O'Shays. With the gargantuan demands of two infants, the couple had not been out since the birth of the little ones. It was a typical wintry night, slick road conditions. They had new chains on the tires, and they knew to be especially careful. The evening had been planned and anticipated for such a long time. They would travel slowly. After all, they were just going to a movie, only one mile away from the house, snow was just beginning to fall. "Don't worry."

The O'Shays were devastated at the loss of their promising first born son and their "sweet-dah-ling" daughter-in-law. Patrick put himself on the outside, looking in on such pain, knowing that sooner than they were prepared for, his parents would be suffering yet another parting...his own. He took stock of his family. In anyone's eyes, the O'Shays epitomized success. A letter perfect unit and yet their destinies had been so painfully mapped out for them. All the gold bullion in the universe was not enough bargaining power to buy back the life of their son or change the course of fate.

A nanny was hired on for the little girls and the Benefit Street home became alive again with the sounds of growing children. Guinevere had fallen in love with Meghan and Maggie, relieving

"Nanny" of most of her duties as the twins' governess, much to the approval and elation of Heather. Guinevere bathed them whenever she could, sang to them, walked them in their carriage, and told them stories while sitting in the white nursery rocker, one tiny tot cradled in each arm. They would look up at her, eyes so bright and eager, entertained by her voice. Even though Guinevere knew they did not yet comprehend the long narratives, she pretended they understood every word, pointing to pictures as she read.

On several evenings, Guinevere would find Michael bent over a crib smiling or cooing at one of the pudgy little girls.

"They are beautiful, aren't they" she would comment in hushed tones.

He acknowledged her statement with a wordless nod. "Sometimes I think how such a tragedy could effect so many lives and yet I look at them" he twiddled a fat little toe, "surrounded by so much love and caring. It hasn't deterred their lives one bit. They'll never know what they missed." He never looked up at her.

"They're such happy little people," she echoed his sentiments "so lucky to have us all."

"And we are lucky to have them." He moved over to the other crib mindful to give equal time to each.

Guinevere tiptoed out of the room, unnoticed, leaving him with his thoughts. She knew his late brother was much on his mind.

Patrick was still on the top landing when he was jolted out of his daydreams by his own hearty laughter. He recalled the evening that Guinevere challenged Michael across a table crowded with Moores and O'Shays.

Poor Michael. It had been a shocker!

Year's End

It was a melancholy time for all.

Guinevere's allotted days with her host family were nearing an end. Although the O'Shays spent no time entertaining their studious guest, she had knotted herself to every member of the O'Shay household. Nor did her indulgent year of stimulating research make it any less difficult to culminate her stay.

And the lives she had flavored, they too were not without dejected spirits as the parting date drew near. Without her upbeat attitude there would be a noticeable void in their monotonous routine. She had left her mark on all of them. She would be thought of often, profoundly missed.

Violet and Bart Moore had returned to Rhode Island to gather their daughter and return with her to Washington, D.C. To visit their old friends, would not only be pleasurable, but would afford them the opportunity to voice their gratitude to Heather and John in person, a gesture unquestionably apropos under the circumstances. The O'Shays had been magnanimous in extending their hospitality to the Moore's beloved daughter, for one whole year.

They arrived, as before, in the throws of a winter snow. This time the distance between visits had not been as lengthy and exchanges of friendly prattle quickly commenced, a rerun of the previous year.

On the last evening of Guinevere's sojourn, all were on hand to send their star boarder off on her way in style. Puff had trumped-up a most enticing presentation of stuffed lamb roast with aromatic herbs. Rosemary, thyme, and garlic, wafted seductively from the kitchen, heralding the nearing of the celebration.

The small group drifted into the dining room with no apparent hurry, trying to stall the inevitable parting. They took their places according to the suggestions of Heather, who had planned the seating arrangement with individual personalities in mind. Heather took her usual seat to the left of her husband. She cautiously placed Guinevere and Michael "not too close" guarding against any accusations of match-making. Across the table was a comfortable distance.

Throughout the evening, Guinevere's virtues were extolled, her accomplishments toasted, mostly for the benefit of the Moores, reassurance that the year had been trouble free and enjoyable. The "remember whens" were numerous, light hearted, humorous incidents rehashed to the delight of all.

The horror of John, Jr.'s death and Michael's disfiguring accident were calculatingly skirted. The past years had brought incredible trials to the O'Shays, but this night belonged to Guinevere Moore and there would be no sombrous memories to dispirit the mood.

The grand finale to the wonderful meal was Guinevere's favorite dessert, Crème brûleè. Tonight Puff came from the kitchen with the chilled white porcelain dish and set it before the lady-of-the-hour to do the honors of cracking the hardened toffee that roofed the delicate pudding.

Guinevere picked up a silver spoon. She felt herself salivate, as thin sheets of toffee broke off under her light tapping and slid helter-skelter into the sweet rich cream below.

"I will really miss this decadent dessert" Guinevere joked. "You'll have to call me when it's on the menu. I'll fly in."

Laughter around the table.

Guinevere was fighting to keep her tears in check. How could she leave this place? It had been her nest for a whole year. Grams, when would she see her again? Patrick, the brother she never had.

Everyone was served and compliments flew, praising the cook for a glorious meal.

The chatter had quieted down during coffee. Only a few hours remained. Guinevere looked across the table at Michael, who had been virtually mute all evening and wondered what he was thinking. His eyes were lowered, his right hand rested on the handle of his coffee cup. His dessert hardly touched. She could feel his sadness. Deliberately, he avoided looking her way in fear of displaying any emotion that might tip off his hand. She was sure he wanted her, as much as she wanted him. They had become such incredibly good friends.

"The stubborn bull!" Guinevere's ire was boiling inside of her. "Why doesn't he make a move?"

Tap-tap-tap.

She was delivered of her anger by a knife lightly drumming the side of a glass at the opposite end of the table. All heads turned toward

John O'Shay, who was on his feet with his wine glass raised.

"I would like to make a toast to our lovely house guest." All followed suite and crystal stems lifted in salute of the honoree.

"We have enjoyed your company, my dear...your wit...your presence in our home. I only wish we could talk you into staying a bit longer.

"Hear ye! Hear ye! How about it, girl?" Patrick egged her on.

The applause faded from her ears. All she could hear was her own heart hammering against her ribs.

An uncomfortable deathlike silence had blanketed the table. All, awaiting her reply.

The next thing she realized, she too, was on her feet, facing Mr. O'Shay who had reseated himself. She felt a flush of fire race to her cheeks. Blushing-red was not her choice of color for the moment. She hardly wanted to portray a timorous maiden. Fighting to command every ligament in her body to remain at attention, she spoke. She was solemn, unsmiling.

"I will accept your offer." Surprised murmurs speed around the room, sporadic applause, hesitant, questioning. The puzzled group quieted down. The girl had more to say.

She repeated "I will accept your offer to remain...under one condition." she spoke clearly. She picked up her Madeira, securing it at the end of a rod-straight arm. Slowly, Guinevere turned away from Mr. O'Shay and pointed her half full glass directly at Michael.

Michael had just positioned himself comfortably for the first time in the entire evening, sitting sideways, one arm resting casually over his chair. He was taken back by her menacing stare. What was she doing? He stared back at her for lack of being able to do anything else.

"I will remain in the family only as ... as ... as Michael's wife."

Drop dead quiet.

GOOD GOD! What did she say?

Before she was able to give any thought to the consequences of her words, they had spewed out over the table like hail stones, spattering wildly in very direction.

All movement around the table ceased. All eyes were on Michael, waiting for his reaction. Any reaction. There was none.

As he stared at Guinevere, who at the moment looked oddly like Joan of Arc, his eyes protruded in glaring disbelief, becoming wider and wider until she was sure they would roll down his shirt.

The characters around the table duplicated a display in a wax museum. No one dared to breath.

Michael, poor Michael. One might have thought he had been wacked on the head with an iron skillet.

How could she present him with such a ludicrous proposal in front of their parents? Had she gone mad?

For a long time, Michael studied her determined posture, until it suddenly all became clear to him. She had, of course, done her homework, and well. She was offering to take the damaged goods "as is."

The room was being suffocated by an eerie pall of silent confusion. The drama heightened. Who would initiate the next move?

Guinevere and Michael stared, eyes frozen. She was still standing statue-like before him, the liquid in her glass trembled. Without removing his eyes from hers, he slowly removed his arm from behind the chair, methodically wiped his mouth with his napkin, set it on the table cloth, stood and slowly picked up his glass. He held it out, almost touching her outstretched arm, which by now was feeling like granite.

For a moment he said nothing.

A chair creaked at the end of the table.

Her heart wedged higher in her throat threatening to cut off her airway. She remained resolute.

Never losing the line of eye contact, Michael spoke almost inaudibly.

"I accept your offer," his voice cracked. "I ask you to stay. As my wife." he remained standing. They were alone now, just the two of them, on some whirling planet above the realm of earthlings.

Neither smiled. Their words needed digesting.

She felt the marrow leave her bones. She was about to drop, but he remained standing with his glass still outstretched to her. She was forced to hold on.

"I, too, have one condition." His voice came from a very special place, louder, clearer, more in control. "That we adopt Megan and

Maggie, as our own.

Guinevere's knees buckled, sending her backwards into her chair, emotionally whipped. Ecstatically happy!

"Yes! Yes! Yes!" It was more joy than she had bargained for.

Upon impact with the hard seat, the red wine from her glass splashed up, splattering her white cotton blouse and face with tiny rose-colored droplets.

"Crimminy! Look at me, what a mess!" She broke out with nervous laughter and held up the few remaining drops of wine that survived the jolt.

There was no mention of love. It would have been superfluous.

He was at her side of the table within seconds. They kissed to cement their words, to a background of deafening applause. Bart and Violet Moore, still semi-comatose, looked at each other in disbelief. Grams seemed to be the only one who was at ease with the whole exchange.

As the couple exited the room, hugging and laughing, they left the table of onlookers reeling, trying to decipher the last few minutes of stunning dialogue.

The two lovebirds were almost out of sight, when Guinevere came running back into the dining room and graced Grams with a warm endearing embrace.

"Thank you" she whispered. "Thank you, thank you, thank you" and fled back into the hall shadows.

Patrick couldn't believe his ears! Yes he could. He turned to Grams with an incredulous look.

"Why you conniving old gal!" Patrick pestered in fun, "did you put her up to that?"

"Just a little bee in her bonnet" Grams twinkled.

"Well, well now, aren't you proud of yourself," he needled.

"I am that." Patrick reached for her hand.

"Another Grams miracle?"

They both enjoyed the moment.

Patrick descended the stairs with his lips still curled in a smile. The stirring events of those remarkable years always conjured up heart-felt memories.

The happy Michael O'Shays and their darling twin daughters moved to Cranston, in a nice middle class neighborhood with a fenced-in back yard, a green station wagon, and two Labrador pups.

Michael remained with the firm. He missed John, Jr. as did his father, but nothing was ever mentioned of the loss between the two men. The brass shingle would always remain, O'Shay, O'Shay, O'Shay.

Patrick would catch up with Guinevere and the twins on his next visit. Tonight he needed to spend some time with Grams.

Foxy Ol' Girl

Coming home to this often stifling atmosphere was made tolerable for Patrick, only by the presence of the dear old lady who occupied the third floor pent house. She was his passage into tranquility and he, her only link to sanity.

Grams Halloran understood Patrick's restlessness, his excited love for life, his passion to write, paint, explore his surroundings. To dream. She knew of his inner demons, for she was of his universe. They spent many meaty hours together discussing the mysteries of existence, delighting in the true freedom they felt in each other's company.

"Patrick, you are my springtime" she would tell him and he would laugh and give the old lady a long hug.

"And you, my beautiful lady, are my most favorite gal." Touching her wrinkled cheek, lovingly, with the back of his big hand, he would threaten with a pointed finger "and don't you ever forget it!"

He graced her with his rakish smile and she pretended to swoon in his company, like a love stricken waif, rolling her eyes back and dramatically covering her heart with her gnarled old hands. Both would laugh away their foolishness.

This weekend, Patrick had spent a goodly amount of time with her and yet, an inner voice urged him to see her one more time before he left for Sweetmeadow.

He rang for the private elevator, to carry him to the welcoming, third floor quarters. As he stepped off the lift at the top landing, he was tickled to see posted at her door the whimsical sign that he had painted for her several years ago.

"GRAM'S JOINT" it announced, in bold purple letters.

He knocked his usual staccato rap and could hear her shuffling, with strained difficulty, toward the door.

"Don't run, Grams" he teased loudly. He knew her walk was labored. She loved his unabashed humor and was forever entertained by his sense of the absurd. He made her laugh and forget her pain. He was her best medicine.

She opened the door with her usual 'I'm-so-glad-to-see-you' look and stretched her thin arms up to greet him. The delicate scent of lavender soothed his nostrils. They hugged and she stepped aside to allow him to pass. But instead, Patrick offered her his arm and they walked together, slowly, across the room to the wide cushion-filled chair, whose back and arms were dressed in hand crocheted doilies.

The room was, as usual, too hot for Patrick and he was amazed that Grams always wore a shawl in such an over-heated atmosphere.

He felt pride in seeing the book of poems resting on her night table. He had composed them for her many years ago as a young boy and wondered if she ever read them now, and if they gave her any comfort in her long days.

Patrick was sure these rooms were the most charming he would ever witness. They brimmed with hundreds of endearing mementos and fragrances of the past. Patrick felt honored to be privy to fragments of a bygone era, a time in which he had not participated.

Everywhere that there was a small space, yet another piece of her life was crammed; a letter, a picture, scraps of ribbon, laces, figurines, postcards, dried flowers, theater tickets and a delightful story went with each.

His favorite was a hand-blown glass Christmas ornament, an exquisitely carved, ivory dove floating inside a clear crystal ball. Her husband, O. James, had always teased his wife about being a free spirit and how she should have been a beautiful bird. Patrick recalled the day she had lifted it gingerly from it's red velvet lined box and held it to her cheek. The glass was cold to the touch, the message remained warm. How she had loved her dear husband. "Someday I will fly to him," she had whispered, "we will be together."

Patrick automatically changed the water in the Wedgewood vase holding the wild flowers he had brought to her two days ago, fresh from the fields in Kingston. He returned it to it's resting place on the cluttered gate leg table. Stalling for time, Patrick surveyed for the hundredth time the decades of trivia he found forever fascinating.

He finally settled his long limbs on the worn tapestry covered ottoman on which Grams rested her tiny crooked feet. He looked lovingly at the dear old woman sitting before him. Although the bonnet of red ringlets had turned to gray, her green eyes, sunken now and rimmed in red, were still splashed with mischief.

Patrick was in need of talk this afternoon and she could tell by the intensity of his demeanor, that it was going to be a long one. There had been many such sessions in the past, and she had never begrudged the time nor the length of his visits.

As he drank in the tender gaze of his grandmother patiently awaiting him to initiate the conversation, he perused her deformed arthritic hands and twisted joints. A pang of sorrow enveloped him for this gentle lady shackled by old age, quietly anticipating the end of her life. It was a new kind of battle for Haddie Kelly Halloran, who had always been the one in charge of making decisions.

Patrick heaved a heavy sigh. The dull ache in his head reminded him of his fatal diagnosis; the day the doctor discovered the dastardly tumor in his brain. He had told no one. He still had a hard time believing the accuracy of the tests and found it easier to cope in silence. The burden seemed less serious, if carried alone. But tonight, he knew the time had come to share the insane twist of his life with his dearest, most trusted friend.

Patrick had not moved from the ottoman. He reached out for Gram's hands and lowered his head for a moment. She could not evaluate his expression. He spoke softly.

"Grams, I gotta unload some pretty heavy stuff on you tonight, if you're up to it." He raised his eyes to hers.

"Of course dear ...of course."

She bent toward him and squeezed his hand in reply. By the strength of his returned gesture, his grandmother knew whatever it was, it was of crucial importance.

Patrick suddenly released his grip without a word. The stool screeched on the hardwood floor as he stood. He went to the small stove to reheat the cold tea in a chipped enamel pot.

"Oh make some fresh" Grams offered "that has been there all day." She motioned to the tea canister.

"This is fine" Patrick dallied.

He knew exactly where everything was in the wooden cupboards, for he had shared tea with Grams many afternoons over the years. He looked forward to the bonding tradition they had begun, when he was just a small lad and his "tea" was ninety percent milk.

Neither spoke.

Patrick idled himself with cups and saucers, teaspoons, napkins, sugar, milk. When the tea was hot enough, he divided it between two flowery Limoges cups and carried them to where Grams waited. They sipped in awkward silence, both feeling the tenseness of anticipation.

He started to speak, but his throat constricted, trapping his words. He tried again and still his sentences would not form clearly. Grams patted his arms softly, encouraging him to open his heart, reassuring him of her unconditional trust. She waited.

He stood, set his cup on the nearest table, and as if delivering what sounded like a well prepared speech, blurted out his whole ordeal from the beginning. His words poured over her like hot lead. Patrick was amazed at how effortlessly his thoughts rushed from his heart as he spoke and how much the oppressive weight of doom had lifted, once he was able to unload it on Grams.

He told her of the horrifying uncontrollable episodes of fear, the bellicose nightmares over and over again, grotesques images of the claws of death tearing at his throat while he slept. With the slightest nuance in his voice, he told her of the small scared little boy, who lived within his prison walls, crying out to be let free. He silently begged for strength, for hope. He needed her to assure him, as she had when he was small, that the deafening hiss of anger incessantly boiling up in his gut was justified.

"Grams" he pleaded "You've always been able to make things right. I need your miracles now. NOW!" he demanded. He stared at her.

His words pierced her scarred old heart like jagged shards of flying glass inflicting a pain too intolerable to give vent to. She remained silent. She had all she could do to refrain from gasping aloud. With agonizing clarity, her mind swept back to her son's horrible death, her husband's senseless suicide, and now, yet another untimely parting. Now, at her age, how was she to cope. Did she have the strength?

He stood in front of her, every muscle tensed, looking down straight into her eyes for any hint of feeling. There was nothing.

She was a "tough old bird," as she had labeled herself and would not give in to her bursting heart. This was not the first tragedy she had been dealt in her long life and she could not allow it to get the better of her.

Grams closed her eyes. She rested her head on a lacy antimacassar that covered the faded floral print of her armchair. She needed time to gather her wits. She must adequately offer her vulnerable grandson the dose of courage he was begging. Grams knew she would have to crochet her words with the finest of threads.

"My God, My God" she silently prayed. "What are You asking of me? If You choose to send such agonizing problems into my life, I beg of You be gracious enough to send along the solutions."

She remained silent, for what Patrick thought was too long. He kept staring at her blue veined lids for the slightest inkling of movement.

Finally she stirred. Grams narrowed her eyes into threatening slits. If ever she had to stay strong, this was the ultimate test. Her heart was pumping much too fast for a woman of her years. She feared it might betray her. She did not falter.

In slow motion, she leaned forward again in her chair. She straightened her torso as erect as she could manage and faced Patrick head on. She did not offer him sympathy. She did not console him. She did not pity him. Grams was wise enough to know, that if she allowed her torn heart to speak, he would crumble under her pain, and weakness was not on her list of admirable traits.

She intensely glared at him.

"So, Patrick, what are you going to do about it?" She hurled her words at him. A direct shot. Undeniably calculated. Cold.

He stepped back, as if slapped in the face by the hand of a giant. His eyes widened. His face flushed with anger, mouth agape. Grams did not flinch. Her eyes were riveted on him. Unyielding. An outward sheet of calm curtained her inner torment.

Patrick swung himself away from her and stomped heavily around the room.

"That really pisses me off!" he blurted out, an expression he knew Grams detested. He was miffed! Livid! He was confused. Why had she shown so little soul?

For several minutes Patrick paced over the worn pieces of carpet, his head shaking, arms flailing. The whole while excoriating Grams under his breath for her blatant lack of concern.

He stopped short! Like air bursting from an over-inflated balloon, Patrick exploded into fits of wild laughter. He ranted on, with uncontrollable force, until all his energy was spent.

The laughter turned to anger. The anger to tears.

Grams had not relaxed her position. She did not join in his amusement, as she normally would. She remained stoic, unsmiling, pretending to be unimpressed with his one man show. Sweet Jesus, how she ached for him.

Long after he managed to curtail his convulsive gasps, Patrick fought for breath, a tell-tale sign of his deep hurt. He wiped the tears from his face on his bare arm.

Gram's heart stung with pangs of sorrow.

The young man sauntered over to where his grandmother sat and loomed over her. He noticed that her hands were relaxed on her lap, her lips soft, her look serene. Had she not heard him? Had she no feeling for what he was experiencing?

Patrick bent over the old lady, rested his palms on the arms of the overstuffed chair, his face inches from hers. She could feel the hostility in his forced breathing. He was still infuriated with her lack of coddling.

She was so out of character. But why?

After a tense interval of time, he straightened his body.

Standing tall in front of her, as if he was the performer and she his private audience, Patrick dramatically held his arms out to his sides in a chiding manner.

"'Well Patrick'" he sarcastically mimicked her words, "'What are you going to do about it?'." He sing-songed in a belittling tone.

"WHAT?" he bellowed, his face flushed and contorted. "Not even 'oh you poor thing' or 'you're too young and handsome to die'." He swung around, acting out his ridicule." He watched her. "Come on Grams, you can do better than that!"

She sat patiently, allowing him all the time he needed to play out his little drama.

He bent over her again, sweat pouring from his brow, half crying, half enraged. "Is that all you have to say to me? That's it?"

The two had never exchanged harsh words and she loathed the strained interaction of emotion.

She spoke.

"It is God's will. We must —"

"GOD'S WILL? BUNK!" he screamed, pouncing on her words in the heat of temper. He flung his arms up in despair.

"God! What God!" Patrick raved.

Grams remained unflinching. The wise old woman was aware that her role was that of listener tonight, not preacher. She allowed him to retch his soul. He needed that, as part of the healing process. The self-pity, the anger, the horror of reality, they must all be exorcized. She knew the process well.

"This so-called benevolent God of yours, why does He impose His wrath on His people? Because He is so kind? Why?" The muscles on Patrick's face were contorted into ugly folds. His jaw locked. "I think He is a demonic god! He blinds us, cripples us, infests our bodies with tormenting diseases," He whipped around and stared at her. "In the name of love?"

Moments later, the force of energy seemed to seep from his bones. He slumped down on the wide stool in front of her and buried his face in his hands. His uncontrollable sobs filled the room.

How she wanted to reach out to him and cradle him in her loving arms, hold him close to her heart, as she did when he was a baby. She must not let him see her weaken, not even for a moment. She had no choice.

Patrick stood and walked to the window. His back was to her. She could not interpret his expression.

Grams dared to speak.

"Our stay on this earth is infinitesimal in the realm of eternity. I believe, we, who do our penance in this life are allowed to have a more gentle transition into everlasting peace." Grams wasn't sure he was even listening and waited for him to turn around.

She heard him chuckle.

In a span of a few minutes, to Patrick's own astonishment, he had gone from total devastation to mild acceptance.

"You foxy ol' girl!" he smiled sheepishly.

Wise Grams. She had always known, instinctively, how to cope with the impossible. She had selflessly given him the gift of slaying his own dragon.

He wrapped his arms around her, bathing in her strength.

Grams flashed an unnoticed "thumbs-up" sign to the heavens while her grandson, once again, settled himself on the ottoman.

After a spell of quiet, they began a powerful exchange of thoughts, chatting long into the evening. Grams offered little. She listened to him expound on his feelings, his choices, his decision to leave college and pursue his artistic talents in his few remaining years. They spoke of death. Patrick told her of Angie and dear ol' Molly, of the Huntingwells, of Sweetmeadow. He chose not to mention his intrigue with the lady of the manor.

Haddie watched her rugged grandson intently. The fire of life radiated from his pores. He was so young, so full of spirit. It was impossible to digest that the vultures of death stalked his soul.

The evening had been a draining one. Patrick took his grandmother's cold hands in his. They exchanged smiles. His, one of gratitude, hers, of compassion. He leaned over to kiss her forehead and readied himself to leave.

"Patrick dear, before you leave, I have something I would like you to have." He couldn't imagine what it might be.

The Claddagh

"There, over there." Grams pointed her cane to the dark mahogany bureau near the door. "There now, remove the bottom drawer."

Patrick followed directions.

"Feel way back and you will find a small reticule."

Patrick's hand swept over the vacant cavity until his hand rested on a beaded purse. He retrieved it with great care.

"Bring it here," Grams instructed.

The intricately crocheted sack had a tightly knotted drawstring closing, a long tassel hung from the bottom. Over the years, the ecru threads had acquired the inevitable age stains, only adding to its antiquity and intrigue.

He placed the fragile looking little bag softly into Grams' open palm. Before divulging its secret, she fingered the contents for a few moments with sensitive, exacting movements as if to discover whatever magic it held for the first time.

Grams forced her painful fingers to knead and palpitate the purse for several minutes, working to loosen the knot. Patrick wanted to offer help, but felt her need to achieve the task herself. After a struggle, she was able to free the tightly fixed threads. Reaching in, she removed a short twisted chain which held the most unusual pendant he had ever seen. Grams arranged it across her lap for him to view in full glory. A circle about an inch and a half in diameter, obviously hand carved from beech wood and highly lacquered. Designed into the bottom of the open circle was a crowned heart, protectively cradled in the open palms of two adjoining hands.

Not waiting for him to comment, Grams spoke.

"This is called a Claddagh. As you can see, it is a pair of open hands gently holding a heart, the symbol of one's love for another."

She paused for a moment, glancing up at him, assuring she had his full attention before going on.

"It is an old Irish custom, a rather romantic legend, believed to bring blessings of good fortune to those who possess it. It is passed from heart to heart, from lover to lover, mother to daughter, father to son, friend to friend, or from grandmother to grandson." She stole a hurried peek at Patrick to assess his attentiveness.

"You will notice," she held the talisman up to him for closer scrutiny, "that the heart and hands are set on a circle." She traced it with her crooked finger. "The circle represents eternity...the heart, love...the hands, friendship...the crown, loyalty." She glanced at him over her spectacles to await his evaluation.

"That's a beautiful piece, Grams." He was much taken by the simplistic artistry of design and what it all represented.

She took hold of Patrick's hand and lifting the Claddagh by its tarnished chain, lightly set it in his large palm. She folded his mannish fingers over her treasure, as if to lock it in for safekeeping.

Patrick was at a momentary loss for words. Grams spoke with feelings that could only pour from an overburdened heart. For the first time that evening, he was hearing the familiar ring of compassion in her voice.

"We all have our secret prison, Patrick." She paused. "We must learn to scale its walls, each in our own way. Ours is not meant to be a painless existence of ecstatic pleasures and constant rewards, you know. I have found that life is a journey of restrictions, rules, confinement, of pain. And yes," she smiled, "the way is deceptively softened by a few strategically placed interludes of pleasure and accomplishment."

She looked away before going on.

"We are all, in one way or another, prisoners of our fate. Some of us are bound by strict religious teachings, some held captive by an all-consuming talent, many rendered powerless simply by the color of their skin, others by paralyzing pain, or lost love. Something, as simple as fear could be a prison for the sufferer."

Grams continued in almost a whisper.

"There are those of us who are bound by the chains of old age and others," she placed her hand over Patrick's, still holding the Claddagh pendant, "strangled by the symptoms of an insufferable disease. We are all prisoners, confined in different cells, for different reasons."

There was comfortable silence for a spell. The old woman's demeanor brightened.

"But with it all, dear boy, there is always the rebirth of spring…moments of great satisfaction that make our spirit stay fresh and alive. Times such as we have shared this evening. The heart can always reach out in love under the most tragic of circumstances if we grant it the freedom to do so."

She squeezed his hand. "Yes?"

Patrick nodded. What she had said made sense. It would take time to digest the fullness of her words.

Grams perked up. She could not allow this meeting to end in despair.

"This pendant was given to me by my mother and father. I have cherished it all these years, not as a possession, but as a dear memory of the sweet love they held for each other and for me." Patrick opened his hand to admire the piece and turning it over, noticed the letter T on the back. They assumed it was the initial of the carver. It was.

Haddie Kelly Halloran had worn the necklace for many years tucked under her shirtwaist, until a few years ago when her stiffening fingers no longer could open the tiny clasp. Now, she was thrilled to be entrusting it to this young, powerful heart, who would know more suffering in his few years on earth, than most experience in an extended lifetime. It was with the most unselfish of unselfish love, that she surrendered her treasured keepsake to Patrick. It was time.

"My fondest prayer for you, Patrick, is that you will somehow find the strength to carry on. Take the power of my love. Use it as fuel."

Patrick assumed she had finished and made a move to leave.

"And remember, Patrick, there really is a God, just waiting for you to call upon Him."

She winked at him. He returned her gesture with a tongue-in-cheek look.

"Yeah, sure, Grams."

She had always been his anchor. She accepted him, exactly as he was, never once trying to program him into a mold that would suffocate his style. She honestly recognized his urgency to fly free. She wished she was young enough to soar with him.

With the aid of her grandson's strong hands, Grams rose from her chair. Patrick curved his arms around her stooped shoulders and they walked together toward the door. He had no way of adequately thanking her for the evening's unfolding and simply said "I love you, Grams. You're quite a gal."

"Oh, go on now, you blarney-talking young fool," she chided. She playfully poked at him with her cane in mocked annoyance.

Her heart bled for him. How she ached! If only she could brew some sort of magic potion that would cleanse his body of its contemptuous infestation. But a weathered old mule she was and had trod a pretty bumpy road herself. She knew he would not crumble in the arms of adversity. She hated a quitter and took great peace in knowing that her grandson had inherited her tough genes. He would drink in life to the end. He was, after all a fighter, as was she.

"Good night, Grams. Thanks."

Patrick lightly kissed her cheek and warmed her with that wonderful crooked smile that flickered across his sun-tanned face. How she loved him.

"Patrick!" she called after him.

He turned, responding to her voice.

"We Hallorans do not buckle under!" Her fist raised in emphasis. "We walk tough! Remember that."

He laughed out loud.

Standing tall, clicking his heels in Gestapo fashion, he returned her high fist.

"THOU SHALL NOT BUCKLE UNDER" he echoed loudly.

Stepping into the elevator cage, Patrick gave her the usual "thumbs-up" sign, as he always did when he left her and slowly dropped out of sight. Before he reached the ground floor, the Claddagh was around his neck.

Tonight's exchange of heartfelt emotions would lay softly upon his soul, silently offering him comfort for the rest of his days.

Haddie Kelly Halloran was never told she had been adopted eighty years ago. All records of adoption, in those days, were destroyed.

Nor was she cognizant of her conception in a foreign land, the product of a mindless rape. Grams was uninformed that her Irish grandfather was a turner and he was the one who had carved the Claddagh for his darlin' daughter, Sarah, her birth mother. It was Sarah, who had insisted that the beautiful token of love, go with the baby, her baby, the fragile little heart she was forbidden to see before the child was adopted and Sarah sent back to Ireland.

Sarah's father carved only one other Claddagh pendant before he died. For his first, legitimate grandchild, Grams' half sister. A sibling, of whom Haddie Kelly Halloran had no knowledge.

Night Artist

Grams closed the door and secured the safety latch, an unnecessary habit she had become a slave to when she lived alone. She walked, with difficulty, back to her sitting room. She positioned herself in front of the tall window and waited.

Patrick walked out of the house into the balmy night air. There was not much light left in the day. The sun was sluggishly dropping from the sky, tinting the heavens with musty shades of purple and mauve. Gossamer puffs of clouds remained...floating aimlessly. The earth was still.

He came to the end of the cement driveway to await the cab he had called to carry him back to Narragansett. He turned to look back at the lovely home that had oddly enough, managed to offer him a comfortable sense of safety.

He had spent a good part of his life in this fashionable east side dwelling, the homestead that Grams almost lost in the Great Depression. He never tired of hearing the colorful old tales she told, of the "goings on" within its walls. Some delightful adventures, others tragic accounts of her dramatic life.

His departing ritual never altered. Patrick took that last look up to the third floor apartment to find Grams peering from her window, watching him leave. They made a formal pact years before, never to say goodbye in any form. No words. No waves. No sign of finality. It would become much more difficult now for they both were painfully aware of life evaporating at an accelerated rate.

Patrick stared up at the ashen lady, framed dwarf-like, in the tall narrow window. Dark shadows of evening had transformed her beautiful, crinkled face into an eerie, ghoulish-looking, corrugated mask. Tall black shutters stood grimly guarding each side of the macabre portrait, emphasizing the littleness of her wispy silhouette. Tonight she looked very old.

A shudder ranted through his body, bringing with it a momentary tremor of sadness. He continued to hold his eyes on the daunting picture before him, bothered by its disquieting effect.

Patrick saw Grams step back into the darkness of her room. He could no longer make out her form. The night artist had once again painted the window canvas with his blackest pigment.

"Good night, sweet lady."

On the other side of the window, Haddie Kelly Halloran shuffled to her small bedroom and looked up at the faithful crucifix that hung by her iron bed.

"I do not understand. I do not understand." Shaking her head, "I do not understand," she humbly confessed again and again to the persecuted body on the cross. "Where is the justice in snuffing out a promising young life so full of anticipation, just beginning his journey, and leaving a withered old coot, like I, to plod on?"

She paused. "For what reason? For what reason." She shook her head.

Grams gazed at the heavy wooden cross. She remembered how many times it had comforted her over the years. She moved in closer and stretched her finger tips up as high as her stiffened spine would allow. She was barely able to touch the pale alabaster form of the crucified man.

"I know, I know," she consoled, as she patted the blood stained feet. "You have enough of your own problems. Forgive me."

218

The old woman ambled around her bed. With great effort, she knelt down on the thread-bare kneeler to begin reciting her nightly rosary, aloud, as she had done faithfully since she was a child. On the window sill nearby, her collection of holy statutes stood in silent reverence. They were her friends.

The prayers over, Grams painfully crawled onto her bed. She did not pull back the hand-quilted comforter nor did she bother with her night clothes. Not tonight.

She welcomed the comforting softness of the down pillow. She could not focus her thoughts. She was too drained to think. Her brain was numbed with disbelief.

"Thy will be done" she conceded to a higher power. Hopefully, in another world, she would be granted the wisdom to solve the mystery of faith.

Grams lay awake for hours, mesmerized by the stark whiteness of the ceiling above her. Images of her grandson's fate fitfully punctured her half-conscious mode, producing an array of emotions all muddled together. The pain he would endure, the love she held for him, her helplessness to alleviate his suffering.

She begged mercy for his young soul.

Unaware of how many hours had passed, Grams turned awkwardly toward her bedside lamp. Using her last drop of energy, she gave the tiny chain a tug. The elaborate glass beaded fringe on the shade tinkled in response to her touch. It was the first time, since the death of her beloved son years before, that Haddie Kelly Halloran allowed darkness to enter her quarters.

She was silently acknowledging that the flame of life was going out within her. She would exist now, for Patrick, only as long as he needed her.

It was then, in the pitch aloneness, that tears of compassion burned a path down the rutted old face.

Summer's End

It was Wednesday, the 26th of August, 1954.

Telltale signs of summer's end had been in evidence for the last week, everywhere around Sweetmeadow. The big travel trunks were quietly brought down from the storage attic and placed in the wide second floor hall for packing. Some of the wooden shutters in the guest rooms were already closed up. The lovely gardens were not being replanted.

The staff was ready for their trek back to the the city. It was always a melancholy time for all. Although New York was home, they cherished this beautiful ocean estate, with its country charm and warm summer days.

Tonight, was also a poignant parting for Patrick and Thad. The Huntingwells were planning to leave on Friday to winter in New York. Spontaneous "veranda talks" were an integral part of this unlikely relationship and both gained pleasant satisfaction from their lively exchanges. This evening, it was later than usual and Thad had an early morning tee-off time, with the governor.

"Let's call it a day, Patrick." Thad suggested with an extended hand and a playful slap on the shoulder. He truly loved the young man as a son. He had filled a hole in the older man's life that Thad himself was unaware needed filling.

They both were aware of the winter separation, but neither chose to bring it up.

"Think I'll walk into town. I'm not ready to turn in, yet." Their verbal sparring always stimulated Patrick's thought process and he wanted to mill over the theories they had discussed. It was like therapy to him and whetted his insatiable need for answers.

"Say, how'd you like to take the Jag for a spin? Runs like a charm. Great night to take the top down."

Thad reached into the pocket of his white slacks and before Patrick could react, softly tossed him the keys."

"Sounds great! Thanks."

They turned and went their separate ways, just like any other evening. It had been an especially meaty debate. Some very "heavy stuff" was discussed.

Before leaving, Patrick picked up one of the wicker rockers and carried it to the forth floor storage attic, to be stored away from the harsh winter elements.

On his way down, he decided to cut across the third floor hall, where the servants quarters were and go out the back entrance to the carriage house garage.

As he passed Molly's room, he was surprised to see her light still on. The door was half open, and he noticed that Molly was on her knees, bent over the floor in a state of agitation. It alarmed him. He rapped on the door as he entered the room, not to startle the high strung woman. The room was no larger than a closet. Scattered around the servantess was an array of trinkets and jewelry. In packing, she had removed the scratched little box from the marble top bureau and it had slipped from her aging fingers. Molly was so focused on retrieving the run-away contents, that she ignored his presence.

Patrick perused the tiny area. It seemed ludicrous that the little lady employed in a mansion brimming with uncountable wealth, proudly held her world of assets in an 8" box. She worked hard and asked for little. Again, where was the justice of it all.

He did not have time to linger on that thought. His eyes were unexpectedly drawn to an object that lay on the floor amidst Molly's chattel.

Patrick was dumb-founded! Unable to speak, he found himself fighting an urge to lunge at the piece and ask a million questions. The only noise in the room was Molly's mutterings as she examined each treasure lovingly for breakage. He bent to look at the shape closer.

A claddagh! Just like Grams'! The one she gave him that he kept looped over his bedrail. The clasped hands holding a heart, hand-carved from one piece of wood. His heart was pounding.

Patrick managed to kneel down next to Molly and put his arm around her shoulders in gentle comfort.

"Here now, let me help you." His voice stayed calm. "You really must be more careful not to throw things on the floor," he teased.

Molly continued her clean-up without a word.

As he gathered the few pieces out of her reach, Patrick's hand went to the wooden pendant. He was mesmerized by the overwhelming feeling of walking into something he did not understand. It was indeed, the very same thing. He turned it over. There was the initial "T" scratched into the base of the circle. He could not believe what he was holding. Was there an untold story? Was he part of it? It was baffling, unreal. He squelched his need to ask Molly how she had come by the unique piece. Instead, he would run up to Grams' place and tell her of his discovery. She would have an explanation. She would not mind the late hour.

Still in shock and bewildered by the experience, Patrick helped Molly to her feet and bid her goodnight. Goodbyes would be exchanged in the morning. He left her in possession of the greatest mystery of his life. Was there a link between Grams and Molly? If Grams and Molly were … then she was his …it was all too absurd. Grams would sort it all out.

Patrick ran down the back stairs, through the kitchen and out into the clear night. The balmy air, sweetly scented from the tuberoses that Angelo planted, was being deliciously enjoyed by a million dancing fire flies, competing with the stars for center stage. Crickets rejoiced in song.

What an evening! The kind of which poets write.

Patrick's mind was in turmoil. How grateful he was that Thad offered him his car. Tonight of all nights.

It had been months since Patrick's hands had touched a steering wheel. Patrick felt energized with the thought of confronting Grams about the discovery of Molly's pendant.

With caution, he turned out onto Ocean Drive. The posh red convertible skimmed in silence over the familiar road. Patrick felt the luxurious plush leather wrapped around him like the hands of a master masseuse, pampering his body with ultimate comfort. Amazing what money could afford one. The radio was on low, complimenting the flawless night with background music for its grand production.

What an incredible summer it had been!

WHAM!

Excruciating pain ramrodded through his skull, piercing his head like a jagged steel pipe.

"OH GOD!" Patrick howled. His hands instinctively shot to his temples in a vain effort to erase the torturous stabs of anguish.

"GOD, HELP ME!" His eerie cries of help evaporated into the stillness of the night.

Patrick's head exploded in raw agony an instant before his merciful red chariot careened off the road, smashing head-on into a hammock of unyielding old oaks.

Peace had come instantly.

Springtime

The funeral was a simple one, as Patrick had requested. Only weeks before the grisly accident, he had confided in Grams his wish for an unpretentious farewell. He voiced his desire to be earthed in an obscure country cemetery where his spirit could run freely among the field flowers, he so dearly loved.

There were to be no frills. He was insistent. No garish costly coffin left open for curiosity seekers to gawk at his expressionless remains. No eulogies from prosperous business clients of his father. No gaudy floral wreaths sent by dutiful secretaries upon orders from their bosses.

Patrick abhorred the prospect of long lines of parading over-dressed positioned friends of the family who would feel obligated to attend the rites for the sole purpose of being seen.

He hoped that only the few people in his life, who truly cared for his presence, would walk a little way with him, bidding him peace on his journey to wherever he was going.

They were all there.

Some cried openly, others sorrowed an inward grief. But each savored a special memory of their irreplaceable friend. He had left them with their own unique gift of love, each in a different way, but all touched forever, consciously or unconsciously, by the inextricable magic of his being.

His mother, father, Michael and Guinevere, Puff. All in somber disbelief.

Angie, her heart broken, bitterly trying to accept the sudden stilling of her love.

The Sweetmeadow staff; Nigel, Max, Angelo, Cook, Tillie, in their most formal attire, grouped together. Silent, heavy-hearted.

Thaddeus Tilton Huntingwell clasped his wife's gloved hand. He stood stoic and strong, accepting with sadness, the loss of his exuberant young friend. Death was a part of life. We must go on.

Prunella Catherine Huntingwell, appearing perfectly poised and self-contained, yearned torturously for the nearness of him. Her free hand, almost motionless, soulfully caressed the throbbing heart that lay veiled beneath a layer of ivory silk, zealously guarding their sacred moments, preserved forever by the silence of death.

Across the hollowed out pit, apart from the small gathering, two diminutive gray-haired ladies stood arm in arm. They met today, for the first time, through the commonality of a young man's heart. The older, in obvious poor health, was a lady of moderate wealth, the younger, by her dress, a servant.

The illusive truths connecting these two women, would never be told. They would remain ignorant of their blood ties. Sources were unavailable to inform them, of being birthed by the same Irish mother. Nor, would their loving Grandfather Thomas, ever be credited with carving the two wooden pendants, before he died in Ireland.

Molly wept softly. She had developed a soft spot in her heart for the dear lad who could always spare a smile and a kind word for his "darlin' Molly."

Grams remained calm, clutching the stems of wild flowers he had brought to her just last week.

He would be painfully missed by both.

Grams Halloran, bent with age, had taken a small step forward, positioning herself at the very edge of the open grave, still attached to Molly's outstretched hand. She wore a slight smile on her bluish lips, as she viewed the rough hand hewn box, softly cradled on a mattress of moist earth.

Grams shed no tears. There was no need for them. She and Patrick had voiced the things that needed to be shared before death had stripped away their sweet elixir of companionship. They would always be tethered by a heart string. She warmed in that lovely thought and in the knowledge that she would be joining him soon.

Before leaving the site, she dropped the scraggly bouquet over the plain box that held the pulse of her own life.

"Fly from your prison, dear boy, you have found your peace. Rest now...rest."

Molly sensed Grams' need for solitude, and quietly removed herself from the gentle woman, without an inkling that the cold bony hand she had clung to was of her own flesh. The unsuspecting sisters exchanged a long, poignant gaze. They shared a depth of compassion for the sadness of the day. The loss of a common love.

With the help of her cane, Grams left, ambling laboriously over the uneven ground toward the waiting cars. She broke out in a private laugh, shaking her head and wondering what sort of devilish prank Patrick might be playing on poor Saint Peter.

Her own life was very nearly over. She could feel the cooling of her blood. As she trod on, she bore witness to the millions of gloriously dressed wild flowers, humbly paying homage to their departed companion.

The old woman was not alone. She could feel him walking beside her, egging her on. Now, it was her turn to call upon the strength of his love, to contend with her final days.

After Grams left, the mourners randomly dispersed. Mamma Zaffini, a fox fur resting loosely over the shoulders of her all-black mourning dress, came forward. It mattered not that it was August, the heavy wool attire was standard garb for all funerals.

Frankie walked a short way with his mother.

She timidly walked to the side of the grave. From her bulky black pocketbook, she removed a small paper bag, the top rolled down to form a neat little package. She bent down, careful to negotiate the little parcel onto the unpretentious coffin. Her wet eyes turned to meet the sad eyes of her son. Frankie smiled in acknowledgement of her tender act of love.

The bag contained a few of her "famous" biscotti, baked fresh for Patrick, early this morning. They were his favorite. The simple gesture was all she knew to do, to send a part of her heart along with him...her Irish son.

Frankie held his mother's arm tightly. He was not embarrassed to cry with her. The emotions were pure. The loss painfully real.

A gentle breeze whispered softly over the meadow, announcing to the universe that wherever the unteethered spirit of Patrick Sean O'Shay deigned to roam,

surely it would be springtime.

GB